Illustration by Arthur Rackham from
The Pied Piper of Hamelin by Robert Browning, 1934.

Sorrow

Is a strange flower

More secret than

The tulip's velvet mystery

Unfolding and unfolding

Nobly ordained

Eloquently pure

Beyond affectation

And always

With the promise

Of an ensuing wisdom

When it has bloomed its fullest

And lies most tenderly wasted

Beside its sweeter sister

Joy

Other Books by Mariah Robinson

Love and Other Illusions

SISTER SORROW, SISTER JOY

MARIAH ROBINSON

Brandylane
PUBLISHERS OF BOOKS SINCE 1985

ISBN: 978-1-9399309-9-6

LCCN: 2017953756

Cover Image: Shutterstock.com
Stock illustration ID: 312657062 (Anna Ismagilova)

Printed in the United States

Published by

Brandylane Publishers

Brandylane
PUBLISHERS OF BOOKS SINCE 1985

For Jim and Eric

"Chaos, Cosmos! Cosmos Chaos!
Once again the sickening game;
Freedom free to slay herself and dying
while they shout her name."

— Alfred, Lord Tennyson

MARCH 1987

"Now, here, you see,
it takes all the running you can do,
to keep in the same place."

— Through the Looking-Glass

He awakens to Richmond rain – an undifferentiated sound of steadily running water – and to his Dobermans pacing the hallway – clockwork dogs trained not to whine or fawn. He yawns, stretches, reaches for the phone, dials and waits.

"Yes?"

"You took forever to answer."

"I'm still asleep."

"What's on your agenda today?"

"A ten o'clock appointment with yet another art conservator."

He reaches for his pocket watch. "It's eight fifteen. You'll never make it."

"I'll make it."

"I'll take you to lunch after your appointment."

"Maybe. I'll call you."

"Say yes now."

"I can't, George. I need to spend the afternoon researching an Audubon folio Skinner's auctioning on Saturday."

"I'll pick you up at noon. A quick lunch. I promise."

"All right."

She replaces the receiver in its cradle – languid from sleep, longing for coffee. She closes her eyes to ponder her options and, when she opens them, it's nine fifteen.

The art conservator is standing in front of the gallery's showroom when Ann pulls up. A long-ashed cigarette dangles from the left corner of her mouth. She observes Ann's approach without shifting her stance.

Ann waves. No return wave from the art conservator. The woman's appearance is surprising – drab skirt and jacket, indifferently paired, Top-Siders worn without stockings, short bottle-blond hair – totally without chic. The telephone voice had suggested otherwise.

She locks the car door and walks briskly over. "Good morning. I'm Ann Cabot."

"Maggie Lambert," the conservator replies in a gravelly voice and gives Ann's extended hand a brief shake.

"I'm so sorry to have kept you waiting, Mrs. Lambert. Eleanor had a dental emergency. She manages the gallery and she's never late except for this morning."

"It's not a problem, but please call me Maggie."

Ann unlocks the gallery's double doors and turns off the alarm. "May I take your jacket, Maggie?"

"I'll leave it on."

"How about a cup of coffee, or tea?"

"No thanks."

"Then let's have a look at the paintings." She leads the way to the gallery's holding room and watches as Maggie examines the four small canvases – front, back, and sideways. Her eyes linger on a pair of robustly painted seventeenth-century florals in elaborately carved and brightly burnished gold-leaf frames.

"Thirty-eight hundred to restore the four of them."

"How long will it take?"

"Two months. Maybe less."

Ann considers. The last conservator had wanted forty-two hundred and half a year to complete the work. "That works well for me," she affirms. "Eleanor will draw up a contract if she survives the dentist's chair." She smiles at Maggie. "In the meantime, shall we toast the contract with coffee?"

"I take mine black, three lumps of sugar. I'll wrap these in bubble while you're brewing. I have a roll of it in my van."

Ann walks back to the kitchenette and turns on the coffeemaker. Maggie is checking out the gallery's coffered and paneled sitting room when she returns with the tray. They sit on French fauteuils, an Irish mahogany tea table between them. Maggie reaches into her jacket pocket and pulls out a pack of cigarettes and a handsome gold lighter.

"Mind if I smoke?"

"It's allowed in this room," Ann walks over to the sitting room's double doors and closes them, removes a shallow enamel bowl from the Jacobean sideboard, and places it on the tea table, next to Maggie's cup. "More coffee?"

"No thanks," Maggie replies. She removes a cigarette from the pack, affixes it to the left corner of her mouth, lights it and takes a long drag. The smoke exits in twin streams from her finely chiseled nostrils. She acknowledges the ashtray Ann has provided with a nod. "Who exactly are you?" she drawls and leans back into her chair, head to one side, appraising.

"What do you mean?"

"Tell me about yourself."

"I'm a born-and-bred Richmonder and I own an art gallery from which you've accepted a consignment. What else would you like to know?"

"Something more personal. Are you a married born-and-bred Richmonder?"

Ann starts to reply but instead flashes the diamond wedding band on her left hand.

"I see. Well, that settles that."

"What settles what?"

"I disavow relationships with married women."

Ann stares at her. "That's a an odd comment. What about unmarried women?"

"She'd have to be spectacular." Maggie arches an eyebrow at Ann.

Ann arches one back. "What's this about, Maggie?"

"It's about you."

She regards Maggie uneasily. "Surely you're not expecting me to take this banter seriously?"

"The banter, no. Me, yes."

Ann's unease intensifies. "Well, I'm sorry to dash your expectations, but I'm not what you're ... what you're ..." She shrugs incomprehension.

"You're not what I'm *what?*" Maggie asks, ever so gently, and her face softens and shapes itself into an unbearably precious boyishness. She pushes back her chair and stands up. "Thanks for the coffee. I'll call when the paintings are ready." She reaches across the table and, lightly, with her right index finger, touches the side of Ann's hand. "Bye now." She turns away and walks to the front of the gallery where the canvases are bubbled and stacked.

"Wait a moment. I'll help you carry them to your van," Ann calls after her.

"No need," Maggie replies. The gallery doors close behind her.

Ann and George lunch at Lemaire. Caesar salad with sautéed jumbo shrimp, crispy polenta croutons, a superior Merlot, dessert, and strong black coffee. George scoops up a generous mouthful of Ann's blackberry tart. "What's up? It isn't like you to fall behind on one of Bundy's pastry chef's specialties." He puts down his fork and scrutinizes her. "How'd your appointment with the conservator go?"

"It was adequate to the occasion."

"Did you like her?"

"Nope."

"Why not?"

"She was," Ann frowns, "she was nosy."

"What did she want to know?"

"My marital status, for one thing."

"For what reason?"

"She ... well ... I'm not sure why."

"Women thrive on gossip. Wasn't it Ben Franklin who quipped that three women may keep a secret if two of them are dead?" He nods approval. "I'm glad you don't have that propensity."

"My mother hated gossip. But I don't think this woman's a gossip. She's ..." She shrugs.

"Finish what you were saying. You've got me curious now."

"I was going to say that she reminded me of my mother, but then I realized that she and my mother are nothing alike."

"Hmmm. She's nothing like your mother but you dislike her. How come?"

"She's pushy." Ann's voice drops. "And predatory."

"Predatory as in she asked you to pass out her business cards?"

"It was more of a ... a personal nature." Her color rises.

George notes the blush and considers several possibilities. "Tell me she didn't make a play for you—good grief." He reaches across the table and clinks her dessert plate with his crest ring. "If she did, don't hire her." He eyes Ann quizzically. "Well? Did she or didn't she?"

"Did or didn't she what, George?"

"Make a pass at you."

Ann starts to give the easy "yes" but something rouses her to caution. "No, she didn't." She reaches for her cup and takes a swallow of tepid coffee. "You promised a short lunch and it's already after two. I must get to the museum library before three."

He signals to the waiter. "When he brings the check, add an eight-dollar tip and sign for me. I'll pick you up at the main entrance."

Ann watches his departure, brisk walk, head tilted in thought. She is, for the second time this day, disconcerted by a sensation she can't identify.

Ann has just driven back from a weekend of planting tulip bulbs and reconciling spars between Edwin and Amory when Eleanor phones the Richmond townhouse to say that the restorations are done and awaiting her inspection at the gallery. The paintings are placed in various light-gathering sites in Ann's spacious office and Eleanor and Maggie are discussing their merits and deficits when she arrives. She gives a gasp of delight at the floral bouquets.

"I was surprised myself," Maggie concedes. "They're gorgeous."

"You've *made* them gorgeous. I've fallen in love with them all over again." She writes out a check and places it, face down, on the desk. "Thank you. Your work is amazing. And in less than a month's time! Are you taking the Boldini today?"

Maggie puts the check into the breast pocket of her green leather jacket. "No, my studio's too full, but I'd like to take another look at it."

They walk back to the gallery's holding room where the painting is hung. The portrait is of a young lad. His stance and expression convey hauteur. He's dressed in a black velvet suit with elaborate festoons of lace on the collar and wrists of the fitted jacket and on the cuffs of the knee-length pantaloons.

Ann watches as Maggie examines the canvas. "Do you like it?"

"Oh yes, it's museum quality. What do you think of it?"

"I find it intriguing that one so young could be so haughty."

"He looks like a snotty little prig."

"I agree, but what lies beneath that snotty priggishness?"

"Too psychological for me. Not to mention that I couldn't care less. What about the floral bouquets I restored? I have an idea you're going to keep them."

Ann looks at Maggie curiously. "How prescient of you. I've been toying with the notion of hanging them in my dining room."

"Where is your dining room?"

"It's ... well, it's in Hampton. I live primarily in Hampton. The Richmond house is mainly a convenience because of the gallery. Why do you ask?"

"I'm interested. Do you mind?"

"It's unsettling."

"You don't look unsettled."

"I didn't say I was. I said *it* was. There's a difference."

"For sure," Maggie drawls. "Maybe you're anxious."

"I'm ill at ease, if that's what you mean."

"In what way?"

"My mind's racing and a racing mind is madness, according to Lord Meher."

"Lord who?"

"Lord Meher."

"Do I know this person?"

"I don't think so. He died almost two decades ago—in January of 1969."

"Why do you call him 'Lord'? Was he royalty?"

Ann smiles. "More than royalty. His devotees believe him to be God-realized in the same way Christ was."

"Do you believe that?"

"I'm not big on belief, but I'm open to the possibility that it's true."

"Where was this Lord Meher from?"

"He was born in India."

"Have you been to India?"

Ann hesitates. "Well, yes. Several trips actually."

"You're a different little creature, aren't you?"

"Aren't we all?"

"We're not all beautiful." Maggie evaluates Ann's features. "But you certainly are."

"I'm not even close."

"You're Vivien Leigh with gloriously thick auburn hair, a more generous mouth, a wider and more softly rounded forehead and—" Maggie sighs approvingly. "You even have her dimples. I've never seen a lovelier face."

"I doubt that's true."

"How cynical of you."

Ann shakes her head as if to clear it. "What exactly are we doing here?"

"We're playing, Ann. Playing like the little lost lambs in the parable. Don't you like to play?"

"I hate being lost and I like to know what I'm playing, Maggie."

"Let us be proper or die," Maggie teases. "Junior League to the bone."

"I'd say I'm more in the Junior League than *of* the Junior League."

Maggie searches Ann's countenance. Her eyes register a frank gathering-together of impressions. "But I know what you're like, Ann. I knew the second I saw you. And I will confess that you took me totally by surprise—which *never* happens to me."

Ann's pulse quickens. She feels the old press to flee—to hightail it to the warren. She tries gamely for humor, but nothing comes to mind. Then she remembers the beauty of the restored floral bouquets. For that perfection of skill, she will handle this woman. For that perfection of skill, she *must* handle this woman. Her jaw tightens. "What exactly is it that you want from me, Maggie?"

"To know you."

"In what way?"

"In whatever way I can. In whatever way you'll let me know you."

"I'd like you to know me as a business associate."

"Nothing else?"

"Perhaps we could schedule lunch together. Or dinner."

"Oh, okay Ann, we'll *schedule* lunch together." Maggie saunters into the showroom. "We'll schedule lunch and dinner together and maybe a few other things together." She waves an airy goodbye over her shoulder.

Ann shudders. "You are not wise," she murmurs.

She awakens to the drone of muffled engines. She's strapped into a narrow seat and her hands and feet are bound with cords. The uniform of the tall captain standing before her is crested. His boots are dark brown and brightly polished. The spurs are studded with jewels. In his right hand is a riding crop with a large gold knob.

"Who are you?" he demands.

She declines to answer and shuts her eyes at the approach of the crop.

The blow raises a searing welt across her cheek. She wills herself to find a mental pathway beyond the pain, but the agony from the lash is too great, her fear too overwhelming. Tears escape from the corners of her eyes.

The captain kneels before her and begins to unbutton her dress—a seemingly never-ending row of buttons—and then slides the bodice over her shoulders and onto her lap. He places his hands on her breasts, her white camisole the only barrier between his flesh and hers. "You're lost. Tell me who you are and I'll take you home."

Her mouth forms the answer but she is voiceless.

He removes his hands from her breasts and cups her face. "Tell me."

She tries again.

And again.

And again.

Soundless words—soundless words—soundless words.

Ann awakens with a start. The bedroom is pitch black. She sits up, turns on the bedside lamp, and peers at the jeweled dial of the small enameled clock on the nightstand. It's four thirty. She struggles to recall what she was dreaming before she awakened. Her body is tense and damp with perspiration and the walls of the room seem to be reverberating with the violent beating of her heart.

Ann and Maggie are having dinner at a newly opened bistro in Shockoe Bottom. No reservations accepted and the place is mobbed. Ann requests a booth, for which the wait seems interminable. Finally, the maître d' motions to them. Ann walks ahead of Maggie, her heels clicking determinedly on the ivory terra-cotta flooring. She is aware of Maggie's scrutiny of her—every aspect of her—hair, clothes, shoes, jewelry, her wedding band. She recalls a recent phone conversation during which she had reluctantly revealed to Maggie that Max and she were divorced. A lengthy silence had ensued followed by a snort and then Maggie had drawled "Whatever" and changed the subject.

Ann scans the menu and decides on crab cake with raspberry and lime rémoulade. Maggie orders a New York strip, well done, and a baked potato with chives and sour cream.

After the waiter brings Ann's Beaujolais and Maggie's double Manhattan on the rocks, Maggie settles into the cushioned back of the booth.

"Well?"

"Well what?"

"Have you been thinking about me?"

"Actually, I have, but in an abstract way."

"What have you been abstractly thinking?"

"That consciousness is distinct from the organism it occupies, but must undergo its vicissitudes."

Maggie shrugs. "A highly stylized art deco way of obscuring the obvious. What are you abstractly trying to say?"

"That I don't know you at all, Maggie…"

"I have every intention of remedying that, Ann. I'm just waiting for your acceptance."

"Don't do that."

"Don't do what?"

"What you're doing."

"What's wrong, Ann? Why are you so uneasy tonight?"

Ann takes a swallow of wine before replying, "I don't know." She smooths a strand of hair behind an ear and looks around the dining area. Her eyes settle on a couple at a nearby table. They are talking animatedly. Relaxed. Flirtatious. Heterosexual. Her face reddens. "I feel like a child in the wrong sandbox," she says in a low voice.

"You're in my sandbox tonight. Does that make you uneasy?"

"Very uneasy."

"I wonder why."

"Perhaps it's because I sense that you have something you want to accomplish," she says and waits for a counterattack, but Maggie lets the remark pass without comment. She lights a cigarette and smokes in silence, observing Ann all the while. Ann endures the scrutiny until she can bear it no longer.

"What?"

Maggie's expression is a composite of wry comprehension and feline playfulness. "I was thinking," she muses, "that in some ways you're a mere snip of a girl, walking around in her mommy's high heels, but determined to be very different from her mommy for reasons she doesn't like to think or talk about."

Ann's fingers tighten around the stem of her wine glass. She looks at Maggie and then away.

"You're perturbed by what I said. Did I hit the nail on the head?"

"It may have contained a measure of truth but it was too ..." She searches for the source of her discomfort. "Too personal, perhaps."

"I wouldn't call that personal, Ann. I'd call saying that you're a sexually unfulfilled woman personal."

"Maggie, please!"

"We're only having a conversation, Ann. That is, unless you have something more personal in mind."

Ann shoots Maggie a look of barely contained animosity. "I'm beginning to think that having dinner with you wasn't a good idea."

"Why is sexuality such a taboo subject for you?"

Ann drains her glass of wine, catches their waiter's attention, and motions for another. She is aware of Maggie's relentless gaze but she waits for clarity before responding to Maggie's question. Finally, she clasps her hands together and looks up. "Maggie?"

"Yes, Ann?"

"Have you read the *Bhagavad Gita*?"

"Parts of it. Why do you ask?"

"It tells of a spiritual journey—the spiritual journey of Arjuna, a lover of God, guided by Krishna, an incarnation of God in human form. Krishna reminds Arjuna throughout the journey that all of life is clouded by desire." Ann gives a grateful nod to the waiter and takes a deep swallow of wine from the glass he places before her. She looks intently into Maggie's eyes. "Desire is never-ending and it's never the bottom line. Surely you know that."

"What I know," Maggie retorts, "is that desire is a necessary catalyst for the medium of human sexuality and what I *should* have known is that you'd come up with some ancient out-in-the-ozone-layer book like the *Bhagavad Gita* to back away from talking about sexuality."

"Well, I'm not going to back away from pointing out that sexuality is the wrong medium for you and me."

"Don't disparage that about which you know nothing."

Ann is spared a response by the appearance of their waiter with dinner. She eyes with pleasure the oversized red earthenware plate he places before her. The crab is succulent backfin, crisply golden brown, with no filler that she can detect. The raspberry sauce has been piped, spider-web fashion, around the periphery of the crab cake. Atop the crab cake is a spider with a raspberry head and body and caper eyes. She smiles at the young man, black tie, white pleated tux shirt, small gold hoop in left earlobe. "What a clever presentation!"

He smiles back and nods. "I'll pass it on to the chef."

"How's your steak?" she asks, glancing down at Maggie's plate.

"I'd have preferred a prosciutto and Damascus fig pizza with toasted pine nuts, seared red peppers and fontina cheese, but at least this less-than-tender cut of beef isn't lowing."

Ann eats several bites of the crab. It's tasty, as is the sautéed coleslaw with chunks of caramelized apple.

Maggie puts down her fork and pushes her plate aside. She has eaten none of the broccoli and less than half of the steak. "I recall your saying that you'd spent time in India. Why India?"

"I was ..." Ann pauses in thought. "No, I *had* a melancholy of spirit, or perhaps of mind, that belied the bounty of my life—two wonderful children, a successful marriage to a good husband and father, endearing friendships, a burgeoning business—" she sighs. "A seemingly perfect recipe for contentment, but I was plagued on a daily basis by a host of anxiety-laden questions that begged answers since the deaths, less than a year apart, of my father and Uncle Lawrence." She glances at Maggie. "Unanswered questions can be anguishing."

"What were the questions?"

"Oh, the usual imponderables—were the experiences of one's life random or not random? What happened after the spirit left the body? Was there life beyond the grave? Why was so much of life characterized by suffering? And, on a more narrowed-down level, had Uncle Lawrence reincarnated in human form as he thought he would or attained God-consciousness as he hoped he would? And, perhaps most pressing— would I ever again see my father?"

"Tell me again who Lord Meher was."

"He was a man of Persian descent who claimed to have achieved God-consciousness."

"God-consciousness? What exactly did Lord Meher mean by God-consciousness?"

"He meant that his state of consciousness and God's state of consciousness were one and the same."

"Nobody other than you, Ann, has, to my knowledge, ever heard of the man. How'd you find out about him?"

"From Uncle Lawrence, my mother's older brother and only sibling. Uncle Lawrence had been engaged to an actress who was interested in Eastern mysticism. She'd loaned Uncle Lawrence a book she'd been given by Stanley Kubrick, the movie director. It was entitled *God Speaks* and was written by a man living in India who called himself Lord Meher and claimed to have achieved God consciousness. After reading *God Speaks*, Uncle Lawrence traveled to India and met with Lord Meher. It was an experience that changed Uncle Lawrence irrevocably. He told me once— he and I were close—that in *God Speaks* he found understanding, and in India he found serenity."

"What was your uncle's profession?"

"Uncle Lawrence was a history professor. He died of lung cancer. I never saw him without his pipe."

"Where'd he teach?"

"Princeton. "

"And do you believe this Lord Meher was God in the same way that Christ was?"

"It's not a question of belief for me. The things Lord Meher has written and is reputed to have said feel true to me in the same way that the teachings of Christ feel true to me. Belief can be a barrier to truth."

"I don't see that. How can a belief be a barrier to truth?"

"By standing between us and the truth we want to know," Ann replies. She pauses in thought. "When we were children, we believed in Santa Claus and that belief blinded us to the impossibility of flying reindeer, a sleigh with endless gifts, and a bearded and rosy-cheeked old man who lived in the North Pole and traveled the globe every Christmas Eve to deliver those gifts to good little boys and girls."

"Yep," Maggie concedes. "Santa Claus remains one of the major heroes from my childhood but I must confess I'm starting to doubt." She lights a cigarette and settles back into the cushioned booth. "Tell me more about your trips to India."

"My first trip was with Max. We left for India two days after Thanksgiving and returned home two weeks before Christmas. The day after we returned, I became violently ill. It took a week for my body to mend but my mind remained out of kilter. I somehow managed to get through the endless round of parties, Christmas Eve dinner, Christmas Day brunch, New Year's Eve, our traditional New Year's Day open house, Edwin and Amory's holiday events, gift lists, grocery lists, Christmas card lists, Christmas caroling, midnight Mass, but I went through the events and tasks as if I were an actress playing an unfamiliar role and I attributed my altered state to what I had experienced in India ... a taste of ... I don't know ... perhaps a taste of God being as intimate as one's own breath. A taste of God existing within oneself." She places a finger to her temple, closes her eyes briefly. "Actually, I didn't understand what was happening to me. I knew only that I had to return to India and so, after Edwin and Amory were back in school, I closed the gallery for a month and arranged for Eleanor to come to Hampton and help Max and our housekeeper,

Hattie, with the children during my absence. I stayed for three weeks and, when I returned, the sensation of otherworldliness had greatly eased and the vibration in my head—it was akin to holding a conch shell next to one's ear—had dissipated."

Maggie lights another cigarette and leans forward. Her intense blue eyes bore into Ann's. "Why did you agree to have dinner with me tonight?"

The abruptness of the question takes Ann by surprise. "I find you to be intelligent, witty, very talented, and . . ." she returns Maggie's gaze, "I'd like for us to be friends."

"Please. I have too many friends already."

"What an impertinent thing to say."

Maggie nods. "I know it was and I apologize." She takes a puff from her cigarette, tilts her chin ever so slightly and floats, from softly rounded lips, a smoke ring that undulates above the table and lingers. "I've always believed," she reflects, pensive of voice and expression, "that there was someone who was a perfect fit for me exactly as I am and am content to be. I want to find out if you're that person." She looks at Ann intently. "I'm not casual about relationships. I was when I was younger and less particular. Now I wait. I watch. I listen. I invariably say 'no.' You're the exception, Ann."

"Why me?"

"Partly because of your physical beauty. I won't deny that," she acknowledges and leans forward, elbows on the table, hands folded. "You have a marvelous gait, you're high-spirited, you possess a keen head for business, and your art gallery is outstanding." She reaches for her cigarette, taps the long ash into the logoed metal ashtray and inhales deeply. "Not to mention that you're a genuine class act, forgive the wordplay."

"Please," Ann demurs, "no more flattery."

"I've barely begun."

"No more," Ann insists.

"But I haven't told you how much I enjoy the way you think and express your thoughts, your sense of humor, the elegant width of your amazingly unlined forehead, your amusing slacks, your finely arched feet in their trendy little slingbacks. The way you walk in those slingbacks." Maggie's face melts. "You're adorable, Ann. Absolutely adorable."

"What's amusing about my slacks?"

Maggie's smile widens. "I knew that would be your first question."

"Just tell me what's amusing about my slacks."

"Well, you wear them a little too large for your body, which makes them flap when you pace the gallery showroom. And then there's your adorable pacing. I could write a villanelle about that."

"You pay attention to everything."

"No, Ann, I pay attention to you."

"Quite frankly, I would prefer moderate admiration," Ann replies. "It's less discomfiting."

"Admiration's a waste of time," Maggie says dismissively. She motions to their waiter for the check.

"Why is admiration a waste of time?"

"Because it's a substitute for the real thing."

"Which is?"

"Love, of course."

"Perhaps admiration is a precursor to love."

"Whatever." Maggie stares into Ann's eyes. "Are you involved with someone?"

Ann shrugs, "Yes and no—more no than yes."

"More no than yes? What the hell does that mean?"

"It means, Maggie, that 'involved' encompasses too many possibilities to give a casual yes or no answer."

"I'll narrow it down. Are you in love?"

"No."

"You should wait for love."

"Wait for love? What the hell does *that* mean?"

Maggie stands up, dinner check in hand. "I can't tell you how much this evening has meant to me." She touches the side of Ann's hand delicately, with her index finger. "Goodnight, dearest," she murmurs and then turns and walks away.

Ann shakes her head ruefully at Maggie's unexpected departure, catches her lower lip between her teeth. She had intended to call George before driving back to Hampton, but she knows now that she won't. "Damn," she murmurs, "damn." She's not ever going to spend time with that woman again. She'll simply handle her by telephone or let Eleanor deal with her.

Ann awakens to the telephone. Only George would call this early and let it ring six trillion times. She decides not to answer, then abruptly reaches for the receiver. "Yes?"

"Good morning, darling."

"Good morning, George."

"I waited for you to call me last night," he tells her, "and when I finally called you, several times, the line was busy."

"I'm sorry," she replies, "I had intended to call you but I was too exhausted. I called home and spoke with Edwin, who complained about the sheer length of Amory's phone conversations with one of her totally ignoramus friends, and then I spoke with Amory, who complained about the ever-increasing volume of Edwin's never-ending and totally gross Madonna albums, and then I got the straight dope from Hattie, who also informed me that Belle had brought a live baby possum in through the doggie door and chucked it in the dogs' toy box from whence Edwin, heavily gloved, cautiously retrieved it, carried it hurriedly outside and then released it into the boxwood maze. After I hung up from that phone call, I took a hot shower, brushed my teeth, and went to bed."

"We need a long cruise on the *Queen Mary*." His whispery tone of voice suggests clandestine days and nights of endless duration.

"Sure, George. I'll put the children in an orphanage and the gallery on hold while we sail the seven seas."

"Charming response. I must have called too early."

"You always call too early."

"What's wrong, Ann?"

"Nothing."

"You're not yourself this morning."

"Oh? Who am I, then?"

"A prizefighter looking for a contender?" The laugh he hopes to elicit is not forthcoming. He exhales audibly. "Well, am I going to see you today?"

"Not with that tone of voice."

George's voice coarsens. "I'm going out to get some breakfast. Call me back when you're feeling better."

"I feel better now."

"Will you call me later, Ann?"

"You can call back if you want to talk to me."

"I don't enjoy talking to you when you're like this."

"Then don't call back."

He heaves another sigh and tries again. "You realize that you're purposely trying to pick a fight, don't you?"

"What I realize, George, is how relentlessly you bear down on me when I'm out of sorts."

"So you admit you're in a bad mood!"

"No, George. I'm not in a bad mood. At least I wasn't until I answered your phone call."

"Jesus H. Christ. I'm going out for breakfast!" he shouts and hangs up.

Ann throws the receiver on the nightstand, gets out of bed, and begins to pace the long span of bedroom, hands behind her back, fingers intertwined. She acknowledges that it's the energy of her racing thoughts that propels her in such a driven manner and tries to quiet her mind by chanting the attributes of God.

God the Compassionate—God the All-knowing—God the Eternal—God the Beloved—and her favorite—God the Obscure—obscure meaning hidden, deficient in light, not easily understood, remote. She knows because she'd looked the definition up the first time she'd heard the phrase chanted as an attribute of God.

In the Name of God the Obscure.

Memory transports her to India. She sits on the edge of her canopied bed and tries to remember what had elicited such serenity during her stay in India and when she remembers, she cries.

APRIL 1987

"It is the quality of our sins which sets us apart."

from *A Price Above Rubies*

A spill of late afternoon sunlight dapples the Hampton River, casting pools of golden amber upon its calm surface. Ann stands beneath the branches of a huge gnarled magnolia and watches the dogs scour the foot-high ivy beneath it in an attempt to sniff out the ancient resident tortoise she has just released into the safety of its dense foliage. She shrieks with laughter as Belle's elegant long snout tunnels furiously through the undergrowth, while Liza, who is as tiny as Belle is huge, stalks the border of periwinkle that encircles the tree's expansive drip line.

It's been weeks since she last set foot in Richmond. Her departing phone call to George was perfunctory. His rage and ensuing hurt were no surprise. He has called several times since, but he is disadvantaged by her remoteness. She won't fight with him and he longs for a fight—for anything that will assuage his misery over her absence.

Ann endures George's calls because she can't rationalize refusing them. But she doesn't miss him. She's content with the children, the dogs, and the river.

"How are you spending your evenings?" he asked plaintively the last time he telephoned.

"Contentedly," she replied and he snorted contempt at her insensitivity.

"Is it over?"

"Is what over, George?"

"Us, Ann. You and I. We. Us."

"I'm taking some much-needed time away from the gallery. You seem to have completely forgotten Edwin and Amory. Children need more than a housekeeper and each other. They love it that I'm here."

"Well, I damn well don't love it. It's been three weeks, for godssake! How much more time do you need?"

"I don't know."

"Are you ever coming back?"

"Eventually."

"Are you coming up this week?"

"No."

"Well, when?"

"I don't know. I'm sorry to be so indefinite, but I just don't know what to tell you."

"Just tell me this, Ann. Do I need to find someone else to be in love with?"

"That's entirely up to you, George." She had answered icily, so icily that he roared impotent outrage.

"Damn it, Ann, what in hell is wrong with you?"

And then Ann had disconnected the line and left the receiver off the hook where it remained until Hattie replaced it the next morning.

She glances at the square dial of her Piaget. Max should be along any minute now. He had cancelled his last two afternoon appointments so that he and Amory could watch Edwin's final soccer game of the season— Amory and her current best friend, Joan Boatwright, a skinny, freckle-faced carrot-topped minx with impeccable brashness, a mouthful of braces, and eyes the color and shape of copper pennies.

"Mommy," Amory asked at breakfast this morning, "guess what caption we're putting under Joan's yearbook picture."

"Veni. Vidi. Vici," Ann replied, deadpan.

Edwin had lifted his face from his bowl of Raisin Bran and leered knowingly. "That means 'I came, I saw, I conquered,' runt."

"Spare me your superiority, utero head. It's what Julius Caesar said after he conquered Gaul, most totally stupido brother."

"Don't call your sister a runt, Edwin, and utero head and stupido are vulgar, Amory," Ann admonished. "What caption's going under Joan's yearbook picture?"

"I suggest 'Keep your nose to the grindstone, twit—it might improve your looks,'" Edwin chortled and then provided his sister with a gaping-mouthful-of-cereal leer.

"Mommy, make him stop!"

"Stop it, Edwin, leave some for others."

But, in spite of Ann's admonishments, Edwin and Amory's mutually hurled and frequently humorous barbs had continued throughout breakfast and carpool. Ann had been everlastingly grateful when her beloved progeny exited the station wagon, mere seconds before the school bell sounded. Joan, waiting for Amory at the curb, had flashed Edwin an adoring metal-laden smile, giggled, and whispered something that sent Amory into peals of girlish laughter.

Ann looks at her wristwatch again. Six o'clock—the day gone in a blur of morning garden club, lunch, and afternoon bridge. "Come on, girls. Let's go inside." The dogs follow her obediently to the double doors of the sunroom, but she doesn't go inside after all. She sits instead on the cool brick steps and waits for Max and the children to arrive.

Belle waits beside her, ears pricked in anticipation. Ann is not the only one who looks forward to Max's visits. Belle begins to howl before the tires of his BMW reach the driveway. Max's favorite ploy is to chase Belle around the magnolia relentlessly until she comes to an abrupt halt and collapses onto the soft mossy lawn in a stupor of exhaustion. Occasionally he trots Belle down to the yacht club to fraternize with the Thursday night Rotary Club boys. One night he returned Belle home slightly tipsy. She had lapped beer with the best of them. Ann hadn't thought it amusing but Max did. He flashed his MD badge of authority to override Ann's concern that Belle might get sick and he alluded to his being a Jungian psychoanalyst to highlight the futility of Ann's trying to monitor his relationship with Belle, a creature that he, in point of fact, had given Ann. That particular dialogue culminated in a particularly unpleasant finale to what began as light-hearted banter.

Taking a stance against Max is always fraught with tension, she muses. Had she ever succeeded in persuading him to her point of view? No. His was an aura of one invariably certain that his was the more enlightened perception— the nobler intent—an aura that many women found tantalizing. It intrigues Ann that, in spite of the availability of several appealing Mrs. Maxwell Cabot wannabees, Max insists he will never marry again. "How could I ever find anyone to compare to you?" he teased, in a happier conversation. He remains coolly indifferent to Ann's relationship with George, whom he refers to as "Wile E. Coyote." "You'll never marry George. We both know that."

"Why won't I?" It was a question she didn't really want to ask but she was curious to hear his answer.

"Because you couldn't respect someone who's beneath you in spiritual awareness."

That pronouncement had laid the foundation for Ann's dismissal of George as a serious contender. Oh, yes, Max was a savvy opponent in that he seldom struck, but when he did, the blow was lethal.

She hears the dull clink of the wrought iron gates being unlatched and looks up. Max is heading down the brick walk that leads to the river. He catches sight of her and waves. She waves back. Belle has already overtaken Max and has her huge forepaws on his shoulders. Max chuckles and strokes her fondly, then reaches down and pets Liza. He walks over to where Ann is sitting and kisses her cheek. "I dropped the children off at the yacht club. They'll walk home after supper. Edwin's celebrating the defeat of St. Alban's with some of his team members and Amory wanted to see the Wednesday night regatta come in. I told them no later than eight thirty. How wonderful you look! How are you?" Only the tiniest flickering back and forth of his eyes reveals his scrutiny.

"I'm fine."

"And how are things at the gallery?"

"Things are fine at the gallery."

"Where's Wile E. Coyote these days?"

"Busily engaging in legal debate at the Richmond halls of justice, I would imagine."

"Who's managing the gallery during your absence?"

"Eleanor and Brandon."

"The uptight and the uppity."

"Eleanor's cautious if that's what you mean by uptight, and I'd call Brandon upscale rather than uppity," Ann retorts crisply. "Eleanor's a natural. The clients adore her."

"They accept Eleanor. They adore *you*."

"You're wrong, but thanks for the compliment."

"Let me give you another. You're lovelier than ever. With your hair pulled back in a ponytail the way you're wearing it now and with no lipstick and barelegged." He touches her cheek. "You look just like Amory, and not a day older. How in the world I managed to outmaneuver those persistent young swains vying for your affection, I'll never know. I've often wondered why you decided to give your hand in marriage to me."

She captures his eyes with hers. "Don't you know?"

"Well—" He teases a smile. "You said I was the first man you'd met who was more intelligent than you."

"I don't recall saying that. Perhaps I said *as* intelligent." She grins. "I'll bet you can't remember the first real fight we had."

"I can give it to you in one word. 'Parsimonious.'"

She had used the word incorrectly. She thought it meant eclectic. Max had told her that it meant excessively frugal. She had refused to admit her error and they had ended up scrabbling like caged animals in her father's library.

Well, yes, she had shrugged, of course it meant frugal, but it could also mean eclectic in the sense that if one were frugal there was a certain eclectic quality of character involved in being so tight-fisted. Anyone with a drop of intelligence could see that.

After Max had gone to the dictionary, located the word, and read the definition aloud to her several times, she had marched over to where he was standing and sent the dictionary crashing to the floor—so forcefully that the base of the stand splintered and the book's spine separated from its leather binding. And that was when she'd slapped Max and he returned the favor.

"Admit you were wrong about the damn word," he ordered, low and contemptuous of voice, twisted of mouth, red in the face. "Pick up that beautiful mahogany stand you deliberately damaged and that vintage dictionary your father's so proud of and let's move on to something else, you spoiled brat."

"Pick it up yourself. Move on wherever you wish. Why should I give a damn about someone too benighted to see the point I was making about 'parsimonious'? God, how I loathe you, you parsimonious prick!" And then she burst into laughter. And then she burst into tears.

Ann looks up. Max is watching her intently.

"So tell me," he asks her, "how did I wean you away from your other suitors?"

She tilts her head and considers the question. "Smoothly and with the appearance of ... of not really caring if you lost me." A knot of anxiety forms but she tamps it down, beneath conscious thought and away from his all-seeing gaze.

"Hmmm." Max nods self-approval. "How astute of me."

"Why astute?"

"Because you would have become indifferent in proportion to my caring."

"That isn't true!" she protests. "I was in love."

"Ah yes. Love!" His eyes narrow. "We mustn't forget your broken vow of eternal love."

Ann is taken aback by the suddenness of his attack. "Should we forget your broken vow to forsake all others?" she rallies.

He scans her face before replying. "We should *forgive* it because 'though truth and love can never really differ, when they seem to, the subaltern should be truth.'"

Her eyes glint. "How predictable of you to justify what you did with a scrap of ambiguous poetic subterfuge."

"Truth doesn't require justification, Ann, and Auden's assessment of truth and love isn't a subterfuge."

The condescension in his voice infuriates her. She regards him with disdain. "The subterfuge is not in what Auden so eloquently states, Max, but in your misappropriation of his prose to support the insincerity of your behavior. You handled me instead of—" She pauses in thought. "Instead of just—well, just being in love. Do you understand?"

Max retrieves a well-worn soccer ball, half hidden in the ivy, and kicks it toward Belle, who takes off in rapid pursuit, with Liza following behind as quickly as her stubby legs will permit. "I understand that you think depth of feeling should be measured by behavior, much of which is contrived," he counters. "Feigned indifference is part of the mating ritual. The animal kingdom does it. Birds and insects do it. It's too obvious to debate."

"I certainly never pretended indifference to you," Ann scoffs.

"You didn't need to. I feigned indifference because it heightened your infatuation with me, a suitor older than those crew-necked college lads jockeying for your attention."

"I was not infatuated." She levels the word at him in syllables. "I was in love. You were insincere."

"I was more sincere than you in that I married the person I sincerely wanted whereas you didn't sincerely want the person you married."

"Oh. I see. And I guess you think that's why you were unfaithful and why I ..." She can't bring herself to finish the sentence.

"Why you divorced me?" His eyes darken. "So tell me, Ann, now that you've divorced me—did it get Daddy's little girl what she wanted?"

"The dissolution of our marriage was never what I wanted," Ann replies.

She turns away from him and walks down the path that leads to the old greenhouse. Max's rejoinder was a lancet of finely honed steel—a shaft of piercing sunlight. It blinded as it drew blood. She glances back at him. He's watching Belle bound after the soccer ball—completely unconcerned—carefree in the moment. Her anger wanes at the sight of him, tie and jacket tossed heedlessly onto the lawn, shirtsleeves rolled, cavorting with the dogs.

He's a child—a beautiful, nobly browed child. Why can't it be enough for me that I'm a part of what he loves?

But, even as her heart softens, her mind gives vent to avenues of retribution.

Maggie sounds surprised to hear Ann's voice on the other end of the line.

"Why are you in Hampton?"

"I live in Hampton, remember? The Richmond house is merely a business convenience."

"It's hard to visualize you lifting crab pots and sailing a Hampton 1 in those weekly Wednesday regattas. I mean, really, Ann." Maggie's voice drips drawl. "Hampton is downright provincial, not to mention redneck."

"It's a wonderful old city—the oldest continuously English-speaking settlement in America. I'll bet you didn't know that."

"Didn't know and don't care to know."

"You must be smoking. I just heard a match being struck."

"I boost Virginia Slims sales by one carton a week." Maggie exhales into the receiver. "But enough about me—tell me something fascinating about that son you dote on."

"Edwin scored the winning goal this afternoon. It was the last game of the season. His teammates carried him off the soccer field on their shoulders."

"Marvelous! What position does he play?"

"Center forward. He's rather aggressive. Lots of fouls."

"I'm big on fouls as a defense strategy," Maggie states. "'If your enemy is superior, invade him.' From *The Art of War.*" She clears her throat. "What about little Amory? What blood sport does little Amory play?" She gives Amory's name three musically distinct syllables.

"Little Amory," Ann answers, "is into telephone sport these days."

Ann's last phone bill listed forty-four charges for star-sixty-nine, all stemming from one Saturday. It didn't take her long to figure out it was the Saturday night of Amory's slumber party. She laid down the law to Amory, who then blamed Joan Boatwright for most of the redials. Ann was firm. "I don't want you calling boys on the telephone, Amory. It's tacky and you'll get a reputation for being boy-crazy."

"But all of my friends do it, Mommy."

"I don't care what your friends do. It's in bad taste and you may tell Joan I said so. Not to mention that it added more than twenty dollars to the phone bill. Why in the world did you call star-sixty-nine so many times?"

"Because," Amory replied in a tone that suggested Ann was clearly daft, "Robby and Baxter kept calling and then hanging up when we answered."

Maggie interrupts her reverie. "Are you still there?"

"Yes, I'm still here."

Maggie's voice drops a decibel. "I want to see you. When are you coming to Richmond?"

"I don't know for sure," Ann replies.

"For *sure?*" Maggie mocks.

"I *might* come up tomorrow."

"*Might* come? What the hell does that mean?"

"Don't curse."

"Why the hell not?"

"Because it's in bad taste."

"Forgive me. I didn't realize I had Emily Post on the line." Maggie's voice softens. "I've been thinking about you a lot, Ann."

"All good things, I hope."

"Only good things. Now, when are you coming to Richmond?"

"I'll come tomorrow. Would you like to come by the gallery for a cup of coffee?"

"I'd rather you came to my studio."

Ann's throat tightens. She means to say that she can't, but the image of Max indifferently cavorting with the dogs rears its head. "What time should I come by?"

"What's the earliest you can manage?"

Ann computes. Breakfast, the children off to school, a few errands, half a dozen phone calls. "I can be there by two."

"I'll see you at two then."

"All right," Ann confirms and disconnects the line. She leans back in the desk chair and gazes through the bay window at the undulating blackness of the water, partially obscured from view by a massive

Southern live oak, whose lowest thickset branch trails the river at high tide.

As a child, she had relished the thrill of play coupled with danger. Her two-wheeler without hands. The high-diving board at the club before she knew how to swim. The most difficult mount at Blaise Summerhill's Riding Academy.

"Give Gibraltar to Ann. She can handle Gibraltar!"

And she could, too. She would nudge Gibraltar on, beyond the restrained gallop—the fear of falling outweighed by the exhilarating rush of wind filling her lungs, whistling past her ears.

After the ride, after Miss Summerhill's gentle scolding for Ann's recklessness and Gibraltar's lather, Ann would croon to Gibraltar while she rubbed him down. She would murmur his name and stroke his corded neck and Gibraltar would turn his head and nuzzle Ann's mantle of damp and tangled hair, nibble her earlobes with his fleshy lips, paw the ground, shake his mane and let loose a low and tender nicker of longing—of affinity.

The memory elicits a respondent affinity in Ann. She stands, pushes back the heavy desk chair, switches off the lamps and chandelier, walks into the hallway, and peers into the sunroom. Belle and Liza are sleeping side by side on the tiled floor.

She removes her sandals and tiptoes soundlessly past them, opens the sunroom doors, and steps outside. The night air is deliciously cool, the lap of waves against the seawall rhythmic and familiar. A sudden ruffle of wind sets the newly arrived fireflies into a flurry of motion. They randomly flicker, disappear, and then flicker again—tiny flashing lanterns of soon-to-be summer—tiny helter-skelter beacons of cautionary yellow in an unfamiliar sky.

Maggie has unlocked the front entrance gates and is waiting outside when Ann pulls up.

"Are you invariably late?" she asks with a wry smile.

"I was two weeks late getting myself born," Ann retorts, "and even then I had to be induced." She does a double take at the heavy iron bars on every window and door. "This place is like Fort Knox."

"Lots of museum acquisitions have spent time here. You'd be surprised at what the insurance on them costs. Those bars lower my premium." Maggie eyes Ann appreciatively. "Nice jacket."

"Armani."

"Classy."

"Thanks."

"What may I get you to drink?"

Ann considers coffee but decides against it. She has a notion that Maggie knows nothing about brewing decent coffee. "I'll have a glass of water," she replies. "And no ice," she adds.

"Now that surprises me. I'd have figured you for ice."

"Are you going to get my water or stand here jibing about how I drink it?"

"I beg your pardon?"

"Forgive me. I'm out of sorts today. "

Maggie eyes her curiously. "Why would that be?"

"I couldn't get to sleep last night. Sleep deprivation makes me as tense as a coiled snake."

"Maybe you can uncoil while I'm getting your water without ice. I've got to make a phone call, so have a look around. There's lots of interesting art here. The John Singer Sargent belongs to the Chrysler."

Ann explores the studio with frank curiosity—an expansive double-storied room with two sets of copper washtubs sporting tall brass gooseneck faucets. The side of the room that faces the street has four morning-light-bearing windows with wrought iron grills on the inside that unlock and swing into the room. Although they have a Gothic handsomeness, they impart a cell-like quality to the massive space. She counts three seventeenth-century refractory tables, upon which rest an assortment of dental tools, apothecary jars filled with multicolored solvents, rolls of cotton, various-sized brushes, and paint knives. One of the room's brick walls is covered with framed newspaper clippings, yellowed and curled-with-age photographs, theater and concert playbills, cleverly matted cartoons, antique padlocks with keys, steel and copper engraving plates, roulette wheels of various sizes—an eclectic assemblage of handsomely displayed memorabilia. The studio floor appears to be smoothly worn cement, painted forest green and heavily lacquered, with a large brass drain in its center. The several pieces of furniture scattered about are oversized and inviting, including a pair of nineteenth-century, polished-steel, campaign daybeds with crimson, yellow, and black plaid cushions. There are numerous floor lamps, several with multi-colored glass shades, and, as Maggie promised, an abundance of artwork – oils, watercolors, gouaches, etchings—on the walls, on display easels and in numerous antique folio stands.

Her gaze settles on a large canvas in an egg-and-dart gilt frame. The painting, early nineteenth century, is of a mother and child. The similarity of their faces is subtle but distinct; their features and attire are precisely rendered. They are looking, not at each other, but into an unknown vista—intent of expression—mother and child physically so close as to be one flesh, but their proximity, notwithstanding the child's hand resting possessively on the full roundness of her mother's breast, exudes an impersonal quality. The brass plaque on the frame reads, "Lady Cornelia and daughter Isabella."

Maggie returns with a tumbler of water. "Drink your water and then we're leaving."

"Where are we going?"

"To visit a friend."

"Who is it?"

"John Brooks Archer. He's one of the finest behind-the-scenes restoration artists on the East Coast. I've known him for years. He has a horse farm in Hanover. I know how much you love horses. You'll enjoy it."

"Is he expecting us?"

"I told him I might bring you by."

Ann hesitates. "Well, all right, but I'll drive."

"How come?"

"Because I prefer to?"

"What if I prefer to?"

She shrugs. "Then I'll drive with you."

Maggie gives her a probing look, then her startling blue eyes resume their normal opacity. "No, it's fine. You can drive. Do you want more water?"

Ann drains the glass and places it on a Henry VIII coaster—from a boxed set of eight—the six wives plus Henry and his daughter Elizabeth. The museum gift shop carried them and Ann purchased a set for her father-in-law. "I believe everyone I know owns a set of these overpriced Anglophile coasters," she comments.

Maggie emits a low whistle. "You *are* out of sorts today. What kept you awake last night?"

"I thought you'd never ask." She walks to the door, keys in hand. "Come on. I want to see those horses."

"I'm right behind you, but you didn't answer my question, Ann."

"And if you're going to smoke in the car," she snaps, "open the vent window."

The farm is a tucked-away, three-hundred-acre site in the heart of Hanover County. The macadam entrance, more than half a mile in length, terminates in a circular drive before a freshly painted white clapboard farmhouse of considerable size. Ann assesses its age to be late eighteenth century. Several hounds gather around the station wagon. They're happy to see Maggie and curious about Ann.

"Gracie, Chowder, and Fred. Meet my bravest friend, Ann."

"Why bravest?"

"It's in proportion to your anxiety."

"What's the proportion of my anxiety?"

"Significant."

"And how would you know that?"

"In so many ways."

"Name one."

"The way you drove your car."

"Whatever do you mean?"

Maggie shakes her head, her eyelids shudder closed. "That geezer in overalls, who was jaywalking up and down Broad Street for donations, tossed his money cup, jackknifed onto the curb, and then presented you with a finger gesture of tribute befitting the experience of that amazing right-hand turn."

Ann bursts into laughter. "Why in the world would he do something so vulgar?"

"Hey," Maggie shrugs incredulity, "a trio of Jehovah's Witnesses gave the man the high-five sign and some ninny with 'God is Love' tattooed on her forearm further endorsed the gesture by giving it to you with both hands. Folks have no regard for a pricey Mercedes wagon these days." She arches an eyebrow at Ann. "I assume you saw me gripping the burled-walnut and hand-stitched leather dashboard with my teeth."

"Of course I didn't," Ann retorts. "I was intent upon my driving, which got us here safely and surely in record time—those two factors being the reasons for the purchase of that pricey station wagon, in point of fact."

"Whatever," Maggie answers and directs Ann toward a weathered stone path that leads to a large barn. "This is where we'll most likely find John." Her voice is, as always, Deep South hauteur.

Ann looks at Maggie sideways. "What have you told John about me?"

Maggie claps her hands. "Chowder, get out of your owner's prized English boxwood. You know better!" The dog, old and heavy, pays no attention. Maggie saunters over and takes hold of his collar. "I told him that you are beautiful, intelligent, and affluent."

"What else did you tell him?"

"What else did you have in mind?"

"Nothing in particular."

"He knows I'm taken with you."

"You told him that?"

"He knows by my bringing you here."

"You and he must be close." Ann feels a wash of relief. She looks at Maggie covertly. The planes of her face, vivid in the sunlight, highlight a high-cheekbone attractiveness that men would find compelling. She adjusts her sunglasses higher on the bridge of her nose and examines Maggie's features more carefully.

"What's going through that energetic little mind of yours?" Maggie teases.

"I was wondering if you and John were ever romantically involved," Ann confesses.

"Yes, dearest, we were."

"What changed it?"

"It's a long story and John's around somewhere."

"I'm glad that you and John had a relationship."

"I thought you might be."

"Why would you think that?"

"Because it's reassuring to you."

Ann acknowledges the insight without protest. Why deny truth, even when it is unfavorably self-revealing? Or is it unfavorable that she would not want Maggie to be ... her mind tamps down before the rest of the thought swings into play. It's a thing she's not willing to name. Her eyes darken with pain.

Maggie reaches over and touches Ann's hand lightly with her index finger. "What are you thinking now?"

"I'm thinking that you're very knowing."

"Do you like that?"

"I do like it."

"A similar strain of soul thing between us?"

"Well, in point of ... well ... yes."

"What a guarded little creature you are," Maggie murmurs. "Here's John now."

Sitting beneath a copse of pecan trees, beside the barn—Venetian red and original to the house—Ann has ample opportunity to examine John Brooks Archer. He is patrician of feature, tall and angular of frame. He's wearing jeans, a navy turtleneck, and a pair of seriously worn riding boots. He's as attentive to Maggie as she is indifferent to him. They have similar mannerisms. They walk at the same languid pace and speak with similar easy drawls. They could be brother and sister except that anyone can see that John's in love with Maggie.

John interrupts her thoughts. "I'm wondering if you'd like to saddle up one of my horses and ride, Ann."

"I'd like to very much," she says and glances down at her slacks. The linen is durable. Her jacket is perfect. Her flats will just have to do. "You're not going to insist I wear a riding helmet, are you?"

"Of course he is," Maggie retorts.

John stands up and motions to Ann. "Saddle or bareback?"

"English," Ann replies.

"Ann," Maggie interjects and shakes her head no, "are you sure you want to ride today?"

"Of course I am." She rises from her chair and follows John into the barn.

He stops at the third stall and looks in. "I think you'll be safe with Missy. She's a sweetheart."

"Oh, safe is not a problem for me," Ann tells him. She gazes into an adjacent stall. A magnificent dark-brown steed, easily seventeen hands high, is munching hay. He tosses his head and whinnies, then gazes insouciantly at Ann. "What about this glorious creature?" she asks John.

"Balthazar's a favorite of mine but he's a bolter, easily spooked and not always polite when being reined in."

"I like the challenge of an unexpected bolt. Don't we all?" She reaches over the stall gate and gently strokes the side of Balthazar's strong neck.

"Are you a seasoned rider?"

"Since I was six, so there's no need for a saddle. That was to appease Maggie. I'm a natural and I adore riding bareback. I'll be cautious."

John unlatches the gate of Balthazar's stall and steps inside. "Well, young fellow, it seems this is your lucky day. This lovely creature is Ann. Remember that you're a Hanoverian and treat Ann like the lady she is." He attaches the reins to Balthazar's bridle and escorts him out of the stall. "You need a helmet," he reminds Ann. "There are several hanging in the tack room."

"I'd rather not. I don't plan on taking any jumps or falls."

"I think you should, but it's your call," he replies impassively.

He cups his hands and assists her to mount. When he passes over the reins, their eyes lock briefly and Ann gets a hint of the intensity of John Brooks Archer.

"Enjoy your ride," he says quietly.

"Oh, I surely will, John, thank you." She urges Balthazar into a restrained trot, past Maggie, still sitting at the iron filigree table, teacup in hand. John walks up behind her and rests his hands on her shoulders. She can feel their gaze upon her and the sensation is unsettling. Balthazar accelerates into a canter, through the open pasture and then across a span of broad acreage bordered by a dense expanse of uncleared land, through which, almost dead center, she spies the wide pathway Balthazar seems intent upon reaching. She considers tightening the reins to slow down his gait. Her attire mandates it, she has no helmet, no boots, and no saddle and she knows nothing of the path, which is somewhat shrouded by a thick overhang of variegated foliage. But she can't bring herself to rein in. She leans forward, loosens her grip upon the reins, tightens her thighs and calves against Balthazar's barrel and then wraps her arms around his neck, her face pressed so firmly against his dampening flesh that horse and rider appear to be one.

She does not see the porcupine, traversing the path a few yards ahead, until Balthazar rears up and slightly back, but by then it's too late. She's lost her grip and her balance. She's going to take a fall. The fear wells up but she moves beyond the fear, relaxes her body, releases the reins and rolls quickly to the rear and off. The ground takes her hard. Tears of shock spill onto her cheeks, her lungs empty of air in a painful exhale, and she loses consciousness.

She awakens to footsteps followed by the sound of a key being turned in a lock. The captain enters the cell. He gazes at her solicitously. "Ah! You're awake. Good. Don't be afraid. You're fine. You weren't injured by your fall."

She sits up. "No, not injured at all." The heavy woolen blanket on the cot is hot and scratchy against her bare legs. "Why am I here?" she asks.

"You must answer that question for yourself, but for now you need to wake up."

She struggles to remember why she is here. "I am here because I was—" She gasps for breath. "Because I was taken unguarded of this hard ground and—" She tries to open her eyes. "There were blinking yellow caution lights on the horizon because this way is forbidden ... only I forget why," she murmurs.

The ground air feels cool, but the glittering prisms of light piercing the umbrella of emerald are blinding her. She tries to remove the painfully tight helmet from her throbbing head, but there is no helmet after all, only an amber-colored ivory pointer with a bejeweled gold sovereign handle. Yes—there it is—tucked away smack in the middle of Grandmummy's best parasol collection. She reaches out for it, but now she's gone blind again. She gives a yelp of fear.

"You're safe," he tells her, "only open your eyes, open your eyes open your eyes ..."

Ann opens her eyes. John is kneeling beside her, his face full of worry. "You took a hard spill," he says in a low voice.

"Not too hard," Ann replies gamely and sits up, the weight of her torso supported by both elbows.

"You little fool!" Maggie comes up behind John. Her eyes are wild with fear. And fury. "Who the hell taught you to ride like that?"

"I'm sorry."

"Tell it to Balthazar."

"Stop it, Maggie," John says calmly. "Balthazar's fine."

"No thanks to Ann!"

"I'm sorry," Ann repeats.

"As well you should be." Maggie looks Ann over apprehensively. "Can you get up?"

Ann struggles to her feet. Her head is throbbing and her side hurts, but she's not about to show it. She takes several steps, her gait measured but steady.

"Let's go up to the main house and drink some whiskey," John suggests.

"I'm taking Ann home, John, before she gets into any more trouble."

He doesn't protest. The three of them walk back to Ann's station wagon in silence. The dogs are nowhere to be seen.

"Do you want me to drive?" Maggie asks.

"No. I'm fine."

John extends his hand to Ann. She takes it gratefully.

"I hope you'll come again."

"Thank you."

He opens the car door. "Next time we'll ride together."

"I'm sure you'll not want me near your horses again."

"Don't be silly."

Maggie snorts. "She's not silly. She's fucked in the head."

The outrageousness of Maggie's insult dissolves the tension and the three of them burst into hysterical laughter that escalates, dies down, and begins again.

Ann steals a glance at Maggie.

The anger is gone from Maggie's eyes but the reprimand remains.

Ann stops the car in front of Maggie's studio.

"Park here," Maggie directs. "The city and I have an arrangement. It's a 'no parking, loading zone' for everyone but me and just for now you get to be me." She allows a tiny play of a smile before her profile settles into its ritual inscrutability. She lights a cigarette and holds it out to Ann.

"No, thank you."

"Take it, Ann."

"I don't like to smoke in cars."

"Why don't you?"

"I just don't." But she takes a puff anyway and hands it back. "This cigarette is overwhelmingly mentholated."

"Are you really all right? Are you hurting anywhere?"

"I'm fine, Maggie, and I can't stay because the children are expecting me tonight. But, I want to ask you something before I go and—"

"And what?"

"And please don't say it's none of my business."

"What do you want to know?"

"What went wrong between you and John?"

"Why do you want to know that?"

"I don't know why. Only that I do."

"It's personal, Ann—something personal between John and me. If you press me about such matters I'll do the same with you."

"I realize that."

"He revealed a flaw in his character that I couldn't get past."

"What was it?"

Maggie regards Ann as if she were taking the measure of her soul. Her face grows hard in recollection. "He struck a filly with his fist—so viciously that..." She exhales a pain-laden sigh. "So viciously that I have yet to completely forgive him for it." She takes a long drag from her cigarette, opens the window, and exhales the smoke into the air. "I shrieked bloody murder and burst out crying. And then I made a fist and hit him as hard as I could—school ring and all. I hit him so hard that he had tears in his eyes." She shudders, shrugs, takes another long drag and tosses the cigarette onto the sidewalk. "That was the end of our relationship. I wouldn't see him or talk to him for years and then one day we crossed paths at a Van Gogh exhibit at the Virginia Museum. We chatted briefly, impersonally. And then he stopped in at the studio a couple of weeks later. And a few months after that we began restoring art together again."

Ann lowers her window and breathes in the fresh air. "What he did was dreadful and yet he seems a man who loves his horses. Why did he strike that filly?"

"I never asked why."

"He's still in love with you."

"So he says. But he's too proud a Southern gent and too restrained, at least in that respect, to make a fuss. We were a couple for more than two years."

"Did he ever try to make it right?"

"Ann dearest, one can't make something like that right. It was between us. It could never again not be between us." She sighs. "I happened upon John abusing that sweet little filly and my love of John bit the dust because I knew him to be a man who was cruel to animals—a man who was perfectly polished but fundamentally insensitive." She looks over at Ann. "Do you understand?"

Ann nods. "Am I sensitive?"

"Sensitive and stubborn, yes you are." She reaches over and touches the side of Ann's hand. "Will you call me later?"

"If I can."

"*If I can?* What the hell does that mean?" She gets out of the car, shuts the door, and leans into the open window. "Well?"

"I'll call you after Edwin and Amory have gone to bed."

"But only if you want to." She waves an airy good-bye, fingers curled, and walks to the front door of the studio.

Ann turns the key in the ignition and pulls slowly away from the curb. She's relieved to be on her own. She feels like a fish that's been out of water a few seconds beyond comfort. She turns to where Maggie was sitting only moments ago. Implausible as it seems, she misses Maggie's presence in the car. She snorts as she has heard Maggie snort, a nasal exhalation of mockery. She should not have called Maggie last night and she should not have ridden so heedlessly this afternoon. She, Ann Cabot, was spinning out of control—cultivating an ambiguous friendship with a difficult person—someone Ann's mother would have never permitted Ann to have as a friend. She would have thought Maggie too bold—too knowing—too improper. Maggie would *not* have been invited to Ann's birthday parties and she would most definitely *not* have been invited for sleepovers. The image elicits a burst of laughter.

"*I'm going to rein you in,*" she whispers.

George waylays Ann as she is locking the front door of her townhouse.

"Hello, George."

He brushes aside her greeting with a contemptuous sweep of hand. "You've been in Richmond and haven't even telephoned me."

"George, I—"

"George, I what?"

"I'm sorry," she says quietly.

"What are you sorry for? What's going on in your life that you find so hard to disclose? And, please, don't allude to that pathetic fight you contrived over a month ago." He regards her sorrowfully. "I'm in love with you and have been for two years. You can't keep things from me in the face of that. What aren't you telling me?"

"There *are* things I don't tell you, George."

"Such as?"

"Such as, what's happening to me at this point in my life is something I might want to keep to myself. Something I might not want to subject to your scrutiny."

"Why do you refer to my interest as scrutiny?"

"Because you constantly scrutinize me. You treat me as if I were a witness on the stand, being interrogated for the sole purpose of supporting your case. Well, it won't work in this particular—"

"Particular what?" he prods.

"No more questions, George," she says tersely. She walks toward her car and then stops and turns back around to him. "Listen to me, my dear, for what it's worth, you're right. I did provoke that fight. It wasn't because of you. It was because of me. I wanted some time alone. I wanted to be free to—" She considers for a moment. "I can't put it into words because I really don't know what I'm trying to change about myself or my life because I don't understand or trust what I'm drawn to."

"What you're drawn to? What does that mean?"

"I don't know what it means. It's just something I said," she murmurs and averts her face. She cannot bear the pain in his eyes.

"Ann, look at me. Please. I want to ask you something."

The tired sadness in George's voice hurts her. She feels small and selfish. She looks finally into his eyes. They connect and she realizes that, whatever it is that he is going to ask her, she must either respond truthfully or decline to answer. She resists the impulse to bite her lip. "What?" she asks but he remains silent. "What?" she presses, "just ask me."

"Are you in love with another man?"

"If you mean other than Max, then no. I'm not."

"You're not in love with Max. You're addicted and guilt ridden. I've been trying to get you to marry me since the day you divorced that pinstriped prick." He reaches for her hand. "I'm sorry. I know you hate vulgarity."

He's relieved by her answer. Relieved that nothing is different. He can handle anything with Ann except another man or another trip to godforsaken India. He touches her face tenderly. "Come on, darling. Let's have dinner together tonight."

"Not tonight, George."

"Yes, tonight. Please don't refuse again. I'll bring you home early."

"If I go, I want to drive myself."

"Why?"

"Is it necessary for me to have a reason? I don't belong to you," she protests.

"But I want you to belong to me. I want you to marry me."

"No, George."

"No, what?"

"No to marriage and no to dinner."

"Yes to dinner and not yet to marriage."

"Where do you want to have dinner?" she asks resignedly.

"How about the Commonwealth Club?"

"I don't want to go there tonight."

"Where then? You choose, darling."

"La Petite France ... no ... Traveler's."

"Good choice. I'll make a reservation. Is seven good?

"Six is better." She offers a slight smile. "I promised the children I'd be home by nine. Traveler's is three blocks from the interstate."

"Well, more than three blocks, but whatever you say." George returns Ann's smile, tilts her head, and kisses her tenderly. His lips are firm. Familiar. He slips his hand against the small of her back, lightly fits his body to hers, and kisses her again. "It's a good thing I'm taking you out to dinner," he states in a cool voice, "you need it."

"Why do I need it?" Ann releases herself from his embrace and gets into her car.

"Because you've lost weight," George replies impassively. He watches as she pulls away from the curb but he does not return her wave.

Ann and Maggie are having an argument of sorts. Actually, Ann muses, she's defending against Maggie's defense of herself.

"You're being unfair about this," Ann continues.

"I don't see it that way, Ann."

"I'm trying to be straightforward without offending you, Maggie."

"You're not offending me, dearest. You're telling me how you want me to talk and be. Those things are up to me."

Ann sighs. "I want us to have a platonic relationship."

"And that's what we have. But I'm not satisfied with it and you aren't either."

"But I am."

"I'd say you're conflicted."

"Why would I be conflicted?"

Maggie lights a cigarette and leans back into the tufted chesterfield. "Because you know I'm in love with you and you're astute enough to realize that I'd like to physically express that love."

"That would be *your* conflict. What's my conflict?"

"Maybe you're afraid of love between two women or think it's immoral." She looks intently at Ann. "Well?"

Ann regards her solemnly. "I do fear it. I suspect virtually everyone does because it's considered aberrant and therefore not the highest good. I'm not sure how I feel about it morally. I've never really considered the moral implications but it's probable that at some level its morality would be dubious."

"Well then, step away from it." Maggie rises from the couch and reaches for her jacket.

"Wait a minute, Maggie."

"No, dearest. You need to come to terms with this on your own. I could take you there, of course. I could debate and shred every point you might present to defend your mindset and I do understand that your mindset is traditional and sincere. But if I were to do that, somewhere down the road you would say that I had persuaded you."

She reaches down, pulls Ann to her feet and gathers her gently into her arms. "I want to unbind you—to set you free." She nuzzles Ann's hair with her chin. "Not only for you, Ann, but for me too—only—" She kisses the palm of Ann's hand. "I do require one thing."

"And what would that one thing be?" Ann asks.

"That you accept."

"I must think this through," Ann whispers.

The drive from Richmond to the river house is a stretch of highway more than familiar to Ann.

She turns on the stereo, inserts a tape of *Goldberg Variations by Glenn Gould* and lights a cigarette, the second of three she now allows herself daily and justifies because of having read years ago, in one of Max's medical journals, that three cigarettes a day barely increased the risk of lung cancer.

Max, who smoked infrequently and entirely without trepidation, was of the mindset that obsessing about a vice was more insidious, health-wise, than the vice. Maggie had nodded agreement when Ann shared Max's perception about smoking and had added, with thinly veiled intent, that obsessing about *anything* was unhealthy.

The late afternoon sun is a glorious ball of vibrant coral, its hugeness and proximity reminiscent of the way the moon dominated the night sky in Ahmednagar—so seemingly low to the ground—so seemingly close, that it appeared to be a reachable-by-walking part of the landscape.

For two evenings in a row, Ann had attended meetings that were visited by that moon. One of the guest speakers, a dark-haired brooding engineer from Bombay, who had traveled the globe to lecture about Lord Meher, had recited a quatrain from Hafiz that compared the moon's purity to the purity of God-consciousness.

Someone in the audience had suggested that purity was not a problem for the moon, because, for the moon, sexual desire did not exist.

"The moon brings the woman to the man." An elderly bearded scholar, wearing a turban, had told the audience. "Ah, yes, well, that makes it less tempting for the moon than for those hot-blooded lovers she brings together, eh?" a youthful male voice had quipped. Heads had danced side to side, a frivolous suggestion had been heedlessly added, and the audience had roared laughter.

Those comments and the images they elicited had stayed with Ann for a long time.

Post divorce, past midnight, wide awake in her solitary marital bed, she would ascribe a fully developed consciousness to the moon—pristine, celibate, aloof.

The feminine concept of "moon" eluded her. Was the moon a sensate entity? Did it experience desire? Ache with hunger for the masculine warmth of the sun? Or was it merely an uncomplicated simplicity of mindless sun-reflected light—an ancient satellite, indifferently steadfast to planet Earth. An entity unclouded by sexual desire.

For reasons not fully explored, Ann had determined to refrain from a physical involvement with George and she had told him so at the beginning of their relationship.

George had sat quietly in thought for several moments. "Why not?"

"Because I'm not past my marriage vows," she had replied.

"You're guilt ridden because you divorced your husband. You'll feel different down the road, my dear."

"I'm only interested in us as good friends, George," she had insisted.

They began attending social gatherings together and having dinner together when Ann was in Richmond. Often they dined out and occasionally Ann cooked. And then one night, less than two years down the road, after one of her finer meals and two generous snifters of finely aged Armagnac, Ann had acquiesced.

"Enjoy yourself," she had murmured in a sensuous voice.

George had telephoned the following morning and recounted the evening in low, husky tones. "I couldn't believe it ... you—pulling me into your bedroom—removing every last stitch of clothing and climbing stark naked onto that massive poster bed. Ann, darling, you do have style."

Ann had no idea what she had but style was not the noun she would have chosen to describe what had taken place on that bed—a passion of sorts, a fondness of sorts—but minus the vulnerability that had rendered lovemaking with Max complete.

And now—Ann winces—but now—she has Maggie's dogged and escalating sexuality to come to terms with—the most salient sticking point being that Ann's proclivities are clearly not the same as Maggie's—a sticking point that, overridden, would most surely destroy their friendship.

She lowers the window, takes several breaths of fresh air, and carefully releases the remainder of her stubbed-out cigarette onto the highway. That's what she's going to have to somehow convey to Maggie, except she instinctively knows that blunt truth will not be the best approach in this situation. No, she'll have to take another tack—perhaps tell Maggie they need a year of pure friendship uncompromised by sex—one year of Ann and Maggie at their best. She'll just have to persuade Maggie to that alternative somehow because ... because being sexual with a woman is a line she wouldn't cross even if she wanted to, which she doesn't—and she doesn't because—she swallows hard and acknowledges that deep down she considers it improper—worse than improper—just plain wrong.

And yet—and yet—a significant portion of humanity was that way and, not because it was a sexuality they chose, but because they were born that way or had irrevocably evolved that way. So how could it be—and why would it be that an expression of sexuality—freely shared between two consenting adults—was immoral—wrong—bad?

There's nothing in the world that's good or bad but thinking makes it so.

Shakespeare at his most facile and much too glib for this conundrum—but the quote lingers in her consciousness. Neither good nor bad, apart from the mind determining it so. Was it a true, a valid perception? She remembers a quote from the teachings of Lord Meher.

Those who understand nothing condemn everything.

Those who understand everything condemn nothing.

A crystalline beam of lightning-quick insight infiltrates the barrier of conditioned thought and permeates her consciousness. She experiences the freedom and residing calm of a nonjudgmental mind and heart. There but for the knowing. There until the ego protested, the pointing finger accused, the crowd condemned—there until the old stance was resumed—the circle of exclusivity was re-entered.

Charted. Insular. Safe.

In childhood, her parents had charted that circle. In marriage, Max had charted that circle. She had not resisted until she came to see the disparity between what Max said and did.

Forget what they say. Watch what they do.

Her hands tighten on the steering wheel. She knows precisely when that understanding had dealt a staggering blow to their unity.

She has not shared with Maggie the reason for her divorce from Max, but she is certain that Maggie's assessment of Max, and of Ann for continuing to care about Max, would be contemptuous if Maggie knew what had prompted the dissolution of their marriage.

But a habit of relationship was hard to disavow, partly because all relationships, bitter or sweet, were ultimately of the same dynamic.

Ah, Yes! The hidden and fearsome dynamic of relationships. What impelled them? What *were* their points of entry—of exit—their bottom lines?

Her brow furrows in thought. Perhaps relationships were entirely random involvements with no predetermined points of reference as their basis—random involvements whose sole dynamic was an indifferent broadening of universal consciousness by setting into play anything and everything—one drama after another until every conceivable drama had been conceptualized, played out and assimilated.

Or perhaps relationships were entirely karmic—entirely mandated by previous lifetimes—lifetimes impressed upon one's consciousness but not remembered except as an inexplicable sensation of déjà vu. Perhaps karma was the most judicious perspective in that it satisfied every jot and tittle and rendered life equitable for all in that no one was exempt and all came to the same destiny upon the satisfaction of karmic obligations. But the Western mind—and hers was trained to be a Western mind—was conditioned to think in terms of good and bad—saint and sinner—heaven and hell, whereas reincarnation gave no credence to worldly judgments or to eternal damnation. Reincarnation espoused that, when the game was over, king and pawn went back into the same box, experienced the same brevity of respite, and then back to work out residual karma in another lifetime, occupying another body, developing another mind and intellect—but with the same soul. An ancient troupe of souls assigned thousands upon thousands of differing life roles in karmically ordained life plays.

She sighs. There was irony here—the irony being that one could perceive that a thing was true but that perception without unwavering certainty was inadequate to the occasion of perception.

If you want to perceive the truth of a thing, do not be for or against it.

She pulls into the driveway, turns off the motor, lights her final cigarette of the day, and walks down to the seawall. A small fishing boat is anchored straight ahead, so close that she can see the weathered faces of the yellow-slickered men emptying crab pots, hear the clamorous cries of the seagulls circling overhead.

The scene fills her with even greater anxiety. Her life feels suddenly bizarre—convoluted—out of step with the quaint normalcy of the landscape—so much so that she feels a great press to be any place but where she is at this moment.

"I'm totally lost," she whispers, "rained out and in need of temporary shelter." She considers and casts aside several possibilities, and then the sensation of dread lifts.

She'll spend next week with Edwin and Amory and book fare for the following Monday.

MAY 1987

"With the rich and mighty, always, a little patience."

— *The Philadelphia Story*

Ann has been in Ireland for three days. Cool, sunny, mid-May weather and a houseful of guests. Harry and Cookie's estate is in Kilkenny, less than a two-hour drive from Shannon airport. Cookie had met her plane.

"So, darling, what brings you to me this time? Let me guess. You've decided to ignore my advice and marry George."

"No, I haven't decided that."

"You've determined, during one of your guilt-ridden stupors, to return to Max and renew your marriage vows."

"Wrong again."

"What then?"

"I don't want to talk about it just now, Cookie. I'm exhausted from the flight."

"It sounds serious."

"More sticky than serious."

"Why not tell me now and get it over with?"

But Ann had remained silent, although she knew she would not leave Ireland without telling Cookie about Maggie.

The trio of days has been activity filled. Mornings on horseback, late afternoon high teas, never-ending black tie dinners, drawing room bridge, billiards in the game room, charades, dancing, and always with charming escorts to refill Ann's whiskey glass, light her cigarettes (still three daily), and murmur how desirable she is, if she wishes to go that route. She's aware that Cookie is dismayed by her indifference to the attentive bachelors she and Harry have arranged. The baron from Austria has been particularly attentive.

"I adore your hair," he had murmured. "Have you always worn it long?"

"Yes."

"It's beautiful. So many women doing so many foolish things to their hair. Yours is so natural, so glorious." And then he had stroked it with his Teutonic paws, his eyes lingering on her bare shoulders, traveling slowly down the length of her strapless black silk gown. "Will you shoot skeet with me tomorrow?"

"I'm sorry, Victor, but I avoid shooting anything, including skeet."

"Ride with me, then."

"I'm afraid I can't. I've already committed to a day of shopping."

He had regarded her meditatively, measuring the precise extent of her cool dismissal of him. Then, lifting her hand to his lips, he had clicked his heels together, bowed, and joined the others. She had left the billiard room without bidding anyone goodnight. Ascending the great hall staircase, her hand trailing the wide oak banister, she had glanced sidewise and caught a glimpse of the baron, observing her, inscrutable of expression, totally at ease.

She glances at her wristwatch. It's now two in the morning and she's exhausted but not sleepy. It's a good time to call home except that she's edgy from having given Victor the lie of a shopping expedition because now she'll have to quickly arrange one.

Might as well get it over with.

She walks over to the dressing table, runs a comb through her hair, tightens the sash of her bathrobe, opens her bedroom door, scans the hallway, and then walks, barefooted and reluctant of pace, down the hallway and through the archway that leads to Cookie's bedroom.

It's nearly noon, and Ann is impatient to leave for her contrived shopping spree. Cookie had readily agreed when Ann asked her.

"*Of course. We'll be extravagant. Have a marvelous lunch, lots of wine, and you'll tell me your more-sticky-than-serious secret.*"

"*No, Cookie, I just want to go shopping for the children.*"

"*Not a word of protest. Something is going on in that muddled little head of yours. Even Harry has noticed.*"

"*Noticed what?*"

"*How abstracted you are. How you haven't given the time of day to Victor and he trailing after you like a forlorn puppy.*"

"*He's pretentious.*"

"*Of course he is! He's the great-grandson of an Austrian baron.*"

"*I suppose he's divorced.*"

"*He is.*"

"*More than one marriage?*"

"*Two or three brief marriages. What does it matter?*"

"*It matters, Cookie.*"

"*Darling! He's tall, good-looking, and charming. And he's besotted with you. 'That American cousin of yours with the magnificent hair and eyes,' he said to me, 'I must take her back to Vienna with me.' I was so delighted for you, for the two of you. And what happens? You turn up your nose at him. I call that foolish on your part.*"

"*I'm not attracted to him.*"

"*And how that makes his Prussian heartbeat quicken! Oh yes, we'll spend tomorrow together, just the two of us, and you'll tell me everything. Now off to bed. It's after two and I'm exhausted.*"

It's half past noon when Cookie finally descends the great hall stairway. She pauses at the landing, repositions her ivory linen cloche, and continues down, erect of back, gloves in hand. She is elegantly attired—ivory silk sheath, a strand of lustrous pearls that falls several inches below her trim waist, and navy-and-cream spectator pumps that accentuate her shapely legs and perfectly match the belted linen jacket she's carrying. She walks over to the sofa and sits down beside Ann. "I love your outfit."

"You should," Ann tells her. "You gave it to me."

Cookie examines Ann's yellow, short-sleeved bouclé suit more carefully.

"Was this one of mine?"

"A rather pricey one of yours. You bought it at the Valentino trunk show in Milan." Ann teases a smile. "After rather too many cocktails at the Excelsior Hotel Bar. Now do you remember?"

Cookie shrugs. "I must have had you in mind when I bought it. The fabric is divine, but lemon is not one of my colors."

"Whatever." Ann shrugs back.

"Whatever? That's a curt little turn of phrase. Have you tried it out on Victor yet?"

"I'm saving it for the next time he fondles my hair."

"Hmmm. It does impart a certain cachet."

"More than you realize," Ann informs her in a chary voice.

Cookie looks at Ann with dismay. "So secretive and not a bit happy. Come, now. We're off to lunch at Devon's. I've reserved a table and you'll tell me everything." She touches Ann's cheek protectively. "Every sticky little thing Cousin Cookie needs to know about her baby lamb. Oh, no, don't protest. You're completely out of hand and I must know why."

Devon's is crowded. The window table Cookie has reserved is a muted distance from the clinks of cutlery against porcelain, the conversational hums and pauses, the occasional burst of staccato laughter.

Cookie's demeanor thus far has been utterly gracious; full of praise for the perfection of the braised veal, the mellowed-with-age Meursault the wine captain recommended to accompany it, the velvet texture of the lavender crème brûlée.

Hankins had driven them to town in the Bentley—Cookie chatting ceaselessly, mindful of her chauffeur and of Ann's preoccupation with her own thoughts. Clever chatter as only Cookie can maintain, Ann muses. She's waiting for the right moment to pounce. She is so like Ann's mother in that way.

The memory rankles. As far back as Ann could remember, her mother had idolized Cookie. Ann had been jealous—Cookie, blasé. "Aunt Constance has not had to raise me or live with me on a daily basis," she would inform Ann, in patient tones. "Why wouldn't she see me as the perfect daughter? And, in point of fact, since I'm several years older than you, I've had more time to develop a winning routine. We needn't inform Aunt Constance that it was I who taught you how to hold your whiskey, French inhale, flirt without getting a reputation for being fast, sunbathe with no straplines whatsoever ... need I go on?" And she would go on and on until she had Ann in hysterics, her hurt at her mother's blatant adoration of Cookie forgotten.

Ann lifts her chin defiantly. "I do have something to tell you."

"Yes?"

"I'm not sure how you're going to handle it."

"Beautifully, I promise you."

Ann looks around the dining room. "Well, I'm not sure this is the right place."

"Is there a dead body involved?"

"Of course not."

"Are we being tailed?"

"Cookie, be serious."

"Ann, darling, you're serious enough to lead the Good Friday processional at Westminster. Just tell me. I promise I'll help you with it, whatever it is." She reaches across the table and places her hand protectively over Ann's. "Tell me."

"There's a woman in Richmond," Ann begins without preamble, "a talented and interesting woman—her name is Maggie Lambert. She came to the gallery to advise me on some paintings that needed restoring and I hired her. And now she says ... she says she's fallen in love with me."

Cookie's expression remains serene.

"You're not shocked?"

"No."

"What are you then?"

Cookie fingers her pearls. "I'm waiting for you to continue your tale of woe."

"Isn't what I've just told you woe enough?"

"A talented and interesting woman is in love with you, yes?"

"Yes."

"Why would that cause you woe?"

"It's somewhat of a moral dilemma, isn't it?"

"In what way?"

"In the way that she's a woman and so am I."

"Is she a married woman?"

"No."

"And you're divorced from Max, yes?"

"Yes."

"Are you attracted to her?"

"I like her a lot. But I'm not comfortable with her—" She hesitates.

"Her what?"

"She wants a more physical relationship."

"Ah, yes. Now I understand. How far along are we, in point of fact?"

Ann smiles. "In point of fact" is one of Cookie's favorite turns of phrase. She has used it since she was twelve years old. "We aren't far along at all, in point of fact."

"How far precisely?"

"She's kissed my forehead, my hair, and the palm of my right hand."

Cookie regards her thoughtfully. She reaches into her handbag and places a cigarette case and lighter on the white damask tablecloth, a Fabergé malachite case encrusted with rose-cut diamonds and watermelon-pink tourmalines and emblazoned with the imperial cipher of Czar Nicholas II. Harry had given it to her when their son was born. The lighter, a gold Cartier, was from Ann, a celebratory gift in honor of the same birth. Harry and Ann had been ecstatic over the synchronicity of their presents.

She reaches across the table and pats Ann's hand. "Listen to me, Ann. You're making too much of this. This woman, Maggie, if she interests you, if you find her appealing, why not have a fling with her?" She lights a cigarette and exhales. "I don't mean to sound flippant, but it's very chic, very continental. It won't harm you and it most certainly won't harm her. I expect she's quite experienced."

"I don't know if she is or not."

Cookie eyes her coolly. "I'm surprised you've not been approached before. You do have that appeal, you know."

"No, Cookie, I don't know."

"And therein, my lamb, lies the very essence of that appeal."

"Which is?"

"You're an innocent, of course."

"I most certainly am not an innocent. I've been married, I have two children, and let's not forget my relationship with George."

"I'd like to forget your relationship with George. He's the wrong man for you."

"You've never liked George, have you?"

"No, I never have. Nor do I like Max although, foolish little girl that you are, you still harbor the notion that you love him and that he's deserving of your love, which he most certainly is not."

"Why do you dislike Max so?"

"Because he's one person pretending to be another. But I don't want to talk about Max now. I want to discuss another man with you."

"And that man would be Victor, the nobly born and bred baron, correct?"

"Be serious for a moment, Ann. I want you to give him a chance."

"I'm not attracted to him."

"Perhaps because you're titillated by Maggie. She can only be a plaything for you. Nothing serious will come of that. But Victor! I see the two of you together. A wonderful relationship. Possibly a marriage. No, don't scowl, I'm serious. He's charming and genteel. Harry is terrifically fond of him. Please, darling." She taps Ann's hand. "Go riding with him tomorrow morning. Let him see what an accomplished horsewoman you are. And have lunch with him afterward. I'll have Cook prepare a picnic basket for just the two of you. Say 'yes' and I'll give you Mummy's stunning coral snake bracelet with the ruby eyes. You've always loved it."

"Nothing will come of it, Cookie. You'll forfeit that bracelet for nothing."

"It's a risk I'm willing to take. So, is it a deal?"

"I don't want to," Ann barters. "But I will," she continues smoothly, "if you throw in mummy's stunning pair of matching coral snake earrings."

Cookie shoots her a look of grudging admiration. "You're ruthless! It's agreed, then?"

"Yes."

"Good. Now let's go shopping. I want Victor to see you toting tons of glitzy boutique bags filled with expensively wrapped packages when we return. Men need to know these little tidbits about women they profess to adore. And I want you to put this Maggie out of your thoughts until you return to the States."

"I'm not sure I can."

"Oh, but you must. Let me give you some advice, darling, some very important advice. Don't mistake a plaything for a treasure."

"You see Victor as a treasure?"

"Oh yes."

"And Maggie?"

"A plaything."

"But she wants a serious relationship with me."

"I don't think so, but if she does, she'll be sorely disappointed."

"How could you know that?"

"I know you."

"What about me do you know?"

"You are a heterosexual woman by nature."

"Why am I interested in Maggie?"

"Sometimes it just happens that way."

"How do you know *that*?"

"I've heard stories and—" Cookie shrugs.

"And what?"

Cookie takes another cigarette from the jeweled case and lights it. "Well yes ... it did happen to me once. In Paris."

"With whom?"

"You don't know her, dear. Her name's Daphne."

"But how did it happen?"

Cookie's eyes soften in memory. "She kissed me in the powder room at a dinner party for Mimi Winslow. And, for some ridiculous reason, I kissed her back."

"What was it like?"

"It was exciting. She was exciting."

"Were you in love with her?"

"No, but she was the most sensual creature I've ever encountered."

"More so than Harry?'

"Definitely."

"How did it end?"

"Harry ended it."

"You told him?"

Cookie chuckles. "I suppose in a way I did. I shared a certain aspect of Daphne's repertoire with him and he questioned me about it. Somehow I had the notion that he wouldn't mind very much, since Daphne was not a man, after all. In that, my dear, I was as naïve as you."

"What do you mean?"

"Harry was out of his head with jealousy. He threatened to kill us both. With his grandfather's sword, if you can believe it. He threw half my clothes from the dressing room balcony. The servants spent days retrieving underwear from treetops."

"What happened then?"

"I broke off the affair, of course."

"Do you miss her?"

"I miss the divertissement."

"But?"

"But what?"

"You're so casual about it."

"You will be too."

"Oh?" Ann scoffs. "And when exactly *does* casual come into play?"

"When circumstances require it of you. Until then, it's a plaything. You pick it up. You put it down. Pick it up, put it down. Then one day you put it away. One fits such a thing to one's life. One never fits one's life to it. That would be a great folly and you, my beloved cousin and darling friend, are not a fool. Now, let's not continue on with this. I'm beginning to bore myself with all of this serious talk about a very trivial matter. Trivial whether you decide 'yes' to her or 'no' to her. Do you understand?"

"Yes, Cookie. I understand."

"Good girl."

Ann gives Cookie a wry, knowing look. "Good girl, in point of fact, has nothing to do with this."

Victor and Ann are snooping about in Cookie's favorite room—the costume room. It's on the third floor of the manor house and contains dozens of outfits in impeccable state of repair and fastidiously pressed.

It is raining steadily outside—a warm rain that mists the windows and casts a grey pall over the landscape. The entire manor house, even with lit fireplaces and lamps, is dismal.

Ann hates the weather, hates the costume room, the coral bracelet on her wrist, and the matching coral earrings in her padded jewel case. She hates Harry and Cookie, all of their guests, most of the servants, and all but two of Harry and Cookie's seven dogs. She hates herself and she hates Victor. They have been practically melded together for two days because of the downpour's accompanying fog.

Victor has been relentlessly attentive. Cookie was correct in her assessment of him. He is genteel, well informed, and capable of cogent thought. He's also an attentive listener, a better-than-average pianist, plays excellent bridge, drinks a lot but not too much, holds it well, has flawless manners, a great laugh, a warm smile, and is clearly perfect. Ann would like to smack Cookie's smug, square-shaped face. How clever of her to have contrived for Ann to do her bidding in exchange for vintage jewelry. The snake bracelet and matching earrings with their coiled coral bodies and cold ruby eyes were on the coffee tray the very next morning. No note required for tacit understanding. Ann could have sworn that she'd seen the Faustian reptiles slither past the silver creamer on the tray. She had not been a happy camper that morning.

She has spent much of her time with Victor answering his tactful queries about her family. He knows that Edwin, tall, raven-haired, even-featured—a slighter-of-build replica of his father—is sensitive and moody at fourteen and that his great passions are soccer and music, and he knows that Amory, delicate of frame and feature and sporting a handful of worrisome freckles across the bridge of her slightly snub nose, is strong-willed, witty, observant, wise beyond her eleven years, and reserved rather than shy. Of Max he knows little—that he's the eldest of three brothers, that he's a cardiologist turned psychiatrist, that he's fifty-two, that his condo overlooks the Chesapeake Bay, and that he has yet to remarry since his and Ann's divorce. Victor approaches conversation in a "just the facts, ma'am" sort of way, Ann muses. Max would have Victor tastefully stripped bare by now—debunked and accessible—and Ann keeping pace with Max. Oh, the diversity and flow of their conversations. Couples would speak of it enviously, especially the wives. Several of them had, from time to time, fallen in love with Max. Ann had not minded until ... until the time Max had loved back. She had happened upon the prelude to that disaster in Max's study, after a dinner party—Faye, her neighbor and close friend, reclining on Ann's grandfather's chesterfield, her bare back pressed against the tufted seat, the hard leather buttons leaving circular imprints on the suntanned flesh—Max sitting on the floor alongside her, brandy snifter in hand, eyes warm with affection clouded by soft desire—past midnight, Faye's husband long gone, long asleep in their house, snoring obliviously away—and Ann, motioning to Max, pulling the study door closed behind him and whispering in his ear, "You'll have to take Faye home. She's totally trashed."

Victor interrupts her thoughts. "I would like to see you in this." The costume he holds up is a black velvet page's suit, elaborately embellished with lace at the collar, wrists, and knees. It reminds her of the painting at her art gallery—the Boldini Maggie has yet to complete.

"Why that one?"

"It suits you."

"As well as being a suit," Ann quips.

"It suits you perfectly."

"It's rather boyish."

"Yes."

Ann regards him quizzically. "Do you think me boyish?"

"Yes."

"In what way?"

"Your appearance is feminine," Victor replies, "but inside is a little boy."

Ann is stunned by his answer. She turns to the window and presses her forehead against the mullioned glass panes. "My father used to say that about me."

"Your papa must have thought you an adorable child."

"I adored him."

"Is he no longer alive?"

She turns from the window. "He died ten years ago. A riding accident complicated by pneumonia. He had been unconscious for hours before anyone discovered him."

"How sad."

"Yes. His death was a great loss."

"And what of your mama?"

"She died before my father. When I was in my twenties. She had rheumatic fever as a child. It left her heart damaged."

"Was she beautiful?"

"I thought she was."

"And did your papa think her beautiful?"

"My father thought her quite beautiful."

"And your papa was in love with her and you were a bit in love with her also, yes?"

"My father was in love with her. I was in awe of her."

"You will have the pleasure of meeting my mother one day soon."

"I think not. I'm returning home soon."

"I should like for you to visit Mama and me in Portofino this summer. Mama has a villa there, almost at the summit, with a view of the Mediterranean beyond description. I have not asked you, although with your art gallery, I have wondered. Do you paint?"

"Not even a little. Do you?"

"I would like to paint you wearing this."

Ann observes him with heightened interest. "Then you do paint."

"Several of my acquaintances have hanging in their houses portraits I have done of them and sometimes of their children."

"How wonderful."

He holds up the outfit. "May I paint you wearing this?"

"But when, Victor?"

"Now. Before you leave Ireland."

"How long will it take?"

He computes. "Some of this afternoon, all of this evening, much of tomorrow and the following day."

"Will I have to sit absolutely still?"

"I intend to paint you standing but, yes, you will have to be still. I will allow you to read from time to time and to smoke one of your three daily cigarettes."

"Shall I be permitted one each sitting?" Ann barters.

"Only if you're a good little boy."

She grins. "I'll try."

"So we'll begin this afternoon, yes?"

"Yes," she replies.

Although the sittings now number seven instead of the five she had anticipated, Ann is not bored, but she is sick to death of the costume in which she is encased. The heavily starched lace collar around her neck is particularly annoying. On her feet are Harry's black velvet slippers, elaborately crested and outlined with gold-and-silver stitchery. Victor has posed her standing next to the great hall fireplace, holding his own gold-knobbed riding crop in her left hand and an unfiltered Gauloise in her right hand, between her index and middle fingers, close to the knuckles.

Harry and Cookie love the stance, think the costume so very fascinating, and are delighted at the turn of events. Ann suspects they spend every waking moment congratulating each other over how well the Ann-Victor relationship is progressing.

The rest of the houseguests have departed, except for Douglas and Matilda Mowbrey, a dreadfully dull couple from Edinburgh who drink copious quantities of Harry's best brandy and play mediocre bridge endlessly. Harry and Cookie always take each other for partners and, as they are excellent players, have thus far trounced the Mowbreys of hundreds of pounds. How Harry loves money, Ann muses. She lifts her eyes to Victor and catches him in a frown.

"What's wrong?"

"I need for you to look at me directly now," he replies, "and to hold that mysterious unsmiling gaze of yours, yes?"

"I'll try for it."

She rouses her thoughts to the varied treasury of spiritual quotes she has cherished throughout the years: "Lift the stone and you will find me. Cleave the wood and I am there." Jesus, from the Gospel of St. Thomas. "I have esteemed the words of His mouth more than my necessary food." The Book of Job, from the Old Testament. "Thou hast made us for Thyself, O Lord, and our hearts will not find rest until they rest in Thee." St. Augustine, from his personal confessions.

"That's it," Victor says to Ann in a softly jubilant voice, "that's exactly the expression I want!"

Ann returns to her ruminations. Her memory obliges with a treasure trove of profundities from ancient mystics and God-intoxicated poets of the East. "All except God doth perish." "Where is God not?" "Nothing can be hidden from the One who is everywhere present." "He who loves God becomes God." "When was I ever less by dying?" And, her favorite and perhaps the most obscure, from the sayings of the Sufis, "The happiness of the drop of water is to die in the ocean."

Raised an Episcopalian, baptized and confirmed in that restrained but elegant liturgy, Ann had ventured at a young age into the realm of Eastern mysticism. Uncle Lawrence would take her for long walks through the wildlife sanctuary bordering his childhood home. Sometimes they would spread a blanket under the canopy of silver birches and, while they were eating their Sally Bell box lunches, Uncle Lawrence would talk to her about the true nature of God, the purpose of existence, the ultimate destiny of every living entity. Those afternoons were among the most memorable experiences of Ann's childhood.

"And the light shineth in the darkness but the darkness comprehendeth it not."

She was ten when that quotation, read by Father Hagan, caught her attention. As with the delicate strains of Chopin's second piano concerto, those words, the imagery of darkness unable to assimilate the light that dispelled it, had elicited in her a sensation of bittersweet longing and she had rejoiced in the knowledge that rapture could be found in exquisite (harmonies of) sound, in the power of words strung eloquently together, in the artist's masterful rendering of brush and palette to capture on canvas the vast array of life.

It is almost time for the dinner gong to sound when Victor finally releases Ann from her pose. "I have finished all of your face but for a bit more around the eyes," he tells her. "An hour more this evening and we are done."

"Must I wear this again?"

Victor considers. "It will be the last time, but yes."

"I'm going to set fire to it afterward," she threatens.

"Perhaps we shall both do that," he murmurs.

Ann dresses with particular care for dinner. She chooses a sleek midnight-blue Armani—long sleeves, jewel neckline, slightly padded shoulders. She decides on the navy suede slingbacks. They have higher heels than she normally wears, but she likes the way the dress swirls gently around them when she walks. They'll be fine if she doesn't drink too much. She piles her hair casually atop the crown of her head and secures it with a tortoiseshell comb, a technique she learned from her grandmother. On her wrist is the hateful coral bracelet, and one viper sleeps on each earlobe. Her only other piece of jewelry is a gold crest ring. It was her father's and she wears it always on the fourth finger of her right hand. It is the only adornment Victor has allowed for her portrait. He considered it for a moment and then pronounced it "suitable." They both grinned at his choice of adjective.

She is late for cocktails but she relishes her entrance.

Harry whistles and hands her a whiskey. "What a marvelous gown!" he exclaims. He eyes the row of round silk buttons from nape to boldly flared hem. "Somebody went blind sewing those babies on," he quips. "I've counted twenty-six and I've yet to reach," he winks at Ann, "center field."

"Ann, darling," Cookie interjects, "Victor says he's going to unveil your portrait tomorrow morning."

Victor turns to Cookie. "That is for you and Harry and—" He nods at the Mowbreys, side by side, drinking their interminable brandies. "And for Douglas and Matilda. Ann shall see it tonight."

"Is it finished, then?" Harry asks Victor.

"Just a few more details," Victor answers in a tone of voice that quashes discussion.

He has allowed no one to view his work since he began and, and after each of his and Ann's sittings, he has carefully carried the still-damp canvas back to his suite of rooms, leaving only the easel in place in the great hallway.

Ann considers Victor's insistence that she not view it before completion prudent and, despite Harry's and Cookie's boasts that Victor is so very talented, she is prepared for the possibility that the portrait may not be to her liking. But she is terribly keyed up for it and she has noted the intensity of Victor's concentration and his nods of satisfaction when looking from the canvas to Ann or from Ann to the canvas.

It is after eleven when the Mowbreys bid Harry and Cookie goodnight. Victor turns to Ann.

"And now for the final sitting."

Ann nods. "I'll go upstairs and change."

"No, I think not. The suit is unnecessary."

"There is a God!" she whispers.

"But," Victor reaches over and deftly releases her hair from its comb. It tumbles below her shoulders. "Yes. The hair down."

Ann walks into the great hall and sits on the sofa in front of the fireplace. Her face is flushed from the brandy she has been steadily drinking and from the blazing logs on the hearth.

Cookie walks over to the fireplace and turns to Ann. "I'm exhausted. I think I'll turn in. Do you mind?"

"Of course not."

She kisses Ann on both cheeks. "Don't stay up too late now. You have a full day tomorrow."

"Yes, Cookie."

"Come, Harry."

Harry follows obediently.

"Kiss Ann goodnight."

"Yes, dear." He bends down and kisses Ann's cheek. "Goodnight, old girl."

Ann watches them ascend the stairway to their suite of rooms on the second floor. They are perfectly suited, she muses, and shudders at the ever-surfacing adjective she has chosen to describe them. She decides she will never again wear a suit, not for the rest of her life. What will she wear? A grey homespun robe. She'll become a female monk. The children can come to visit her at Christmas and Easter. She'll be abstemious, eat next to nothing, renounce sex, and bequeath everything she owns to the children and the SPCA. Max can provide for the poor, the mentally unhinged, and

Faye Graham. She takes a deep swallow from her brandy snifter. Harry has poured her enough to fell an ox. She suspects his generosity is not completely honorable, not to mention Cookie's feigned exhaustion.

Victor finally descends the staircase with the canvas. He places it on the easel and holds out his hand. "Come and see."

"But our sitting?"

"Come and see."

She takes another swallow of brandy, rises unsteadily from the sofa, and walks over to Victor. He does not take his eyes from the painting as he encircles her waist with his arm. She holds her breath before looking at the painting. She is astounded at how fine it is.

"You've made me beautiful," she breathes.

"You are beautiful."

"And a bit haughty, I think."

"Not haughty, but aloof."

"Do you think me aloof?"

"Yes."

"I'm not as aloof as you've portrayed me."

His arm tightens around her waist. "I am certain of that."

"It's just that I don't really know you."

"You do not know me as well as I know you, but that is one of the privileges a painter of portraits anticipates." He draws her closer to him.

"It's magnificent, Victor."

"I shall have a reward, then?"

She chuckles, a soft girlish chuckle. "As in the fairy tales of my childhood, you shall be allowed *three* wishes."

He closes his eyes. "I have my first wish."

"And for what do you wish?"

"A kiss."

"Granted."

He kisses her lips—a slow lingering kiss.

"Your second wish?" she whispers.

"A second kiss."

"Granted."

He kisses her again.

"And your third wish?" She breathes the question against his throat.

"A third kiss."

When he places his lips on hers a third time, her balance falters. She reaches down and releases one and then the other foot from its shoe, and then places her hands behind Victor's neck. They kiss again and again.

"Victor, wait a moment. I—" She protests but she does not stop him as he begins to unfasten her gown, button after button after button, his mouth relentlessly on hers.

He takes her unexpectedly, masterfully. She means to stop him but it's much too late. She's caught in the motion—beyond thinking or choosing or caring.

She awakens to a tactful knock on her bedroom door. Her body is naked beneath the luxurious eiderdown quilt, her mouth dry and acidic from the aftertaste of well-aged brandy. She slides more deeply beneath the bedcovers.

"Good morning, mum."

"Good morning, Gretchen."

She glances at the silver tray Gretchen places on the tea table next to the four-poster bed. Croissant with butter and bitter-orange marmalade, a pot of coffee, cream and honey, an ivory envelope with her name heavily scrawled in black ink, three unfiltered cigarettes and Victor's gold-knobbed riding crop with one perfect white rose affixed to it—Ann looks more closely—with her grandmother's tortoiseshell hair comb. Her pulse quickens.

Gretchen draws back the heavy damask curtains. Multicolored prisms of light dance on the mullioned windows. "Shall I be hanging those up for you, mum?" she asks and gestures toward Ann's gown, suede slingbacks, and undergarments lying in a twisted heap on the faded Persian carpet.

"No, thank you, Gretchen, I'll be packing them shortly."

She waits for Gretchen to leave before she sits up, drapes the covers around her shoulders, reaches for the envelope, and turns it over. It's sealed with a blob of wax impressed with two swans, a coronet above the head of one. She slides a finger beneath the flap and extracts the heavy card. It too is embossed in gold with the same crest as on the envelope. Written on the card are three words only:

Until Portofino,
Victor

She is already dressed and her luggage neatly packed when Cookie enters the bedroom.

"Guess what I'm holding in my hand?" she announces breezily.

"The deed to the Mowbreys' ranch. It should just about cover their losses at the bridge table," Ann retorts drily.

"Guess again."

Ann raises an eyebrow. "Just show me."

Cookie opens her hand. Resting on her palm are the coral snake earrings.

"Ugh." Ann shudders. "Yet another pair of conspiring vipers."

"Aren't you going to ask me where I found them."

"Where did you find them?"

"One on the hearth, the other winking up at me from the sofa." Her eyes search Ann's. "Was last night as wonderful as I prayed it might be?"

"Prayed, indeed! It was nothing less than a Faustian pact."

"Oh, Ann, how can you say that? You know I care only for your happiness."

"Well, I'm not happy."

"Why not?"

Ann shuts her eyes in disgust. "Because I behaved badly last night. I drank too much. I succumbed too easily and, with Victor's inestimable assistance, I trashed the great hall."

"But, what else?"

"Cookie, surely you can fill in the dots to complete the picture."

"I only want to know one thing," Cookie murmurs and looks intently at Ann.

"And what would that one thing be?"

"Are you in love?"

"Am I in love?" Ann considers the question. "Hmmm. Am I in love?" She walks to the trio of mullioned windows overlooking the side pastures and gazes at a flock of burly ewes, their offspring alongside them, contentedly munching the clover-free grass of the side lawn. She turns around, arms folded against her breast, and faces Cookie. "I hope this won't shock you, dearest," she announces, "what with the trashed great hall and personal artifacts scattered about, but no, I am not in love."

"Well, what are you then?"

"A slut, perhaps? Or, as we used to say at boarding school, just plain fast?"

"Well," Cookie answers, imperturbable of tone, "Victor is most definitely in love."

"Oh? And where is the noble baron at this moment?'

"He left after breakfast. Harry suggested he stay for lunch but he declined the invitation."

Ann winces. "May I tactfully suggest that Victor's not so much in love as he is in a hurry to get the hell out of Dodge."

"But Victor intends to see you again. He told me so."

Ann turns back to the windows. The beauty of the landscape and the early morning quietude, broken only by the wavering cries of softly bleating baby lambs, momentarily lessen the dull throbbing of her temples. "So tell me," she asks Cookie, "what exactly did Victor say?"

"He said, 'We must persuade our Ann to return to us soon.' I don't remember his precise wording, but his intent was clear. And besides," Cookie brightens visibly, "he took your portrait with him."

"Maybe he's decided I haven't earned it yet."

"I don't like your humor, Ann. It's in bad taste."

"If we're going to be honest here, Cookie, what happened last night was in bad taste."

"Guilt from Aunt Constance." Cookie sighs and places a hand on Ann's shoulder. "You're a foolish girl to go on this way and it will cause unpleasant memories for both of us if you continue. You're an adult and you're divorced. You're free to do as you please. In point of fact, you've not given anyone a chance. Walter Redwine was wild for you, do you remember? You turned him down. And Alfred Fielding? My God! He followed you all the way back to Virginia and holed up at The Jefferson for a week. You wouldn't even take his phone calls. And Winston Throckmorton? So many fine men you've turned away."

"Well, I didn't turn Victor away, did I?"

"Victor's special. I'm terribly taken with him and, despite what you say, my sweet, and in your own hidden way, I believe you're taken with him, too. No, Ann, not another word. I can see from the set of your chin that it's the wrong time to talk about this and we must hurry if you're going to catch your plane. Harry's driving with us to the airport and you know how he hates to be kept waiting."

She reaches for the bell pull and gives it a yank. "Come," she says in a kindly tone, "let's go down. Graves will be up in a moment to carry your luggage. Hurry, lamb, and try to look happy, for heaven's sake. We don't want Harry to think his father's best brandy has given you a hangover."

"A hangover," Ann retorts, "is the *only* thing I wasn't given."

Airborne at last and comfortably ensconced in the commodious seat of the first-class cabin, Ann turns off the overhead lamp and tries to sleep. But she can't. Her thoughts keep her relentlessly awake although she is weary beyond the point of exhaustion. She thinks of Victor's riding crop nestled in her suitcase and his note tucked away in her handbag. She wonders what he means to do with her portrait, full lipped, unsmiling, wide browed, intent green eyes looking beyond Victor, beyond Ireland, beyond the realm of illusion.

"But you are a little boy," he had suggested when she questioned his choice of costume. And so he had portrayed her—a young lad—tall, boyishly slim, the incongruous feminine mane of auburn hair outweighed by the addition of the heavily knobbed riding crop and the glowing red tip of the cigarette he had so precisely placed between the knuckles of her fingers.

She contemplates their night of lovemaking. Why had she succumbed? Desire—the painting—the brandy—and yes, Cookie, too.

"Come, sir, and welcome. Cookie wills it so."

But it was for more than all of those rationalizations bound up in a tidy package. It was for the possibility that Victor might reawaken her to the openness—the vulnerability of love—that unguarded simplicity with which she had begun her marriage to Max.

And yet—and yet—despite Victor's measured charm, artistic talent and the magical interlude of their final days together—she was as she had been during and ever since the dissolution of her marriage—un-imprinted and solitary.

She awakens to dappled sunlight shining through the bars on the window of her cell. Her blindfold partially obscures her view.

There is the sound of approaching footsteps, followed by the sound of keys being jangled. The cell door opens. She is no longer solitary. It is the captain. Her heart lifts at his presence.

"I have come to take you away."

"Oh yes, please. I've been waiting for you."

He unbinds her hands and then loosens her blindfold, but does not remove it. He propels her past the cell door. "We must move quickly. This is really not permitted. I myself could be in great danger for taking you."

"Where are you taking me?"

"Home, as I promised I would. Now come. The corridor is empty. There is no one to keep you here any longer. I can take you there because—" He holds out an elaborately scrolled gold key. "I hold the key to your paddock."

He places one hand on her shoulder and the other under her chin. She can see the lambent glow of his eyes through the loose gossamer of her blindfold. "You have no idea how lovely you are, as lovely as Vivien Leigh, only taller. I shall paint a portrait of you one day exactly as you are now but with a cigarette. Will you remember?"

"Yes," she murmurs, "I'll remember."

"And the hair—" He reaches behind her and removes a gold coin from her ear. The mantle of hair tumbles below her shoulders. The captain takes it in his hands, his fingers twining and untwining its dense mass. "The hair," he murmurs, "must be down."

"Down," she repeats. "Yes. Down."

He encircles her wrist with his hand. "Come now—follow me."

But his stride is long and brisk and she loses her balance. She has forgotten to remove her slingbacks. He reaches down and removes them from her feet and then scoops her up and they are suddenly airborne—

*flying through the corridor, through the bars of the chained prison gates
and into the sunlit day.*

*She gives a cry of joy. "I had forgotten this," she whispers in his ear.
"I had forgotten flight."*

*"There is nothing to compare to it. It's what I have wanted for you
from the first time I saw you. Do you believe me now?"*

"Yes," she whispers, "I believe you now."

*"We must remain in this position," the captain announces. "I know
it's unknown to you but we will circle overhead. Can you endure it?"*

*She is too lost in the rapture of flight to answer. Beads of sweat
form on her upper lip and temples as they glide in ever-widening circles,
above treetops, past clouds—beyond the diaphanous overhang of sky.*

*"Almost home," the captain tells her, "but not yet landed. Still
circling—circling—circling—*

Ann awakens with a start. The stewardess is peering down at her.

"We're circling over Norfolk," she says. "The captain is waiting for
permission to land."

"What?" Ann looks at her blankly and places a hand to her forehead.

The stewardess eyes her solicitously. "Are you alright?"

"Yes. I'm fine."

She sits up and adjusts her seat to the forward position, all the while
struggling to remember her dream. She places her fingertips against her
temples. They are damp with perspiration. Her entire body is damp with
perspiration and her eyelashes are laced with tears.

Max and the children are standing next to the car when she exits the terminal.

"I was expecting to see Hattie behind the wheel," she says to Max. "What a wonderful surprise!" She hugs Amory and then Edwin. "I missed you both so much."

"You look great, Mom," Edwin effuses and gives her a second hug.

Max starts the car engine and checks the rearview mirror before pulling into the terminal's exit lane. Ann fastens her seat belt and turns her head in his direction. "How've you been, Max?'

"Missing you." He removes a hand from the steering wheel and trails her face with his fingers. "We've all been missing you."

Ann cups his hand briefly with hers. "Is Hattie worn to a frazzle? Did everything go well at home?" She turns to Edwin and Amory. "Did everything run smoothly while I was away?"

Edwin pats her shoulder reassuringly. "You called and checked things out on a daily basis, Mom. Hattie tattled to you about everything."

"Except that Belle might be pregnant," Amory blurts out.

"What?" Ann stares blankly at Amory.

"Nice work, Amory." Edwin thumps his sister on the shoulder. "You're such a brat!"

"Belle isn't pregnant, Ann," Max says in a calm voice.

"Then why did Amory say that?"

"Because Belle went out the doggie door one evening and didn't return. Both of the property gates were latched so we have no reason to think that she left the property. We called her until we were hoarse and drove around the neighborhood for hours trying to find her. We finally gave up and went to bed. She was waiting at the side porch door when Hattie went out to get the morning paper and she still refused to come in." Max replies. "She's a willful sight hound. She just didn't want to come in. She was probably hoping to outwait that ancient tortoise in the boxwood maze or stalking that witless muskrat she always chases into the river. Belle minds you and me, Ann, but that's pretty much it for her, obedience-wise."

"Could she have been in season?" Ann asks in a quiet voice.

"Hattie said she wasn't and I saw no evidence that she was. We'll just have to wait and see," Max reflects soberly. "I don't think Belle got into trouble. You know how aloof she is. With Belle, it's the thrill of the chase and not the aftermath." He smiles. "Don't worry. Whatever happens, Daddy will take care of it. How was your trip?"

"It was good."

Amory taps Ann on the shoulder. "What did you bring back, Mommy?"

"Lots of presents for my baby lambs."

"Eleanor told us about the painting," Max says to Ann. "That must have added considerably to the pleasure of your trip."

"Eleanor told you about the painting? How did Eleanor know about the painting?"

"She knew because she sold it," Max replies. "Didn't she call you to negotiate a price?"

"Oh," Ann nods. "Yes, now I remember. The Theodore Robinson painting. She did call me. I wouldn't go down on the price but the client bought it anyway."

"You're edgy." Max reaches for her hand and pats it reassuringly.

"Am I?"

"Yes."

"You're fine, Mom," Edwin says protectively. "I'm glad you're home."

"Hattie made Edwin play his stereo low the whole time you were gone," Amory says archly.

"Shut up, runt," Edwin hisses.

"Quiet, both of you, or your mother's going to head right back to the airport and book fare to Africa."

"That's not funny, Max."

Max chuckles. "I thought it was."

Amory wraps her arms around her father's neck. "I thought it was funny too, Daddy."

They are pulling into the long driveway when Amory taps Max on the shoulder and asks in a shy voice, "Daddy, are you going to keep staying here all night and all?"

Ann turns from the window. "All night and all?"

"I've been sleeping here during your trip to Ireland."

"For what reason?"

"How dare you ask me that!"

"Mommy," Amory intervenes, "I asked him to because Belle was always crying and whining and all and she brought in a garden snake and a couple of turtles and Hattie's scared of snakes and she wanted Daddy to leave Liza but take Belle to his place to stay until you got back and all."

Ann cups the side of Amory's face. "Don't say 'and all,'" she says gently. She turns to Max. "I'm sorry, Max, and I'm glad that you stayed here to take care of things while I was gone."

"I was happy to help out and thanks for the apology." He turns off the engine.

The children scramble out of the car. The night air is atypically cool. Moonlight glistens on the river, cutting a wide silvery swath in the very center of its rippling blackness. Max opens the car door and holds out his hand to Ann.

"Oh Max, let's walk down to the seawall. I think I've been homesick for Hampton without realizing it."

The dogs are suddenly upon them. Belle jumps up on Ann, her huge paws on Ann's shoulders, her soft tongue trailing a path down Ann's face.

"Belle, beautiful Belle," Ann croons. She bends down and scoops Liza into her arms. "And sweet Liza."

Belle sniffs Ann suspiciously.

"Those are Harry's hounds you're smelling, you naughty girl!" Ann shakes an admonishing finger. "What did you get into while I was away?"

"It would have been the other way around, I think," Max teases.

"Pray God it didn't happen."

"Why would it be such a tragedy?"

"Because she's a champion-bred Scottish Deerhound and there's no way she could have lucked out and mated with another Deerhound, and because," Ann grins, "I'm still awaiting enlightenment about the desire-laden vanity of pedigrees."

They walk down to the seawall arm in arm. The magnolia is in fullest bloom—its blossoms rendered a luminous white in the moonlight.

"While the slow moon shines, sending silver to the rock," Max recites in a resonant voice.

"That's beautiful, Max. What's it from?"

"A poem I wrote."

"When?"

"While you were in Ireland. I wrote three poems, actually."

"May I read them?"

He steps behind her and wraps his arms around her waist. "I wrote them for you. The second one is about you. They're on your dressing table. I used our old rooms and slept in our bed while you were away."

The ache at the back of her throat is familiar. She watches the dogs tunneling through the ivy under the huge magnolia. "They've caught a whiff of turtle."

He nods. "Belle brought one into the living room yesterday. She kept flipping it over with her paw. I took it from her. The poor thing stayed in its shell for half an hour. I thought it had died from cardiac arrest but it finally poked its head beyond the shell, eyeballed the living room for ten full minutes, made a couple of slow advances to the front and then—faster than Secretariat—it covered the length of your grandmother's Heriz. I sprang from my chair and caught up with it, took it outside, and watched it haul ass into the boxwood maze." He eyes Ann solicitously. "Are you tired?"

"A little. It was a long flight."

"You go on ahead. I'll bring the dogs. Come, Belle," he says firmly. Belle trots to Max's side immediately. Liza follows behind her.

Ann stares at Max in amazement. "Belle obeys you!"

"She's in love with me."

"When did that happen?"

"Belle's always been in love with me, but this was the first opportunity she and I had to really sleep together."

"Did she sleep in bed with you?"

"Indeed she did." His eyes dance wickedly.

"All night long?" She envisions them together and smiles.

"Every night I stayed here except for her one night on the town."

"Well, that one night should have made it clear," Ann teases.

"Not that night, but the next night definitely."

"Why? What happened the next night?"

"She returned to me as I knew she would and she knew she must," Max says matter-of-factly. "Let's go in now. It's getting late and Amory's dying to see what you've brought her from her extravagant godmother. She's hoping for jewelry."

"A gold enameled bracelet," Ann assents. "It was Cookie's confirmation present from *her godmother* and it's a beauty."

"Your earrings are interesting." Max eyes the coral and ruby-eyed snakes appreciatively.

Ann forces a bright smile. "Poker winnings."

"What were you holding?"

She thinks a moment. "A straight heart flush."

"Nice."

"Jack high."

Max whistles. "That *is* impressive. Was Cookie playing?"

"Cookie was most definitely playing."

"What was she holding?"

"She had a full house but she folded early."

"Why would she, with such a good hand?"

"She expected the baron to win."

"What baron?"

"A friend of Harry's. Harry was the first to fold. He held two pairs."

"What was the baron holding?"

"What he wished for. Three aces."

Max whistles again. "Damn good hands."

"Amazingly good hands," she answers wryly.

After the children have been given their presents—after Edwin's nods of approval for the silver link key chain with an enameled soccer ball, the black-and-brown striped rugby shirt, and most especially, Madonna's available-only-in-England latest album; after Amory's delight with the tartan kilt, the antique bracelet, and the Polo alligator belt; and after Hattie's quiet appreciation for her crocheted shawl and Scottish bloodstone cameo—Ann bids them all a weary goodnight and walks upstairs. Max follows her. She notes with pleasure the extravagant bouquet of freshly cut and tidily arranged flowers in her sitting room.

"Are these your doing, Max?"

He shakes his head. "Edwin picked them from the garden and Hattie arranged them."

"How dear of Edwin."

"He missed you."

Ann walks through the bedroom and into the dressing room. Max's poems are on the table. She sits on the gilt bench and reads them.

I

Go now, go, they'll look for you there.
Those who play in the Dapple Down Dare.
Not for a penny they'll look for you there.
 Nor any small kiss from a maiden fair.
The flagon full brimming and nothing to spare.
A hundred years flowing through Dapple Down Dare
Is a small price to pay for the privilege rare
Of shedding your blood in the Dapple Down Dare.
Some may call "sister" or "mother" or "Wife."
They will not stop it—it cuts like a knife.
Through the breast of your woes, the shackles, the strife.
In Dapple Down Dare it's the time of your life.

II

When in the graying of my later thought
I turn to your eyes, your lips, your breasts,
Your fondest unmentioned currents, heartfelt and deep,
A sadness, wild with regret, deep as first love, old,
Steals unbidden to the central place and dwells there.
I have seen it before. Yes. And mourned it
Then as I do now, not knowing its source or goal,
Only that I have known it. An old familiar shoe.
An immemorial feeling that love was once there,
And will be again.
We pursue the past in our thrust,
Like salmon returning to spawn,
Knowing only that we must go where we have been.

III

A Hudson River steamer with its old slow ways
Wends a wide slow path through the bluebottle haze.
The wild jumping stamping of the frenzied and the crazed
In the quiet sliding womb of the deep hull says
"Let us up, let us out, let our bodies run amok
While the moon still shines on the riverside dock!"
The old pool ripples and the water bugs talk
While the slow moon shines sending silver to the rock.
In a slow susurration, like the breathing of a mole,
Just above the sound of the glowing of a coal.
They whisper of a child who fell down into a hole
And an old man crying from the bottom of his soul.
A Hudson River steamer getting smaller through the trees
Makes a far-off sound like twenty million bees.
And the water bugs speak of how an old man grieves
When the marrow of his bones gets cold enough to freeze.

Ann does not, in the moment, separate Max from his writing and longing wells up in her for him as he is in the consciousness of his prose. She picks up the paper and reads again the second poem. His sadness—ah yes, his sadness—the sotto voce accompanist to each of his accomplishments. And the respondent sadness it had elicited in Ann. *"We cannot evade the repercussions of my sorrow,"* he had warned her early in their marriage. His eyes had registered wistful knowing. *"My sorrow is the unanticipated furl of my plumage—the nether end of my joy."*

And so it had been during the final years of their reign as the perfect couple with the perfect relationship, children, house, property, éclat.

She becomes aware that Max is standing in the doorway. She turns around and faces him. "They're magnificent. They're beyond magnificent. I love them." She stands up, walks over to him, puts her arms around his neck and kisses his cheek. "Thank you, Max. Thank you for these glorious poems and for taking care of things while I was away."

"I was happy to be here."

"Do you miss being here?"

Max nods. "Often."

"Do you miss me?" She asks it even as she is determining that she must not ask it.

"I do at this moment."

"And what of the next moment?"

"If you are then as you are now, then yes," he replies.

She looks into his eyes. "And if I'm not?"

"Then you will have whatever comes out of that moment."

His eyes tighten and Ann knows he is remembering old confrontations.

"That was the wrong answer," she tells him.

"Perhaps it was the wrong question."

Their eyes lock—an old stance, preliminary to the familiar dance of their relationship—the outcome as unpredictable as the flip of a coin. Heads, they will part decently. Tails, they will clash, hurt each other—perhaps awaken Hattie and the children. If it lands on its side they will meld—beyond their differences—beyond past injuries.

"Do you have a quarter?"

He reaches into his pocket and holds out a handful of change. She reaches for a quarter but takes a nickel instead. Its edge is wider. Then she flips it gently and lets it fall to the floor. It lands on its side, rolls briefly and then tips over, tail side up.

Max glances down. "Tails," he says and scans Ann's face. "What was your question?"

"What do you think it was?" she temporizes.

"I'm hoping it was whether I should be spared the drive back to my place."

"Anything to make your life less difficult," she replies. "Stay the night if you want. I'm going to draw a bath. I'm so tired I may end up sleeping in the tub."

After Ann bathes, she gives her hair its customary fifty strokes, her mind closed to any thought of Max, sleeping in the guestroom. Nor does she allow herself to think of Victor and the tangle of emotions that had welled up in her upon seeing his ivory crop while she was unpacking the presents for Hattie and the children.

"Wow, Mom!" Edwin had exclaimed. "Is it real ivory?"

"Yes, darling."

"Where'd you get it?"

"I won it."

"From who?" Amory had asked.

"From *whom*, runt."

"From a baron."

Edwin had examined it more closely. "Is this his crest?"

"Is there a crest on it?" Max had asked.

"It's on the gold knob. Two swans. One has a crown above its head."

Max had asked nothing further. Nor had he examined the crop.

"What else did you win, Mommy?" Amory had asked, her eyes alight with curiosity.

"The coral snake earrings I'm wearing. And a painting."

"What of?"

And so she had told them the story of her strange but wonderful portrait—costumed in a velvet suit, holding the baron's crop in her left hand, one of his unfiltered French cigarettes in her right hand and wearing Harry's elaborate velvet slippers on her feet—Edwin and Amory, listening spellbound. Hattie, listening spellbound.

But not Max. All-cognizant Max had walked onto the sun porch and then outside, with Belle and Liza following at his heels.

She decides to sleep, not in the high king-size tester bed, but on the low and cozy sitting room sofa. She takes a pillow and the satin quilt from the turned-down bed and turns off the lamps. She is asleep in seconds.

She awakens to someone standing over her. For a moment she cannot remember where she is. The room is dark, its outlines unfamiliar from where she has fallen asleep. She cries out in fear.

Max sits down beside her and places his hand gently over her mouth. "Shush," he whispers, "it's only me."

She wraps her arms around his neck. "I got lost," she wails in the voice of a child.

He kisses her eyes, her forehead—her lips.

"What time is it?" She whispers.

"It's after six."

"Why are you up?"

"I awakened. Why are you sleeping on the sofa?"

"I didn't want the bed."

"Why not?"

"I don't know," she says mournfully.

He kisses her again, an achingly familiar kiss. Her mouth softens beneath his. She nibbles his lower lip.

"Were you missing me?" he asks, low and tender of voice.

"Perhaps so."

"Do you want me?"

A sigh escapes her. "I don't know."

"Unknowing is a way of knowing."

"Are you unknowing?"

He kisses her again. "Oh, I think so."

She sits up, one hand on the nape of his neck, and nuzzles his cheek. "What creatures of habit we are! I wonder how the children would feel, and—" She chuckles softly. "And what dear old-fashioned Hattie would think about us carrying on like this."

"Edwin and Amory would like it because they would like for us to reconcile and I'm sure that Hattie would approve of my moving back home."

"Hattie thinks you can do no wrong and she usually blames the woman, no matter what the circumstances."

"Does she?"

"Yes."

"Did she blame Faye Graham?"

The outrage is immediate. "For what?" Her voice drips venom.

"For her divorce from Leonard."

"How the hell would I know? Hattie and I never discussed Faye's divorce from Leonard." She pulls away from him and springs up from the sofa. "How dare you bring that woman's name up to me!"

"For heaven's sake, Ann! It happened years ago. Can't you ever get past anything?"

"I've gotten past many things!" she retorts. "But you seem to have forgotten that before you began your affair with her, Faye was my best friend. She and I had a close relationship."

His eyes dart back and forth rapidly. "What *you* can't get past and won't forgive," he says, quiet and dreadful of voice, "is that Faye chose her relationship with me over her relationship with you."

"You bastard!"

"Ann, lower your voice. You'll awaken the entire neighborhood."

"Get out!" she shrieks. "Get the hell out of my room."

The gray shuttered light of early morning reveals Victor's crop on the sitting room mantel where she had placed it the night before. She snatches it and strikes Max, a stinging blow across the face.

He rises abruptly and, with a cry of pain-laden rage, grabs her roughly by the shoulders and hurls her against the back of the sofa, tears the crop from her hand, snaps it in two, and throws the halves at her. "To hell with you," he snarls. "And to hell with your baron." He turns on his heel and walks out of the room. She hears his heavy tread down the carpeted hallway and then the sound of a door being slammed shut.

"Mommy?"

Ann looks up.

Amory is standing in the doorway, her eyes wide with fright. "What's wrong, Mommy? Why were you and Daddy fighting?"

She walks quickly to where Amory is standing, kneels down, and gathers her into her arms. "It's alright, Amory. Don't be scared. Everything's fine. Your father and I just had a little disagreement. Why don't you climb into my bed and sleep with me for a while? It's barely morning."

Amory withdraws from Ann's embrace. "No. I want to go back to my bed." She turns around and walks out of the room and down the hallway to her bedroom and then turns around and faces Ann, who is following helplessly behind her. "Will Daddy be here for breakfast like he promised?"

"I don't think so."

"Why not?"

"Because your father and I had a disagreement."

"I don't like it when you fight with Daddy."

"I know, Amory."

"And Edwin hates it too."

"I know, darling. Shall I tuck you in and sit with you until you fall back asleep?'

"I'm too big for that."

"No you're not."

"Yes I am," Amory says matter-of-factly and shuts her bedroom door.

Ann walks slowly back to her room. She is remembering the prophetic flip of the coin she had taken from Max's outstretched hand.

Breakfast is a dismal affair. Ann nurses a cup of coffee while Edwin consumes a stack of Hattie's buttermilk pancakes, several slices of bacon, and a sizeable wedge of cantaloupe. He finishes with a bowl of cereal. Amory is still in her room. Asleep, Ann hopes. She is relieved that Max left before the children came down. His quiet fury and the telltale gash on his left cheek were not a pretty picture. She did not apologize for the blow. She has never apologized for anything hateful she's said or done that had Faye Graham at its center.

Edwin interrupts her thoughts. "Mom, I need to go shopping for camp."

"I know, lamb. Make a list and we'll go this afternoon."

She had forgotten about camp. Edwin leaves next week for Maine and Amory leaves the following week for Mont Shenandoah. It will be Amory's third summer at camp. She smiles at the memory of Amory's agonized phone call two summers ago.

"Amory, darling, what's wrong? Are you homesick?"

"No, Mommy," Amory had choked out between sobs. "It's not that."

"What is it then?"

"I want to stay longer. Joan and Katie have just gotten here for the middle session. They want me in their cabin because Celeste has chicken pox and can't come. Please, Mommy, can I stay?"

And so, she had stayed for eight weeks without getting homesick even once—self-contained little Amory's first camp experience.

This summer they will both be away at camp for eight weeks. Edwin in Kennebunkport and Amory in North Carolina. She and Max had planned to see them off together and visit them together.

Divorced but together. An oxymoron. Max and Ann an oxymoron.

She walks into the butler's pantry, pours herself another cup of coffee, and carries it out to the sunroom. The dogs are sprawled on the sisal matting in front of the wet bar. The beauty of the natural landscape is as compelling in the light of early morning as it was during last evening's full moon. She had anticipated a summer of such days and nights but she knows now that staying here would be disastrous. She tries to shrug off her disappointment by assembling a mental list of things she'll do instead—devote her time to working at the gallery and attending the summer art auctions in the states and possibly abroad—write to Edwin and Amory every day—fly to Maine for Parents' Weekend with Edwin and then to North Carolina for Parents' Weekend with Amory.

But they'll want their parents together for Parents' Weekend!

The realization sends fresh waves of anxiety through her. This morning's fight—whose fault was it? Who had struck the first blow? She had. Across Max's face and with Victor's riding crop, no less.

She puts a clenched fist against her teeth and presses hard. She is stricken with remorse. She had hit Max with enough savagery to break the skin. And why? Why, indeed.

"It's a scorpion's nature to sting. And when does it sting? It stings the instant it feels threatened."

Her therapist's words. Her therapist's analogy.

Ann had protested. *"If that way of reacting when one feels threatened makes Max a scorpion, then I'm a scorpion, too, Dr. Greenfield."*

"No," he had countered, *"your first impulse is to retreat to a safe distance."*

She wonders what it's like to be a man. To decide what one wants and have the temerity to take it merely for the wanting, as Max had done with Faye Graham. He had taken her that first night in the library and many nights thereafter. Ann hadn't known. She hadn't even suspected. And if Max hadn't finally told her, she would never have known.

"Why are you telling me this?" She had been astonished, then tearful, and finally enraged.

"Because I love you and can keep nothing from you."

"It would seem that you have kept quite a lot from me and that you don't love me at all."

And so she had divorced him. But, not that time. Not after his shattering confession and anguished remorse. She had forgiven him that time. She had presented him with Amory as living proof of that forgiveness. No, it was six years down the road, sitting in his private office, waiting for him to return from a hastily called conference, idly thumbing through an open journal on his desk. There, in his own handwriting, entry after entry. Tender love entries, such as he might have written to her. She had risen convulsively from the chair and when she rose, her knees had buckled beneath her and she had fallen to the floor in trembling disbelief.

She had exited his office abruptly, past his surprised and questioning secretary, the journal still clenched in her shaking hands, gotten into her car, driven a block away, pulled into a shopping mall parking lot and read the entire journal—rich with passion and sex and yearning—and photographs of them together—Max and this woman—this stranger in their midst.

She had divorced him then. She had divorced him and after the divorce was finalized she had burned the journal, page by page, in the sitting room fireplace.

She had not wept once during the entire agonizing procedure, nor any time thereafter. Not one tear until last night, when she had read his poems and her heart, caught finally unguarded, had remembered what she so loved in him.

She is angry afresh now, remembering. Anger was less anguishing than guilt. Anger would get her through the hateful gash on his cheek—through sending the children off to camp without his assistance—through an entire summer without his ambiguous presence in her life.

JUNE 1987

"And then something happens, as you knew it would,
and nothing can ever be the same again."

— *The Quiet American*

Eleanor's smile is sheer pleasure. "Welcome back! I missed you. The clients missed you."

"I hope everyone missed Belle and Liza too, because the three of us are going to be spending this summer in Richmond." She gives Eleanor a hug and presses a monogrammed jeweler's box into her hand. "This is for you."

"Oh Ann, you shouldn't have." Eleanor opens the box and utters a whoop of delight at the pearl-and-emerald circle pin. "It's beautiful," she breathes. "Thank you."

"I'm the one who should be thanking *you*. You've outdone yourself. I'm thrilled about the Theodore Robinson painting."

"So was Mrs. Rutledge. She's wanted that painting for a long time. She said she could have spared herself a lot of agonizing if she'd bought it when she first saw it." Eleanor shrugs incomprehension. "She obviously had the funds to buy it. She wrote out the check like it was nothing. How are the children?"

"I put Amory on the plane this morning."

"Is she excited about camp?"

"That she is. She and Katie and Joan were on the same flight, but not seated together. Joan told the stewardess that if they weren't seated together the three little lost lambs from Tidewater might not survive the trip. I watched Joan's performance in awe. She actually had tears in her eyes."

"Did Joan get her way?"

"The stewardess did some shuffling and seated them together."

Eleanor's brow wrinkles. "I hope the girls don't fight this year."

Ann nods knowingly. "Worrying already?"

"Well, you know how sensitive Amory is."

"I do know that. And you know that if Amory gets so much as a hangnail she'll call her father and me." She gives Eleanor's shoulder a reassuring pat.

"Speaking of Max, how is he?"

"He was waiting at the airport the night I returned. We had a fight the following morning."

"Was it a bad fight?"

"Yes."

"How bad?"

"I struck him."

"With what?"

"With an ivory riding crop."

Eleanor whistles. "Gosh! That sounds kinky. Where'd you strike him?"

"In the sitting room."

"I meant where on his body."

"His face."

Eleanor's mouth drops open. "Did you break the skin?"

"Yes, I broke the skin. Years of working together make it possible for me to relate these personal tidbits to you but I am most eager to forget that incident. I'm letting you know how things are so you won't expect warmth from him if he calls." Ann shrugs. "Or whatever."

Eleanor looks up. "Speaking of whatever, you've had lots of phone calls from Maggie Lambert."

"Who else?"

"She was the most persistent and she was rude to me."

"In what way?"

"When I told her you'd gone to Ireland, she grunted."

"What do you mean?"

"I mean she snarled '*whatever*' and then grunted."

Ann laughs. "I can hear her doing it."

"That woman annoys me."

"Why?"

"Her attitude about you is possessive and domineering. She's your art consultant, not your mother."

"Maggie's not quite old enough to be my mother."

"She's a hard woman, Ann. I find her very unpleasant."

"I find her interesting," Ann replies. "And, as a matter of fact, I have a print I purchased in Dublin that I want framed. I'm going to give it to her. Will you take it to Lloyd for me? Tell him I want it triple matted in a simple gold frame. He can decide on the mat colors."

"What's the print?"

"The *Pied Piper of Hamelin*. For some reason I thought of Maggie the minute I saw it."

"I know why." Eleanor shudders. "That story's about vermin."

"You're awful." Ann averts her face to hide the grin. "I'm going to attack my mail. I'll be in my office if you need me."

Her heels make a clicking jaunty sound on the black marble of the showroom floor—a sound reminiscent of her mother and of Ann clunking about in her mother's shoes, pretending to be her mother.

The memory elicits a sigh.

After Ann has sorted through the voluminous stack of mail, she picks up the phone to call Maggie Lambert, hesitates, and then puts the receiver back in its cradle. She settles into her chair and eyes the room appreciatively. The walls are padded and covered in scarlet damask. The bronze doré chandelier sports three fierce eagles, wings outstretched, and is English Regency, as is most of the furniture, including her grandfather's leather chesterfield and leather-topped partner's desk, a massive affair on which she has carefully arranged her father's George III silver inkwell, his silver and gold vinaigrettes and a collection of museum-quality eighteenth-century enameled patch boxes.

She picks up the photograph she took seven years ago of Amory, sitting on her father's lap, in his oversized wing chair, both of them in pajamas—grinning—relaxed—happy.

The French cartel clock, her grandmother's wedding gift to Max and Ann, strikes the half hour. Twelve thirty—half the day already gone. The phone rings but she waits for Eleanor to take the call. The intercom buzzes.

"Yes?"

"And the bad news of the afternoon is," Eleanor pauses for emphasis, "Maggie Lambert's on the line. She wants to know if you're back from Ireland—heavy emphasis on the 'D'."

"Tell her I'm in my office but didn't answer the intercom."

"Gladly," she retorts and hangs up.

She waits a few moments and then buzzes Eleanor. "What did she say?"

"She said 'thank you.'"

"That's all she said?"

"She also reminded me to cut up your meat at lunch."

"Very funny," Ann retorts and clicks off. The last thing she wants to do today is to handle Maggie. Eleanor can handle Maggie. She takes out a sheet of pale-blue stationery and begins a letter to Edwin. She had been anxious before his flight and Edwin had noted it.

"Don't worry, Mom," he had admonished, in a soft but decisive tone amazingly like his father's. *"Everything will be fine."*

"I'm not worried, darling. I just hate giving you up for the summer. I miss you and Amory terribly when you go off to camp."

"You'll be up in a few weeks and I'll write you a lot, I promise. And you can write me prodigiously. Gosh! That's a vocabulary word I never thought I'd use!"

"But you said the boys ribbed you about getting so many letters from your mother."

Edwin had shrugged indifference. *"Hide them in Hattie's chocolate chips and I'll fish them out unnoticed."*

She finishes her letter to Edwin and glances at the clock. Much too early—the plane will have barely landed. She opens the Sotheby's catalog of nineteenth-century paintings. One in particular compels her. Unsigned and unattributed, its merit lies in the artist's interpretation of the subject matter— "Joseph being sold into slavery by his brothers." The facial expressions are intriguing. The old slave merchant's smile reveals craftiness tempered by rueful knowing. Joseph's brothers' faces are a composite of rage, jealousy, cruelty, and guilt. Joseph is depicted as a tender sapling of a child, slim and pale of limb, aglow with joyous innocence. The heavy sky is lit by a full moon. There are camels and several tents in the background encircling a blazing campfire.

She marks the catalog page and puts the brochure beside the desk telephone. She'll call about it this afternoon. The estimate is surprisingly low, notwithstanding that it has no provenance. She suspects it may be earlier than nineteenth century, although Sotheby's determinations are generally accurate. *Perhaps it's a sleeper!* She acknowledges the adrenaline rush. It's part and parcel of the chase—as thrilling as the first hurdle when riding the hounds or placing a heady bet at the casino gaming tables.

Many times she has been approached before the start of an auction. *"I hope you're not going to bid on that early Demuth watercolor, Mrs. Cabot. I do so want it for my sunroom."* Or, even more outrageous, *"Would you please not bid on the Henry Moore sketchbook? I couldn't possibly compete and you already have a gallery filled with art."*

Ann's demeanor ultimately discourages such chumminess. She's uninformative and solitary at auctions. It's the nature of the beast—a beast whose predatory tension is disconcerting to see in others and difficult to override in one's self, particularly when the bidding has accelerated quickly and far beyond expectation. When hers is the winning bid, she feels heady elation followed by an apprehension of having bid too high for the purchase to be lucrative. But she has yet to regret a purchase— primarily because seeing a client fall in love with fine art she has acquired for resale is a happiness-eliciting experience. She is of the persuasion that fine art ultimately finds its rightful owner—the one who most loves it— respects it—wants it in a museum for the world to see.

The intercom buzzes.

"Yes?"

"Amory's on the line and I'm taking your print to Lloyd and then I'm off to lunch. Can I bring you something back?"

"No, thanks. Enjoy your lunch." She clicks on to Amory's call. "Hi, darling."

"Hi, Mommy."

"How was your flight?"

"It was fine, except Joan hogged the aisle seat the whole way."

Ann chuckles. "I would have expected nothing less. How's your cabin?"

"I got, I mean I have an upper bunk."

"Super! Who's in the bunk beneath yours?"

"Katie is, but she wanted a bottom bunk. I can't talk long. The girls are lined up to call home."

"I miss you already, Amory."

"I miss you and Daddy too. Don't forget to send cookies."

"Hattie's baking them as we speak."

"Wait, Mommy. Joan wants to talk to you."

"Hi, Mrs. Cabot," Joan whistles through her mouthful of metal braces. "I just wanted to reassure you not to worry about Amory. I'm going to look out for her. So I want to thank you now, you know, ahead of time, for those care packages like you sent our cabin last summer. I mean they helped lots with her homesickness and all, you know, I mean especially the food packages. We're not allowed candy here, so it's got to be sent in being as how the food here really sucks—except no candy that gets stuck and all. You know what I mean, right, Mrs. Cabot?"

"I think so, Joan."

"Good grief, Joan! Give me back the phone." Amory's voice drips outrage. "Mommy, ignore everything Joan said. I love you."

"I love you, too. Have fun and call when you can."

"I will. Bye, Mommy"

"Bye, darling."

Ann puts down the receiver and glances at the photographs of Max and Amory and of herself and Edwin taken at Cape May—happy pictures of happy people. Where does happiness go? What brings it back?—The roller coaster of human emotions—*what was it that you were so worried about a year ago?*

She pushes back her chair and walks into the small powder room adjoining her office. Her hair is already tidy but she brushes it anyway, head down, from the nape of the neck to the tip of its long length.

She hears a rap on her office door—Eleanor with a million questions about Amory's phone call.

"Come in," she calls out. "I'm in the powder room brushing my hair for the third time today. What do you want to ask me?"

"How you had the gall to leave the country without letting me know."

Ann looks up. Her hair is everywhere. "Maggie!" she exclaims. "I thought you were Eleanor."

"No, I do not forgive you," Maggie growls.

"For what?"

"You already know for what." She stands in the bathroom doorway, arms crossed.

"Eleanor will be back any minute."

"To hell with Eleanor."

"She said you were rude to her while I was away."

"So what? I was rude to *everyone* while you were away. I sold my cat, put my mother in a nursing home, and flushed my fish down the john."

"You're so irreverent."

"And you, Ann Cabot, are cruel."

"In what way am I cruel?"

"In every way. Even your hair is cruel."

Ann attempts a smile. "That puts me in mind of a line from a poem. 'She has more hair than she needs— in the sun 'tis a woe to me.' Edna St. Vincent Millay wrote that."

"Good for Edna."

"Maggie, let's get out of this bathroom."

"I don't think so, dearest." Maggie shuts the bathroom door and locks it.

"Maggie, please unlock the door. Eleanor will be back any second."

"Don't worry, this won't take long." She reaches for Ann.

Ann steps back. She can feel the towel rack pressing into her shoulder blades. "What are you doing?"

"I'm going to kiss you."

"Maggie, please. Stop this nonsense."

"Wipe off your lipstick."

"I certainly will not."

"You'd prefer it smeared all over your face?" She reaches for a tissue and hands it to Ann.

"I'm not wiping off my lipstick."

"Must I do everything?" She folds the tissue in half and gently removes Ann's lipstick. "Ann dearest, please unclench your mouth."

"I have no intention of kissing you, Maggie."

"I didn't ask you to kiss me. I asked you to unclench your mouth."

"What about Eleanor?"

"I have no desire to kiss Eleanor and I would prefer her mouth sealed permanently shut." She takes Ann's flowing hair gently in both hands. "You're so lovely. Cruel but lovely. Now, give your mouth to me. Give your sweet warm mouth to me."

Ann is conversing with Dr. Houseman when Eleanor returns from lunch. It's the third time he has visited the gallery to examine the large American primitive of a child holding a cat on her lap. Ann is defending its price tag.

"It's charming and its palette is dramatic. Joseph Whiting Stock's paintings command steep prices these days." She gives Eleanor a grateful nod. "Ah, here's Eleanor. I'm afraid I must rush off or I'm going to be terribly late for an appointment."

Once inside her office, she locks the door and lights a cigarette, the last of her daily allotment. She takes a couple of puffs, stubs it out, and begins to pace the parameters of the large Sultanbad, its shimmering milky-rose background a subtle complement to the room's vibrant crimson walls. She paces precisely, heel to toe, stops to remove her cream-and-white slingbacks, nudges them under the chesterfield with her foot and then resumes pacing.

In the name of God, the All-Seeing.

In the name of God, the All-Knowing.

"So, tell me, God, were you there for that unnatural kiss?"

"I was there, Ann."

"What were you thinking?"

"I was thinking that unnatural is a hard row to hoe."

She shudders. "I'm totally lost," she whispers.

She walks over to the desk, sits tiredly down, reaches for the dictionary and looks up the definition of "natural."

Present in or produced by nature. Not acquired. Inherent. Free from affectation or artificiality. Spontaneous. Expected or accepted. Established by moral certainty or conviction.

And its musical definition: *Having no sharps or flats.*

She winces. Maggie's kiss was nothing but sharps and flats. Discordant notes in the key of D minor.

"You don't know a thing about kissing," Maggie had pronounced, shaking her head at Ann in mock sorrow, a half smile playing about the corners of her mouth.

"Too Junior League for you?" Ann had sneered.

Maggie had grinned rakishly. *"You're way at the bottom of that list, my dear."*

Ann slams the dictionary shut and rests her forehead upon its smooth leather cover. She should have taken Maggie to Ireland. Maggie and Cookie would have gotten along just fine because they were, in point of fact, so alike, whereas she, Ann, was so unalike. She lifts her head. Alike or unalike—natural or unnatural—what occurred in that powder room was unpleasant and alarming and she had warned Maggie of its consequence.

"This is going to ruin our relationship, Maggie."

"No, Ann, this is going to clarify our relationship. We need to get past this so we can get to where we need to be."

"And where exactly is it that you think we need to be?"

"Past sexuality."

"I'm already there, Maggie. It's you who can't walk away."

"Perhaps it's that I can walk away but don't want to, whereas you can't walk away but want to."

"How clever of you, but you're wrong. I could walk away."

"Then why are you so angry?"

"Because this is not who I am."

"Ann, dear, I can only be who I am. I can't be who you are. Don't you understand that?"

"You're damn right I understand. I understand that we are at odds over this."

"You don't trust me."

"I don't trust where you're taking me."

"Where am I taking you?"

"You tell me where you're taking me," Ann had countered.

"Home."

"Home? Home where, exactly?"

"Home, Ann, where the real you lives hidden away. Beyond the glitter, the opulent trappings, the pricey art gallery, the failed marriage, the uninvolved relationship with what's-his-name. Home where you can be yourself, unguarded, unbound, unafraid. Don't you want that?"

"Of course I want it, but not this way."

"It's my way, Ann." The depth of her determination had remained impenetrable. *"My way."*

Later that evening, in bed, unable to sleep, Ann reaches for the telephone and reluctantly dials, hangs up before the connection is made, and then dials again. Maggie answers after the first ring.

"Hello."

"Hi."

"How are you?"

"I'm fine."

"Are you?"

"Yes."

"Did Eleanor return before you reapplied your lipstick?"

"No."

"Good. That Eleanor is one nosy broad."

"Maggie," Ann pauses. "There's something I want to ask you."

"So ask me."

Ann hesitates. "I don't know."

"What is it?"

"I hope the question won't anger you."

"It won't."

"Do you know what I'm going to ask you?"

"No, Ann. I won't know that until after you've asked me. So, for the third time, ask your question."

"Why women? It can't be solely because of what happened with John."

"Now that's what I call a seriously personal question, but I'm willing to try and answer it, and yes, John had a lot to do with it. That incident and the hard-assed way John bred his horses, particularly his fillies. But, you're, right it wasn't just because of John."

"What were the other reasons?"

"Well," she ruminates before continuing, "there's a natural tenderness between women that's hard to open up in a man. Also, I guess I'd have to say that I prefer the female response to the male response because with a woman it's lingering, more intense, multilayered and glorious to behold, which is why I prefer making love to someone rather than the other way around. Men can't endure the idea of a woman coolly watching them lose themselves during intimacy but a woman loves it because it's so intimately about her."

She pauses to light a cigarette. "But I'm also open to the possibility that I have yet to experience some of the more awe-inspiring byproducts of heterosexuality."

"For example?"

"Well, for one thing, I've never conceived a child. Some women claim to have known the very second they became pregnant. That's pretty special, I would imagine."

"Very special. That's the way it was with Edwin. I absolutely knew. Name another heterosexual byproduct," she prods.

"I have yet to meet a man with whom I would want to share my life."

"Have you had that with a woman?"

"I thought I had."

"Tell me."

"I can't do that, dearest."

"Why not?"

"Because another person's privacy is involved, and I don't know yet if you're trustworthy."

"What else?"

"I don't know if you can handle my past."

"Why wouldn't I be able to handle your past?"

"You're uptight about anything that involves sexuality. And you were married to a shrink. A still-keeps-a-tight-rein on the former wife shrink. Does he, by any chance, prescribe for you?"

"Go to hell."

"That was meant to be a tease."

"And I am trustworthy."

"I know that."

"How do you know that?"

"In many ways."

"Name three of those ways."

Maggie snorts. "I'll name one. I wouldn't be drawn to someone who's untrustworthy."

"That's about you."

"Your reticence. And you appear to be a very discreet person. That trait goes hand in hand with trustworthiness. There, I've given you two ways."

"You're too bountiful."

"Perhaps I am, considering—"

"Considering what?"

Maggie exhales into the receiver. "I was thinking about your unkind remarks to me."

"Such as? And when?"

"I'll reverse the order. This afternoon, in your charming powder room. You wiped your mouth with the back of your hand and shrieked for a medic and an ice pack."

"Did I hurt your feelings?"

"Yep."

"I'm sorry."

"Thank you, dearest."

"But I really hated that kiss."

"And thank you again, dearest."

"Let me explain."

"I think you already did that this afternoon. Don't you remember?"

"Remind me."

"Well, I've already mentioned the ice pack and the medic. Let's see. What else. Oh, it was an unnatural kiss. It could promote gum disease. It was mussing the grandmother's tea towels."

"I never said a word about gum disease and I never mentioned my grandmother's impeccably monogrammed tea towels."

"*Grandmother's impeccably monogrammed* tea towels! Didn't you? I thought you did."

"Well I didn't, dearest."

Maggie chortles with delight. "Wonderful!"

"What's wonderful?"

"Your natural and carefree banter is wonderful. You're adorable," Maggie whispers.

Ann can suddenly think of nothing to say. The silence lengthens uncomfortably. "It's getting quite late," she says finally. "I think we should say good night."

"I agree."

"I'll call you in the morning. What time do you get up?"

"Around five."

"Do you always get up that early?"

"Every morning I'm home, which is most mornings."

"What do you do when you get up?"

"Feed the birds, drink several cups of coffee, read the paper, relish my two hours of solitude."

"But you live alone."

"No," Maggie replies, "My mother and I share the second floor of the studio."

Ann draws a shallow breath. "Now *that* surprises me."

"We share living quarters, Ann. I have a private life and so does she."

"I think it's sweet."

"Whatever."

"What's your mother like?"

"She's actually pretty cool."

"Do the two of you get along well?"

"We have our differences."

I'll bet you do! Ann suppresses a chuckle. "I'd love to meet her someday."

"You will."

"Will she like me?"

"She'll adore you."

"How do you know?"

"You have those attributes of which she most approves."

"Such as?"

"Lifestyle. Demeanor. Appearance. Upbringing. Intelligence. Sophistication. Children. MD husband..."

"But I'm divorced."

"So was she."

"When?"

"When I was in my teens."

"Who pursued the divorce?"

"She did."

"Are you an only child?"

"The one and only."

"I am too."

"We finally have something in common," Maggie whispers.

"Yes, we do. Were you born in Richmond?"

"Yes."

"That makes two things in common. Who delivered you?"

"I don't know. I'll have to ask Zeke."

"Is Zeke your father?"

"No. My father died. Zeke is short for the prophet Ezekiel. I've been calling Clarissa, that's my mother's given name, 'Zeke' for years."

"I guess I understand," Ann says dubiously.

"You don't really, but it doesn't matter."

"Well, shall we say goodnight now and hang up?"

"Shall we?"

"I think so, lamb. It's really quite late." Ann hurries past the endearment she has inadvertently used. "I'll call you tomorrow."

"Good night then, dearest."

"Good night, Maggie."

She presses the button to disconnect and places the receiver in its cradle. But she isn't sleepy. She hadn't really wanted to end the conversation. She had only done so because it was late. What a strange person Maggie is. Up at five every morning! And she feeds the birds!

And then she remembers something else. She remembers that when Maggie was enumerating the reasons why Zeke would adore her, Ann had heard, for the first time, a mournful note in that musical southern drawl.

Eleanor gives a Cheshire cat grin when Ann walks into the gallery. "You're twelve thousand dollars richer today than you were yesterday."

"Don't tell me Dr. Houseman took the primitive," Ann says in surprise.

"I just got off the phone with him. It's hanging in his study as we speak. He's wild about it. He said that where you suggested to hang it was pure Zen."

"All I said was 'over the mantel.' Where else in that paneled and bookcase-lined room could he have put it?"

Eleanor's brow wrinkles in thought. "Maybe over the sofa."

"Not unless he moves that huge Federal bull's-eye mirror, which will actually reflect the painting since it's on the opposite wall."

Eleanor hangs her head in mock chagrin. "What could I be thinking of?"

"No, you're right. Hang the *mirror* over the mantel. It would change the look of that room dramatically." Ann nods approval. "You should call him and suggest it."

Eleanor grimaces. "I think I'll leave well enough alone. I'm not sure Dr. Houseman can deal with making another painting decision. He kept me here until after five yesterday trying to make up his mind about buying it. So I told him, 'Don't decide today. Sleep on it.' For some reason that comment decided it for him. I don't think he wanted to leave the gallery without it."

"It was the perfect suggestion to make. It's a great painting. And it's amusing. Any other early morning calls?"

"Nobody yet. Want a cup of coffee?"

"It will be my third today, but yes."

Eleanor heads for the kitchen. "So tell me about Ireland. You've hardly mentioned your trip."

Ann follows her. "This will interest you. I had my portrait painted."

"Who painted it?"

"An Austrian baron."

"That sounds special. Where?"

"At Cookie's. In the great hall."

"Well, I hope you were wearing clothes. That monstrosity of a hallway is freezing, even in the middle of summer."

"Of course I was wearing clothes. Are you suggesting I'm capable of posing nude?"

"I think under the right circumstances and with the right artist you could pose nude."

"And what would the right circumstances be?"

"Well, to begin with, you'd probably have to be somebody else."

"And the right artist?"

"That's harder. He'd have to be saintly and you'd have to be so entranced you didn't care. And if you posed naked in the great hall, it would have to be in the wee hours of the morning after the servants had been allowed to go to bed and Cookie and Harry were unconscious from drinking so much."

"You're terrible."

"But am I right?"

"Actually, the time and state of inebriation are partly accurate."

"What were you wearing?"

"A black-velvet boy's suit with a huge and uncomfortably over-starched white lace collar."

"Sounds like that Boldini brat in the holding room."

"Uncannily like."

"What a weird choice for you. I mean with the way you like to dress up and wear high heels and gloves and carry one of your grandmother's fancy hankies. Why did you pick that instead of a gown or something?"

"Victor chose it from Cookie's costume room. Do you remember the costume room?"

"I remember every room in that dreary dungeon." Eleanor's voice drips disgust.

Ann turns away to hide her smile. She had treated Eleanor to a trip to Ireland a few years back, after Ann's divorce. She had taken Edwin and Amory, too. The children had loved it—the daily riding and grooming of the horses, the Bentley, which Harry had allowed Edwin to drive endlessly around the wide circular driveway, the billiards room, the smoking room, the swan fountain that was large enough to swim in. They had been awed by the sheer size of the estate—more than a thousand acres—rolling green sweeps of lawn and pasture, meandering streams, barns and haystacks and outbuildings, hen houses filled with roosting ducks, geese, grouse, and quail, paddocks for the horses, open fields liberally sprinkled with Herefords, Angus, and fancy long-haired French cattle, woolly sheep and bleating baby ram and ewe lambs grazing the gently sloping banks that led to the wide span of sparkling river.

They had spent endless rain-filled hours playing Sardines with other guests and several of the servants in the forty-two—Edwin had counted them—high-ceilinged rooms, many of which had floors that creaked loudly enough to give away really clever hiding places.

Eleanor, on the other hand, had not enjoyed being there at all. She had hated the weather, the ubiquitous servants and the formal dinners that lasted for hours. She had particularly disliked Harry's "lord of the manor" demeanor and she had thought Cookie arrogant and self-indulgent. She had declined Ann's second invitation to accompany her and the children to Ireland. After Eleanor's third refusal, Ann had not invited her again. But Eleanor was always curious about Ann's visits.

"So tell me more about this baron artist," Eleanor says and hands Ann a cup of coffee, black with a hint of honey.

"His name is Victor and he's Max's age and rather nice." She takes a swallow of coffee and nods appreciatively.

"How many hours did you have to pose for him?"

Ann computes. "If you put all of the hours together, probably a full day. But we broke it up into six or seven sittings. It rained endlessly and I was sick to death of playing bridge, so it was a welcome diversion."

"Where's the painting now?"

"It seems that Victor took it back to Vienna."

"Was it good?"

"It was astonishingly good. I would have liked to own it."

"Did he expect you to buy it?"

"Of course not."

"Well, you know. Strange are the ways of gentry," Eleanor says drily.

Another thing Eleanor had hated about her trip to Ireland was that she had lost 160 pounds playing gin rummy with Harry—early on—the second day, to be exact. She had overlooked Ann's warning to beware of Harry's skill at all card games, claiming that she, Eleanor, was a master rummy player, having learned the game at her father's knee. Harry had cleverly allowed Eleanor to win the first several hands and then proceeded to trounce her soundly until Ann prevailed upon Cookie to put an end to it.

Eleanor had written a check to cover the gambling debt and Harry had cashed it on the fourth day of their visit. She had archly declined Ann's offer to pay and Ann had to physically restrain Eleanor from presenting Harry with her driver's license, along with the hastily scrawled check. Eleanor had been as mean-spirited as a wet hornet for the duration of their stay.

The love of money is the root of all evil, Ann muses. Not money, but the *love* of money. That was what Eleanor had recoiled from in outrage—Harry's love of money.

Eleanor looks at Ann curiously. "What were you just thinking about?"

"I was thinking about money. About the love of money."

"About Harry and Cookie's love of money, you mean."

"Yes."

"I guess the baron's rich."

"Surely."

"And unmarried?"

"Twice or maybe three times divorced. Cookie couldn't remember."

"Is he good-looking?"

"He's tall, slim, nice hair, good eyes, wonderful skin tones. Yes, you would definitely think him handsome."

"Did you?"

"Sort of. I'm off to write my baby lambs." She heads for her office, coffee cup in hand.

"Give me a little more than 'sort of,'" Eleanor calls after her.

"Close, but no cigar," Ann replies and shuts her office door.

She writes light-hearted, humorous letters to the children and gives them to Eleanor to post.

"Take the afternoon off," she says breezily. "It's a scorcher of a day. Doesn't your condo have a pool? Go and get yourself the beginning of a suntan."

"Are you sure?"

"Yes, Eleanor. I'm sure. Now off with you."

"Why are you trying to get rid of me?"

"Are you implying that it's impossible for me to give you the afternoon off without having an ulterior motive?"

"Sounds like it."

"Suspicions recoil upon those who harbor them," Ann retorts. She walks past Eleanor to the rear entrance door and gazes outside. Belle and Liza are in the gallery's fenced-in backyard. She had decided against having it paved for additional parking just so her babies could be as they are now—snoozing alongside each other under a leafy mulberry tree in the corner of the lot. One of Belle's ears is turned inside out—listening for unsuspecting cats, most likely.

She turns to Eleanor. "When will Lloyd be finished with the print and why aren't you racing home to catch the tanning rays of the sun?"

"He didn't say and I feel guilty about leaving."

"My better angel has offered you the afternoon off, Eleanor. Do yourself a favor and accept. You deserve a week of afternoons off."

Eleanor smiles relief. "I think I will. I need to do laps around the pool. Work off some of those chocolate egg creams from High's. You're sure you won't mind being stuck here?"

"If I do, I'll close the gallery, put Belle and Liza in the wagon, and go home. That's one of the fringe benefits of being self-employed. Now off you go."

After Eleanor takes off in the crisply stenciled gallery van, Ann paces the floor of the showroom. She can think of a dozen things she ought to do, beginning with phoning George. She has no idea what she will say to him if he happens to catch her by surprise, as he invariably does. The quintessential weapon of a trial lawyer, he had told her once, the element of surprise, a tactic he acquired during his brief stint in the DA's office.

She walks over to the showroom phone and calls Hattie, whose answers to Ann's queries are primarily monosyllabic. Yes, everything is fine. Yes, she's baked cookies for Edwin and Amory. Yes, she's sending them off this afternoon. No, Dr. Cabot hasn't called. No, he hasn't stopped by the house. Yes, Ann has had several phone calls. Mrs. Phillips called to remind Ann of the garden club luncheon. Mrs. Franklin called to say that bridge had been cancelled. The window washers were coming next Monday. And Mrs. Graham called and asked for Ann to call her back.

Hattie's voice barely conceals her dislike for Faye Graham. Ann suspects that Hattie has much more than an inkling of what transpired between Max and Faye, although she isn't sure exactly *how* Hattie knows. She feels the blood rush to her cheeks as Hattie repeats the telephone number Mrs. Graham has left for Ann to please return her call. She takes pen in hand and actually writes it down, although she more than knows the number from memory. It's a number she called daily for years. How could she ever not remember that number?

She thanks Hattie and hangs up, her thoughts in turmoil. Why in the world would Faye be calling her? Could it have something to do with Max? And even if it did, why should she deign to talk to Faye about anything? Would Faye return a phone call from Ann if the shoe were on the other foot?

She remembers how bitter Faye had been when Leonard sued for divorce. Theirs had been a particularly hateful dissolution, filled with acrimony and mutually hurled insults. And Leonard had remarried shortly after he divorced Faye—a perky red-headed lawyer from Louisiana. It had been rumored that Leonard was seriously involved with the perky Louisiana lawyer long before he pursued his divorce from Faye.

Ann's smile is grim. No, Faye would definitely not have returned a phone call from Leonard's mistress-become-wife.

Not then. Not now. Not ever.

Ann calls Maggie at seven, hangs up after the sixth unanswered ring. Dinner had been a hurried affair—rice and lamb for the dogs, shrimp salad on a croissant for herself.

She wanders aimlessly through the house, pauses in the library and then walks over to the baby grand her father had given her for a wedding present. He used to boast that one day his Ann would become a concert pianist but she had discarded that notion her first year at Mount Holyoke. She possessed neither the temperament nor the skill and it was not in her nature to set a goal clearly beyond her reach.

It had taken another semester to decide upon art history. Her junior year had been in Florence. She had thought it the most beautiful city in Europe.

She plays the opening chords of "Clair de Lune," one of her mother's favorites. She would critique Ann's rendition with a dispassionate ear.

Too fast, too slow, too sentimental.

She lifts her hands from the keyboard and acknowledges the restlessness she feels and why. Max hasn't called her and she hasn't called him to apologize for the blow she struck with Victor's riding crop.

What was it that he had hurled at her? *"For heaven's sake, Ann! Can't you get past anything?"* Was it possible that Faye had meant nothing to him? No. Max wasn't like that. Or was he? Perhaps for him it was, as he had claimed, a love that arose only in the moments of passion between them.

Anger propels her from the piano bench and into her bedroom. She walks over to the bedside table, turns on the light, hesitates, and then lifts the receiver from its cradle and pauses in thought. *Don't think about it—just do it.*

Dialing the number elicits piercing anxiety and the unsettling sensation of déjà vu.

Faye answers after the second ring. "Graham residence."

"Hello, Faye."

"Ann! I don't believe it. It's been so long."

Ann remains silent.

"Ann? Are you there?"

"Yes."

"You're not saying anything."

"I'm returning *your* call, Faye."

Faye clears her throat. "Well, I had hoped, after all this time, we might be able to talk."

"I don't see how."

"Ann, please don't make this any harder than it already is."

"How hard exactly is it, Faye?"

"It's more than hard. It's painful. And awkward." Faye clears her throat again. "I'd best begin by saying how sorry I am."

"For what?"

"For heaven's sake, Ann!"

"I'm simply asking what you're sorry for. Surely you can rise to the occasion."

"You're still angry. It's been years and your anger's as intense as if it happened last week."

"It did happen last week. It happened last week and the week before that. It happens every time Max and I are together. It's still that much between us. Do you understand?"

"I do understand. But it's you he loves, Ann. Do you believe that?"

"What I *don't* believe, Faye, is that love has much to do with infidelity."

"Sometimes it does," Faye says in a mournful voice. "I was, please don't hate me for saying this, but I was in love with Max. It doesn't excuse what happened. There's no excuse for what happened. It was just plain wrong and I'm sorry for my part in it. I know I hurt you terribly. I wish you'd try to forgive me."

Ann shuts her eyes and tries to recall Faye as she was when they were friends.

"Ann," Faye presses, "I'm sorry ... deeply sorry and I'm—" Her voice breaks. "I'm pleading with you to forgive me. I'd like for us to be friends again."

"I do forgive you," Ann says, after another awkward silence between them.

"Do you mean it?"

"Yes, I think I do," she answers slowly, evenly. "I don't think you and I will ever be friends again. But at least now I can stop hating you. I'm relieved to have that thorn removed from my heart. Goodbye, Faye."

She places the phone in its cradle and breathes a sigh of relief. Forgiveness was a strange beast. It clawed and tore to shreds in the getting there, but its aftermath was peace.

It's past ten o'clock when Ann tries Maggie's number again. "Am I calling too late?" she asks when Maggie answers

"Not really."

"I called earlier but no one answered."

"I was out."

"Why didn't your mother answer?"

"Zeke never answers my phone."

"Why doesn't she?"

"Because, dearest, I don't want her to."

"So, what was your day like?"

"Very full."

"Tell me five things you accomplished today."

"Five? Let me think. Well, I lined a sixteenth-century painting, very small, I got a haircut, had dinner with a friend, talked with John, who asked about you, by the way."

"How is John?"

"John's fine."

"Do you talk to him often?"

"Almost daily, for the last twelve or so years. You do remember that John and I work together."

"Actually, I'd sort of forgotten."

"Whatever."

Ann chuckles.

"Why the laugh?"

"That word! And now I've started saying it."

"Whatever."

Ann laughs again—a soft, easy laugh.

"You're in a sweet little mood tonight," Maggie says in a low voice.

"I wasn't earlier."

"Dismay, perhaps, over my unanswered telephone?"

"What an egotist you are. No, my dismay was over a complicated Hampton affair, although I did wonder where you were."

"And now you know."

"What did John ask about me?"

"He asked how you were and about your trip to Ireland. We spoke about you quite a lot, actually."

"Did you tell him that you kissed me?"

"Of course not. Did you think I would?"

"I thought it possible."

"Would you have been angry if I had?"

"I would have thought it an invasion of my privacy."

"I wouldn't invade your privacy in that way. Or in any way, for that matter."

"What was the fifth thing you accomplished today?"

"Oh—you'll like this one. I found out from Zeke the name of the doctor who delivered me."

"What was his name?"

"Sterling Rucker."

"He delivered me, too. At Stuart Circle Hospital."

"I was born at Stuart Circle, too."

"Maggie, think of that—after each of us was born, we were first held by the same person."

"Actually, Rucker wasn't supposed to deliver me. Bert Frazier was Zeke's regular OB, but he was attending a twilight-sleep conference in Toledo when she went into labor. I should probably warn you that Zeke has the memory of an elephant. She filled me in on all of this at breakfast. She was really miffed that old Frazier wasn't in town to take out her firstborn and that she was going to be intimately handled by a total stranger, when in walks tall, dark, and breathtakingly handsome Sterling Alsop Rucker, MD." Maggie pauses to take a drag from her cigarette. "She said he sat down on the side of her hospital bed, took her shaking fist in his and unclenched it finger by finger. 'Now, Clarissa,' he said, 'you stop worrying because I'm going to take extra-special care with you.' He called her by her first name right off the bat, can you believe that?" Maggie snorts into the receiver. "I'll lay you odds he'd barely eyeballed Zeke's name on the chart as he was hauling his trim little ass into her hospital room. Zeke said he was absolutely marvelous, an ambassador of a stork. She might have fallen in love with him, for all I know. She's a sucker for physical beauty.

Anyway—" She takes another long drag from her cigarette and exhales audibly. "She never forgave Frazier for being out of town. She stuck with Rucker through all the remaining years of annual exams, Pap smears, et cetera, and when he died, she attended his funeral."

"My mother thought Dr. Rucker was handsome, too. According to her, he wore a white tea rose in his lapel every day. All the nurses were in love with him and terrified of his disapproval. Oh my gosh!"

"What?"

"It just occurred to me that our mothers might have been in love with the same man. I'm sure Mother had a bit of a crush on Dr. Rucker. If it's true, that would have significance for us also, don't you think, in the sense of their both being in love with the same man?"

Maggie doesn't answer.

"What are you thinking about?"

"I'm visualizing you at six. You're in your nursery, deep in thought, trying to sort out, from a truckload of fancy French dolls, the ones you like versus the ones you don't like. Your long auburn hair is held back with a pale-blue satin ribbon, your little dress is white linen with a blue sash that matches your hair ribbon. You're wearing white tights and your soft white kidskin slippers are kicked off. Each time you pick up one of the dolls, you examine it intently, eyebrows drawn together in a slight frown. Is it a 'play with' doll or a 'don't play with' doll? I can see that little girl." Maggie whispers, "And she is so adorable and so adorably intent upon her work. Or is it her play?"

Ann considers the question. "The Zen definition of happiness is that one works and one plays without knowing which is which."

"Hmmm. I like that definition."

"Maggie, do you have a Sterling Rucker navel?"

"Do I have a *what*?"

"A Sterling Rucker navel."

"What the hell is a Sterling Rucker navel? Are we talking about oranges or belly buttons?"

"We're talking about the navels that attached us physically to our mothers."

"Well, how would I know?"

"Tell me what your navel is like."

"Center of the belly, contained, stays clean, seldom needs scratching. Do those descriptions answer your question?"

"Not really. It's not what we're looking for."

"What in God's name are we looking for?"

"Well, first and foremost, we're looking for depth. You should be able to drop the head of a straight pin into a Sterling Rucker navel and have it completely disappear from sight. And the knotted part should not be visible at all unless you peer in it at close range. Is yours like that?"

Maggie's breathing accelerates audibly. "Is yours?"

"Dr. Rucker did mine as well as any I've ever seen, including Cher's," Ann states proudly.

"Good old Sterling, MD must have tied one on in the scrub room before he delivered me. I can't wait to rib Zeke. My navel is nothing like what you're describing."

"Are you sure? His navels were his trademark."

"How do you know this stuff?"

"We used to compare navels at school and at the beach."

"What school and what beach?"

"St. Timothy's and Virginia Beach," Ann replies, "and you never said where you had dinner tonight."

"Was I supposed to tell you?"

"I just wondered what restaurant."

"No restaurant. I had dinner at a friend's house. But I already told you that, didn't I?"

"No. You didn't say where you had dinner or with whom you had dinner. Just that the person was a friend."

"True." Maggie lights another cigarette and exhales. "But I think I should tell you—" She hesitates.

"Tell me what?"

"Never mind, dearest."

She sighs exasperation. "Just tell me."

"I had dinner with Jane Vitello."

"I don't know her."

"I didn't think you would."

"Tell me about her."

"What do you want to know?"

"Everything."

"I don't think so, Ann."

"For heaven's sake, Maggie!"

"She's a pediatrician in her mid-forties. She's smart, articulate, devoted to her patients, and has a great sense of humor."

"How long have you known her?"

"Ten years. Anything else?"

"Were you in love with her?"

"Yes."

"And was she in love with you?"

"She said she was."

"What happened?"

"A lot happened."

"Who ended it?"

"Jane had an affair and I ended it."

"How long were you and she together?"

"Six years, off and on—and now, Jane's married and has twin boys."

"Was it hard for you to end the relationship with Jane?"

"Once I knew she had been with someone else while she was involved with me, my blood ran cold and never warmed, although we eventually reconnected as friends," Maggie replies in a tight voice.

Ann decides to overlook the tight voice. "Were she and John your only serious relationships?"

"Ann, I don't want to share this with you now. The timing is wrong."

"In what way?"

"I want you to know me before you know about my relationships."

"Your relationships are you just as my relationships are me."

"I know next to nothing about your relationships."

"Ask me what you want to know and I'll tell you. That's what friendship's all about, Maggie."

"Is that really what you want?"

"It's what I really want."

"No secrets between us?"

"The complete truth," Ann replies, "or nothing."

"I respect that. Have dinner with me tomorrow."

"Where?"

"At my studio. I'll introduce you to Zeke, if she's home."

Ann hesitates. The notion of meeting Maggie's mother elicits curiosity coupled with trepidation. "Why not at my house?"

"If you'll let me bring a pizza. Do you like pizza?"

"I hate pizza and I love to cook."

"What time?"

"Is seven good for you?"

"It's fine."

"Goodnight then, Maggie."

"Goodnight, dearest."

She presses the button to disconnect and resolutely dials another number.

"Dr. Cabot."

"Max, did I awaken you?"

"Yes, you did awaken me, Ann. It's after midnight."

"I'm sorry. I didn't realize it was so late. I just wanted to let you know that ..." She starts to tell him about the children and camp, but she takes a deep breath and says instead, "I'm sorry I struck you. It was wrong of me."

She waits anxiously for Max to reply but he remains silent and she cannot bring herself to fill the void with trivial conversation. Moments pass. Finally, she can stand it no longer. "I'm sorry, Max. I'm sorry I hurt you."

The tension of his continued silence accelerates. She waits several moments longer and then places her finger on the button and disconnects. She keeps her finger on the button and slides the receiver cautiously over it. The palms of her hands are damp and there are beads of perspiration on her upper lip.

Once she would have wept at the agony of that call. Once she would have waited and waited for his sanction to transport her past guilt and self-recrimination.

Once—but not tonight.

Ann opens the front door before Maggie has a chance to knock. "Welcome to my world, even if you are late."

"You've got nerve," Maggie retorts. She looks Ann up and down. "Nice apron. What am I supposed to do about the front door?"

"Shut it behind you. I have to get back to the kitchen before something burns."

Maggie follows her. "What an amazing kitchen! It's huge."

"It, my bedroom, bath and sauna, the entrance hall, powder room, and the library are the entire first floor."

"What's on the second floor?"

"Three bedrooms, three tiny bathrooms, a laundry room, and five walk-in closets."

Maggie nods approval. "Nicely planned."

"It's perfect for me, Edwin and Amory, and occasionally Hattie."

Maggie arches an eyebrow at Ann. "Why Hattie? I thought Hattie was Hampton bound and bonded?"

"Well, yes but she's also Edwin and Amory's second mother. Amory, in particular, adores her. Amory tells me all of her woes and expects me to take care of things, but she saves her motherly devotion for Hattie."

"Is that true, Ann?"

"In a way it is." She looks at Maggie in surprise. "Why the disapproval?"

"Children need their real mothers to be their mothers."

"Of course they do. What are you implying?"

"Are we going to fight before dinner, dearest?"

"We're certainly not going to fight over how I raise my children. I carry a sufficient quantity of guilt on my own over my mothering deficits so you needn't augment it. How about a glass of wine?"

"How about a beer?"

"I don't have beer. I'm so sorry. I hate beer and I forgot that you prefer it."

"Beer and pizza, two of my summertime favorites, and she hates them both." She emits a plaintive honking noise.

"What sound are you trying to reproduce?"

"The cry a baby duck makes when it's separated from its mother. It's supposed to elicit pity."

"I'll keep beer in the fridge from now on, so stop honking."

"Thank you." Maggie is three years old now, feet splayed, thumb in mouth. "And I prefer Heineken."

"I'll remember that, but for now have a glass of wine."

"I have an aversion to wine. Always have."

Ann brightens. "I forget what's in a Manhattan, but the bar's well stocked. We could probably concoct one."

"Actually, Ann, I wasn't planning on drinking tonight."

"I could brew you a cup of coffee."

"Hmm, coffee—up all night." She eyes Ann appreciatively. "Nice apron."

"You already said that."

"Did I mention the slacks?"

"No."

Maggie nods approvingly. "Nicely tailored khakis with a more bottom-conforming-than-usual-fit."

"Banana Republic cotton. Number-one choice of safari wannabes."

"And your sleeveless blouse?" Maggie circles the scarlet fabric delicately with thumb and forefinger.

"It's silk. I prefer the lightness of silk in warm weather." Ann lifts the lid from an enameled saucepan, stirs, and sniffs appreciatively. "Ten more minutes," she murmurs.

"Magnificent."

Ann turns around and faces Maggie. "What's magnificent?"

"Uh, that stove. I've never seen a stove like that before."

"It's an AGA."

"Good color. Red is a great color for a stove." She takes a step closer to Ann. "Let's not bother with dinner now, dearest. Show me the rest of the house. I'd like to see the library and your first-floor bedroom."

"What about your coffee?"

"I don't think so." She shoots Ann a look of meaningful intent. "I don't think so," she repeats in a tensile whisper.

Ann clears her throat. She can't step back because Maggie is pressing her into the stove. "You're in my way, Maggie. I need to open the oven door and we need to have a little chat. I have something to tell you but our dinner is going to burn if you don't move. I'm making a great dinner. The table's already set. You can have a look at the rest of the house on your own. You have—" She eyes the French Mobilier clock on the kitchen wall, "—until seven forty-five to amuse yourself. We'll meet there." She inclines her head toward the oval mahogany drop-leaf table she bought in Scotland two summers ago, stands on tiptoe, and kisses Maggie's forehead. "Go on, now. Mother's busy in the kitchen."

Maggie walks through the wide alcove that leads into the library. She turns around, emits a plaintive honking sound, and gazes mournfully at Ann—her eyes huge with disappointment.

Dinner is on the table when Maggie returns. "What a cool house," she says. "Who plays the piano?"

"I do, and Amory does reluctantly."

Maggie examines the dinner table. "You're a precise little creature, aren't you?"

"Why do you say that?"

"Well, the symmetry. Each and every piece of silver—beautiful silver, I might add—exactly where its mate on the other placemat is. The same with the water goblets, the wine glasses, the napkins, saltcellars, pepper mills—even the lamb chops are symmetrical, and the vegetables come damn close to being identically laid out."

Ann beams a smile of beatific delight. "You have an artist's eye for detail."

"It's you, dearest. This house is as handsome as your gallery."

"Why, thank you, Maggie." She sits down at the table and inclines her head. "For what we are about to receive and for all the tender mercies of the universe, may we be truly grateful." She looks up. "I hope you didn't mind that."

"I've been known to pray upon occasion." Maggie holds up a forkful of spinach. "This spinach is delicious."

"It's spinach pudding. James Beard recommends it with lamb chops," Ann says. She is conjuring up mental images of discreetly pouring beer at a formal dinner party when Maggie interrupts her thoughts.

"You said you had something to tell me."

"Actually—" Ann swallows a mouthful of baked potato, reaches for her wineglass, and takes a deep swallow. "I have two things to tell you. I've been trying to figure out how to tell you without making a big deal of either of them."

"Are they important?"

"One of them isn't really important. Well, it's sort of ... but—" She takes another swallow of wine. "I really don't know how to answer that."

"Decide what you want to tell me first and tell me that one. Then tell me the second one."

"Do you have any pocket change?"

"What do you want?"

"Any coin that has two sides."

Maggie hands her a nickel. Ann holds it for a moment, her brow furrowed in concentration. "Okay. If it's heads, I'll tell you about us first. If it's tails, I'll tell you about the baron first."

"The baron? What baron?"

"His name is Victor, but wait until I flip the coin." She gulps a mouthful of wine, puts the glass back on the table, picks it up again, and drains the glass.

Maggie stares at her in amazement.

"What?"

"Nothing, Ann. I said nothing."

"I know you said nothing. I was referring to that look you gave me. What did that look mean?" She pours more wine into her glass.

"Flip the coin, Ann."

"Answer the question first."

"Flip the friggin' coin and I'll pour the wine. I wouldn't want you to get tendonitis from that continuous wrist action."

Ann shrugs and flips the nickel. It lands in the butter, head side up. "Well, I guess we'll only be putting sour cream on our baked potatoes tonight."

"The coin came up heads. What about us do you want to tell me?"

Ann bites her lower lip. "Well, first I want to say that ... that ... you have no idea ... that you have no idea how ... gosh, this is awkward."

"Would you please do us both a favor and cut to the chase?"

"What do you mean?"

"I mean cut the prosaic bullcrap. Tell me what you invited me here to tell me and lay off the pinot noir. I expect that of you."

"I have love for you but we're not sexually compatible."

"Go on."

"I cannot be aroused by a physical relationship with a woman."

"Why can't you?"

"It's alien to my nature. It's not that it ... it offends me, although it does go against the grain ... at least for me. It's more that it disinterests me. I'm what you might call a heterosexual turned asexual."

"Did my kiss disappoint you?"

"I didn't enjoy it, if that's what you mean."

"You were rigid and scared to death. Maybe you've never been kissed by someone who knows how to kiss." Her eyes bore into Ann's. "What was the second thing you wanted to tell me?"

"The second thing? Oh ... right ... the second thing. That was about Victor. I met him in Ireland. He painted my portrait and we went riding together. Several times. Actually we spent a great deal of time together and after—" She bites her lip. "After he finished my portrait—"

Maggie rolls her eyes. "For godssake! Get to the point."

"I made love with him."

"When?"

"When I was in Ireland."

"Are we talking about the two-weeks-ago trip?"

"Yes."

"Had you fallen in love with him?"

"No."

"Then why'd you have sex with him?"

"I'd had too much to drink."

"That's not a reason. It's an excuse."

"I don't know why. It just happened." Ann shrugs. "Cookie was crazy about him."

"Then you should've allowed Cookie to perform the honors." Maggie shakes her head in disbelief. "And here I thought you were such a pure type, you know, an Ali Baba devotee and all that spiritual hogwash you've been spouting to keep me at bay."

"Maggie, please." Ann winces. "It only happened one time."

"Don't say 'one time' like it's nothing, Ann."

"It *was* nothing."

"Do yourself a kindness and don't say that again." Maggie reaches for the silver ashtray and then pushes it away.

"Go ahead and smoke. I'll have one with you. I saved all three of mine for this evening."

"I'll wait until you're finished eating."

Ann rises unsteadily and reaches for the dinner plates. She carries them to the center island, scrapes the potatoes into the garbage disposal, and saves the spinach pudding and lamb for Belle and Liza, who are spending the night at Eleanor's. She stacks the dishes into the dishwasher and turns to Maggie. "How about dessert?"

"Do you have ice cream?"

"I only buy ice cream when the children are here. I don't like ice cream."

"I was going to add that ice cream is my third-favorite summertime food, after beer and pizza. I'm beginning to think you're right. We don't fit at all."

"Food and sex aren't everything, Maggie."

"Oh? What's left?"

"Politics? Religion?"

"I'm a conservative Republican. You're a liberal Democrat. I'm a low-church Episcopalian. You've abandoned the Episcopal faith to embrace Eastern mysticism under the tutelage of a Tiny Tim lookalike. I'd say we don't fit in those arenas either."

"What about money?"

"Universes apart."

"Well, what then?" Ann walks back to the table, sits down, and holds out her wineglass to Maggie, who eyes her dubiously. She reaches for the wine bottle and swings it in Maggie's direction. "Want to help me finish this off?"

"This will be the third time, but no, thank you.'"

"What about coffee? I brewed a pot and put it in the thermos."

"I don't think so. Maybe afterward."

"After Ward?" Ann attempts a grin. "Ward who?"

"Not remotely funny. But you do have a sense of humor. That should compensate for something."

"How much should humor compensate for?"

"A sense of humor, along with beauty and brains ... well, I would have said brains before you told me about Victor, so we're left with beauty and humor."

"What about spirituality?"

Maggie shakes her head. "I'm not keen on spirituality, but to the extent that I am, we're miles apart."

"We're also miles apart sexually," Ann retorts loftily.

Maggie regards Ann with barely contained contempt. "Your attitude about sex is pathetic."

"In what way?"

"You engage in sex without love and think it means nothing."

"Are you insinuating that I'm a slut?"

"I hate to dash your hopes, Ann, but you're no slut. That would entail passion."

Ann's color rises, but she remains silent.

"It's clear to me," Maggie continues, "that you're a novice when it comes to physical intimacy. Who told you the facts of life?"

"Mother made an appointment for me to talk with my pediatrician."

"Who was your pediatrician?"

"Dr. Mangum."

Maggie nods. "He was mine too." She reaches across the table and traces the side of Ann's hand with her index finger. "How about something on the piano? I'd like to hear you play."

Ann walks into the library and sits down at the piano. Maggie follows and stands facing her, the Steinway's full length between them. Ann plays "Clair de Lune" in its entirety then lifts her hands from the keyboard and looks up.

"You're too perfect," Maggie whispers.

"Did you like it?"

"I more than liked it. I was moved almost to tears. You play with searing passion tempered by precision."

"Thank you, Maggie." She pushes back the piano bench and stands up. "How about a game of chess or ..." she points to her grandmother's petit point gaming table ... "Or a game of backgammon? Do you play backgammon?"

"Yes, but backgammon is not what I want to play now."

"What do you want to play now?"

"I want to make love to you."

Ann sighs. "We've been through all of that. I've already told you I'm not interested."

"Your interest or lack of interest makes no difference to me."

"Why do you speak to me so callously?"

"Because you let Victor fuck you."

"Please don't use that word. It really offends me."

"The thought of you letting a baron you didn't give a damn about enter your body offends me. It lessens my esteem for you and quite frankly, Ann, it changes things."

"How does it change things?"

"I've been trying to match my dance card to yours. I'm not doing that anymore."

Ann sits back down on the piano bench, hands clenched, legs crossed, lips pressed together—she is suddenly entirely alert—entirely sober—the hare sensing the presence of the falcon overhead—rearing back—and then forward to defend.

If your enemy is superior, invade him. If your enemy is angry, irritate him. If your enemy is angry and superior—irritate him and then invade him.

She folds her arms across her breast—exhales a sigh of exasperation. "Now listen, Maggie, I'm not going to have a physical relationship with you. It isn't that I object to it morally. My cousin Cookie and I had a frank conversation when I was in Ireland and we discussed the moral aspects of ... of same-sex physical relationships ... two consenting adults not bound to anyone else ... it isn't that it's good or bad or right or wrong ... it's ... well it's ... it has a certain neutrality, is what I'm trying to say ... but it's a neutrality to which—" She draws a shallow breath. "To which you're drawn but I'm not."

Maggie's eyes flash annoyance. "How facile—how wonderfully facile of you and Cousin Cookie to have talked it all through. I do hope it was during high tea, with the other aristocrats in dumbfounded attendance."

"But I really do feel that way, Maggie. I'm leaning toward celibacy as a permanent way of life for me. I know I told you once that I had thought about joining a nunnery."

"Yes, Ann, you did mention that, along with the monastic trips to India and the two years of celibacy after the divorce from the anal-retentive shrink. Yes, dearest, we've covered all of that."

Ann nods earnestly. "Then you understand that what you ask is untenable. I want us to be like sisters."

"Like sisters. Exactly. Now get yourself into that fancy first-floor bedroom and wipe off what's left of your lipstick."

Ann stares at her in amazement.

"And get rid of the khakis."

"You didn't listen to a word I said!"

"I listened to every word you said." Maggie walks over to the mantel, lights a cigarette, and throws the match into the fireplace.

"You don't want it. Fine. I accept that. But the problem is that I do want it. You say you see sex between us as free of moral taint and that you're not emotionally or legally bound to anyone else. You say the baron was just a one-night stand, sanctioned by your Irish cohorts and fortified by too much alcohol. No matter, it boils down to this—I say yes—you say no. It's a question of who gets what she wants. I'm asking you to be a big brave girl by allowing me the experience of making love to you—only that—not you making love to me, but me making love to you. You can handle that, can't you?" She walks over to the piano bench and lifts Ann's chin with her middle finger. "Tell me," she asks, "did you undress for the baron?"

Ann doesn't move a muscle.

"Yes, dearest." Maggie nods knowingly. "I thought you might have." She walks back to the mantel, takes a long drag from her cigarette, and taps the ash into the grate. "Either I'm going to make love to you now, this night, or I'm out of here, out of us. Permanently. Never to return."

Ann's mouth drops open in disbelief.

"I mean it, Ann. We've been playing at this for too long. After a certain point it becomes obsessive. It's already that way for me." She gives a rueful nod. "I've become obsessed with you. This is the bottom line and you must decide. Yes or no? Do I stay or do I leave?"

Ann bristles. "You're going to drop me if I don't have sex with you? That's contemptible."

"Maybe so."

"Then why do it?"

"Because I'm weary of wanting you without being able to touch you and I know that for as long as I continue to see you I'll continue to long for you. The physical longing will never go away."

"What about not seeing each other for a while? We could talk to each other on the phone. We could have a more casual relationship."

"Would that be enough for you?"

"I'd manage."

"Someone other than you to be my person, my favorite," Maggie whispers. "The center of my universe. It would be her phone calls I waited for, her body I longed for. Suppose she were a desirable woman like you. Could you manage that?"

Ann's eyes close spasmodically. Her thoughts, born of long and painful habit, tumble back to Faye Graham. She remembers the aching loveliness of Faye's bare back, the tanned skin taut against the white halter-top dress. She had witnessed Max looking hungrily at that beauty the first night of their affair. She thinks of Cookie's infatuation with Daphne and then her thoughts return to Faye and linger—Faye's head thrown back, laughing at Max—her mouthful of white shark's teeth a dazzling counterpoint to her tanned brunette handsomeness—her laughter a chord of endless tiny trills heading out to sea in a beautiful pea-green boat. Oh yes—Maggie too would have thought Faye glorious.

The hot slash of agonizing jealousy catches Ann unawares, and she realizes that she has, under Maggie's excellent direction, fashioned for herself a hell of her own making. She turns on Maggie viciously.

"You're gruesome. You and everyone like you. You compel others to love you and then you have your way with them or you leave them." She scrambles from the piano bench and plants herself in front of Maggie. "No," she snarls, "not now, not yesterday, not tomorrow and not ever." Her fury dissipates as abruptly as it had arisen. "I won't because I can't," she finishes tonelessly.

Maggie takes a final drag from her cigarette and throws the butt into the fireplace. Her demeanor is entirely composed. "Ann, dear, I do understand and it's not a problem. Thank you for your honesty, for dinner, for the truly marvelous evening. I'll never forget how tenderly you played 'Clair de Lune'." Her startling blue eyes lock into Ann's.

The talons tighten.

"What an absence," She whispers. "You have no idea what an absence I'm going to be in your life." She reaches for Ann's hand and holds it for a moment in her own. Then she raises it to her face and presses it against her cheek, releases it gently, and walks into the hallway.

"Maggie, wait—"

Maggie reaches for the brass doorknob and, still holding it, turns around. "Whatever for?" Her eyes are the eyes of a falcon. Hooded. Watchful. Certain.

Ann shudders. Her heart pumps furiously. It is for her as it had been from the very beginning—greater than the sum of all her parts. When was her heart's last such season—its last such capture?

"Wait," she repeats in a tensile whisper. She feels the fear rise up in her but she wills herself, as when she was a child, to not flinch—to not cry. "Don't leave." She looks away from Maggie. "Stay."

JULY 1987

You can't run from the wind.
You trim your sails,
face the music,
and keep going.

— *White Squall*

Max is waiting when Ann arrives at the gallery.

"Good morning," Ann offers. She glances at the flowers he is carrying— roses—not an auspicious flower—and red—not an auspicious color.

"Good afternoon," he replies and offers her the roses.

"Are those for me?"

He nods. "Who else?"

"What's the occasion?"

"An apology."

She looks at him in surprise. "For what?"

"My rudeness last telephone call—which prompted you to finally hang up."

"Thank you for your apology and for the roses. They're very vibrant. I'll have Eleanor put them in water. Where is she?"

"She went to lunch. It's one o'clock. I insisted she go. I told her I'd wait until she got back or you arrived. She was apprehensive, but I reassured her that you wouldn't mind. Do you mind?"

"It's fine. How was Eleanor's mood?"

His brow furrows. "Why do you ask?'

Because I said I'd be here by ten thirty and it's after one and because I've been incommunicado lately and Eleanor has the instincts of a bloodhound.

"She's been ... I don't know ... edgy lately. You know how Eleanor hates hot weather."

"Well, she was her usual briskly uninformative self with me," Max replies.

Ann eyes the pale-pink slash mark on his cheek and her face softens. "I'm so sorry, Max. I'd give anything not to have hurt you like that."

He puts the roses down and gathers her into his arms. "I accept your apology. Don't worry, it'll heal."

"Will it leave a scar?"

"A sexy scar, I hope. It'll make a fine story to tell our grandchildren."

She pulls away first. "Why don't I brew us a pot of coffee? Would you like that?"

"Not really."

"What would you like?"

He considers the question. "Let's just sit down and talk."

"Sure. The showroom has some fairly accommodating chairs."

"I'd prefer your office, if that won't interfere with the gallery's smooth functioning."

She is intrigued by Max's choice of words. "Smooth functioning" clearly encapsulates his demeanor. He wants something. That would explain the bouquet of roses. Hastily bought, no doubt. He must have sensed a difference in her when she called to apologize. She clears her throat. "I called Faye Graham."

He gestures for her to say more, but she observes him in placid silence. It's a tactic she learned from George.

Wait and see where the animal ventures.

"Was it a pleasant conversation?" He finally asks.

"Faye asked me to forgive her," She confides.

Max's eyes search Ann's. "And did you?"

"Yes."

"How wonderful."

"I told Faye it was as if—"

"As if what?"

"It felt as if a thorn had been removed from my heart, but I might not have actually said that to her."

"Has a thorn been removed from your heart, Ann?"

"Yes."

"Perhaps now you can truly forgive me."

"Max, I want to ask a question and I want you to tell me the truth. As if I were your dearest friend or perhaps your therapist, but not your wife. Will you do that?"

"My willingness to be honest with you has been conditioned by years of relating to you as my wife. What I confide to you is limited by my intuitively knowing how you'll respond if I tell you."

"Why not try it differently this time?"

"I'm still bearing the imprint of my last attempt to do that." He puts his hand to his cheek.

She walks over to the gilt bench beneath the Thomas Sidney Cooper watercolor of Queen Victoria's beloved Highland cows and sits down. "So you haven't really forgiven me. I guess that's why the roses were red."

"So you didn't really mean it when you said they were lovely."

"I never said they were lovely. I said they were vibrant. Weren't you listening, dearest?"

"I listened and I heard."

She observes him astutely. "You don't like it that I called Faye, do you? And you particularly don't like it that she asked my forgiveness for her betrayal of *me*."

He gives a shrug of incomprehension. "Why would I dislike something I pressured Faye to do?"

"What did you pressure Faye to do?"

"Ask your forgiveness."

"When?"

"I saw her at the Medical Auxiliary midsummer cocktail party last week. She was with Will Batten. She asked about you and I suggested she call you and try to make amends."

"You said you pressured her."

"Well, Ann, she didn't really want to do it. She thought it would be awkward."

She must have asked him about the gash on his cheek and he must have told her that it was because of her that I struck him.

Shame of self and loathing of Max well up in Ann simultaneously. She resists the impulse to stand and pace. Her eyes search his— inscrutability in his eyes but not in the twist of his mouth. In the twist of his mouth, she discerns the reason for his trip to Richmond. She captures his gaze before speaking. "I hung up on you the other night because you were intent upon making me suffer and I couldn't bear the anxiety of waiting for you to soften toward me. And you, Max, still angry that I struck you, but disarmed by my apology, rushed up here with red roses—flowers you tease me about disliking because my mother loved them so. If you'd wanted to please me—hell, if you'd given a fig about pleasing me, you'd have brought white tulips, my all-time favorites. Or white daisies. Or white lilies. White roses, even. Anything but red roses—the flower of Constance—the flower of war."

She gets up and stands behind the gilt chair adjacent to his. "I think I finally understand the irony of your dilemma. You want love but you're dismissive of the women who love you. That was the question I wanted to ask you. But it's already been answered."

"I'm not clear about what the question was." His smile is hard. "Would you mind telling me?"

"I wanted to know if you pursued Faye because you were in love with her."

"And what was the answer?"

"That the anguish it caused me was the catalyst to your pursuit of a woman who happened to be my dearest friend."

"Did it ever occur to you that it might have been Faye who pursued me?"

"I think I've always known that it wasn't Faye who initiated the affair, but how unkind, not to mention tasteless, of you to suggest otherwise." She manages a shrug of indifference. "I can't stay because I have an appointment to deliver a picture and I'm already late but I want you to know something. I intend to forgive you also, Max." She attempts a wry smile. "Perhaps you only married me because you couldn't tolerate one of those younger swains besting you but, whatever the reason—" She walks toward the gallery doors and turns back around. "Having done so, you were required by a marriage vow to be faithful."

Max puts a hand over his heart. "My sad, spurned, pumpkin-shell-bound wife."

"Neither sad nor spurned and no longer your wife." She gives a sidewise nod of incomprehension. "I still don't understand why you were unfaithful and I was unable to forgive you. Love is bewildering when clouded by sexual longing—devastating when compromised by infidelity. You, of all people, must realize that."

She walks over to where he is sitting, bends down, and kisses him lightly on the cheek, the wounded cheek. "I'm sorry, dearest. Please try to forgive me for striking you so viciously. Ah! Here's Eleanor now." She holds open the gallery door for Eleanor and pats her incoming arm. "I leave him in your capable hands, Eleanor. Do with him what you will."

"Gee thanks." Eleanor rolls her eyes. "And you're leaving me with him to go where?"

"I'm off to deliver a picture. I'll check in with you later," Ann replies and waves an airy goodbye over her shoulder.

Maggie knocks on the car window before Ann has turned off the motor. "I have a delicious surprise for you," she drawls.

"Maggie, please."

Maggie grins. "You should be so fortunate. No, my surprise is a person. Zeke is home."

Ann regards her with apprehension. "Should I come in?"

"Of course you should."

Ann checks her hair in the rearview mirror.

"Don't you dare!" Maggie hisses.

"Don't I dare what?"

"Be nervous. My mother is going to adore you."

"I'm not nervous. I was just tidying my hair." She hands Maggie a large package wrapped in white paper. "This is for you. I bought it in Ireland."

"Before or after the baron?"

"Before the baron." She strides past Maggie and into the studio. "Are you coming or not?" she drawls. "And do be gentle with that package."

"When am I supposed to open it?"

"Before your mother," Ann replies. She follows Maggie cautiously into the elaborate brass-and-wrought-iron elevator. The elevator's ascension is slow and not entirely smooth. She swallows hard and shuts her eyes.

"You want me to open this package in front of my mother? Why, for God's sake?"

"No. I meant before I met your mother," Ann murmurs. Her stomach lurches when the elevator shudders to a halt. She opens her eyes. "But whatever you decide is fine."

"Okay." Maggie locks the elevator lever in place and slides back the brass grill. "Watch your step getting off," she warns Ann, "I never get the damn thing level."

Ann steps onto the old and polished random-width pine floor of the loft. There are faded oriental carpets scattered generously about and the walls are painted a pale robin's-egg blue. The large sitting area's sloped ceiling, more than fifteen feet high and topped by a faceted glass dome, appears to be entirely constructed of sheets of glass framed by wide bands of dark metal. The sheer expanse of afternoon sky is glorious.

She turns to Maggie. "This is heavenly." She notes the fireplace and envisions the room in the dead of winter, late at night, blazing logs, flickering candles, and, overhead, softly swirling snow enclosing the domed ceiling—stars and sky obscured by millions of waltzing snowflakes. She nods approval. "I adore this loft." Her gaze travels down a long narrow hallway. "Where's your mother now?" she asks in a low voice.

Maggie shrugs. "Probably in her sitting room. She keeps her birds there, six at last count, each of them named and sporting diverse personality traits. They're included in her last will and testament. They squawk at her and peck the hell out of her but Zeke forgives them because they're her babies."

"Aren't you her baby too?"

"Her daughter, yes—her baby, no. Here comes Zeke now. Remember to curtsy."

Maggie's mother is even taller than Maggie. Her hair, a thick, lustrous silver, is softly gathered into a coiled chignon at the nape of her neck. She flashes a smile at Ann. "You must be Ann—the 'Ann' I've been hearing so much about," she pauses, "of late."

"How do you do, Mrs. Lambert? I'm Ann Cabot."

"Please call me Clarissa," she replies in an elegant drawl even more pronounced than Maggie's. She motions toward an armchair covered in lavender silk. "Why don't you sit there and we'll have a lovely pot of tea. Or would you prefer iced tea?"

"I prefer hot tea," Ann replies, "but please don't bother on my account."

"It's no bother," Maggie interjects. "Zeke has afternoon tea, followed by her ritual several cocktails, on a daily basis."

Clarissa turns to Ann. "Would you prefer a cocktail? It's a tad early for me, but five thirty isn't written in stone." She glances reprovingly at Maggie.

"Hot tea is fine."

"I'll put on the kettle." Maggie ambles into the narrow hallway and disappears from view.

Clarissa fingers the lace collar of her mint-green cardigan. "Well, I must say you're every bit as lovely as your photograph."

"Which photograph is that?" Ann asks.

"The one in the marvelous silver-and-tortoiseshell frame that Maggie has currently installed on the night table next to her bed."

"I like that frame, too." Maggie slouches into a yellow linen sofa, kicks out one leg, crosses it with its mate, laces her fingers together and slides them behind her neck. "I showed your picture to Zeke so she could see how well some Sterling Rucker babies turn out."

Ann smiles at Clarissa. "I'm sure your mother thinks you turned out fine, Maggie."

"Not entirely fine," Clarissa says and smiles back at Ann.

"Ann dear, I must teach you not to lead with your chin." Maggie wags a finger in Ann's direction. "Particularly when it concerns me."

"This might be a propitious time to open your present, Maggie."

"I thought you were going to leave the timing of that up to me, dearest."

"Maggie, your mother's going to think we don't play nicely together," she remonstrates.

"Playing nicely means 'no punching on the playground,' to Margaret," Clarissa tells Ann. "She's been that way since childhood."

"Being disapproved of by one's mother doesn't generally predispose a child to not punch, Zeke," Maggie scoffs.

"I didn't consistently disapprove of you, Margaret. You had your finer moments. And of course there was always—" Clarissa turns to Ann. "The element of sheer surprise. Margaret's an unusual daughter."

"Only because *usual* is nothing you'd know a damn thing about," Maggie retorts. She picks up a magazine from the coffee table and riffles the pages.

"Be quiet, Margaret, and let me talk to Ann." Clarissa's eyes, the exact blue of Maggie's, bore into Ann's and then soften. "I knew your father, Ann. I had the privilege of working as a teller in his bank my first summer after high school and before college. He was a genuine Bostonian, a true gent and so handsome."

"Thank you."

"He always treated me with kindness. I was such a shy young thing."

Maggie slaps the magazine down on the coffee table. "A *shy young thing*, Zeke? What complete hogwash!"

Ann rises with alacrity from her chair. "I'm sure I hear the kettle whistling. I'll just go and turn it off."

"Oh no you don't!" Maggie hollers after her. "I get to make the tea. You get to come back and be devoured by the tigress."

"But you promised me this was going to be a piece of cake," Ann wails.

Clarissa laughs. "Come back here, Ann. I like your spirit. I'll be nice. Margaret always likes to get this out of the way—this attitude nonsense. It's a habit she developed during her rebellious teenage years. Come sit by me in this chair and tell me all about yourself. I want to have a look at those marvelous earrings you're wearing. I'll bet everything I own they're vintage Cartier."

"They *are* by Cartier," Ann assents, "and they make for an interesting story." She pauses. A story that Maggie, heading back from the kitchen, tea tray in hand, will surely not applaud. "Actually," she continues, "the handsomest piece is at home. A matching snake bracelet. I'll wear it the next time I visit."

"Tea time, girls," Maggie announces.

Clarissa removes the magazines and a large marble ashtray from the coffee table and places them on the floor next to her chair. She catches Ann's gaze and holds it with her own. "The prospect of a return visit from you pleases me, Ann, and I'm sure Margaret feels about you as I do. Is that not true, Margaret?"

"Not true, Zeke."

Clarissa and Ann eye her reproachfully.

"I'm sorry," Maggie drawls, "to once again be so *unusual* but then again—" She places the tea tray on the coffee table. "I'm not. Where's that damn package you brought me, Ann? I think I'll open it now."

Ann and Clarissa watch as Maggie releases the picture from its sheath of white paper. Ann observes the look of surprise on Maggie's face. She holds the picture at arm's length, then leans it against the sofa, backs away several paces, and examines it again, head tilted, chin in hand.

Clarissa breaks the silence. "How interesting! And how tastefully matted and framed! But what is it of?"

"It's the Pied Piper luring the children of Hamelin into following him," Ann explains. "What intrigued me most about it was the entranced expressions on the faces of the children and the ecstatic twitching of their hands, contrasted by the sheer dismay of the nanny, who is not enthralled. One is awestruck by the event—besieged by numberless possibilities. What were the children hearing? How did the piper come to know of such music? Were the children forever ecstatic once inside the mountain where the Pied Piper led them?" She pauses in bemusement before continuing. "The original is by Arthur Rackham—a late-nineteenth-century British illustrator. I was thrilled to find this reproduction in Ireland."

"It's great," Maggie breathes, "but such an odd picture to have chosen for me."

"You remind me of the Pied Piper a bit," Ann teases.

"I was just thinking the same thing," Clarissa says in a quiet voice. Her eyes travel from the picture to Ann. "Here's your cup of tea, my dear. Do you prefer lemon or cream?"

"Neither," Ann replies, "and no sugar." She takes a shortbread cookie from the plate Clarissa proffers and bites into it. "These are delicious. I adore shortbread. Thank you."

Clarissa arises majestically from her armchair, the mate to Ann's. "Ann dear, I always read to my birds in the afternoon. I'm a creature of proper and usual habit, I'm afraid. It's been a pleasure to meet you. You so remind me of your father. I do hope you'll come again." She reaches over and touches the side of Ann's hand lightly with her index finger and walks over to Maggie, who is still examining the picture.

"How curious," she says reflectively, "that you would give Margaret a picture of the Pied Piper, and I agree that this is an intriguing depiction of the tale." She points to a little girl with a mane of tousled, straw-colored hair, rosy cheeked, hands a-tremble, eyes glistening. "That naive slip of a girl reminds me of you, Ann." She eyes Ann coolly. "I have a notion that you too could be seduced into blindly following after an experienced Pied Piper with a mindset to do just that. Don't you agree, Margaret?"

Maggie's mouth drops open. She stares at Clarissa's retreating form in mute disbelief.

It's the first time Ann has seen her at a loss for words.

Ann is already at the gallery when Eleanor arrives. She eyes Ann's sleeveless black linen sheath and matching espadrilles.

"Who died?"

"Why in the world would you ask that?"

"It's early for you."

"I'm here early sometimes."

"Rarely and you're wearing black." Eleanor smiles. "Are you carrying a black hanky?"

"Of course," Ann admits, "but no one died. At least no one I know. However, Amory has acquired six stitches in her left arm. That's the news of the morning."

"What happened?"

"She fell into a window and it shattered. Actually she was lucky. The doctor who stitched her arm said she just missed a tendon. Nicked it slightly—lots of blood, according to Joan, who accompanied Amory to the emergency room. Her best friend, you know." Ann sighs. "Amory is completely enamored of Joan. You should have heard her singing Joan's praises this morning." She acknowledges Eleanor's knowing nod. "Yes, it was early this morning. Anyway, Amory's fine. The girls are making up her bunk, helping with her meals, and opening doors for her, because her arm's in a sling. Guess who called to give me the news."

Eleanor shakes her head in disbelief. "Not Joan!"

"None other ... from the hospital ... on a pay phone. She reversed the charges. The operator informed me that she had a very distraught little girl on the phone. I almost fainted from fear. Can you believe that child?"

"You've always said Joan is just like her mother."

"She's worse. She observes no boundaries whatsoever."

"When did you say you talked to Amory?"

"This morning, after the stitches. The camp director called, too. She was very on top of everything, including Joan, who made the mistake of informing Mrs. Hollingsworth that she had already told the hysterical mother the terrible news and that the camp should pay for the stitches

because all of the cabin windows were ... and I quote, 'grossly negligible.'"
Ann grins. "Mrs. Hollingsworth and I had a good laugh over that one
and over Miss Joan Boatwright who is confined to her cabin for tonight's
campfire, for speaking so rudely to Mrs. Hollingsworth and then refusing
twice to apologize."

Eleanor frowns. "Knowing Joan, she'll probably take it out on Amory.
I'm getting a cup of coffee for myself. Want one?"

"No thanks. I'm a little queasy this morning. Too much talk about
spilled blood."

"So, did you ever give Maggie Lambert the picture?"

"I did."

"How'd she like it?"

"A lot. She thought it was interesting. I met Maggie's mother, by the
way. We had tea together."

"You met her mother?" Eleanor takes a sip of coffee. "Where?"

"At Maggie's loft. She and her mother live together."

"Maggie Lambert lives with her mother? You can't mean it!"

"Why are you so surprised?"

"Maggie looks like a woman who requires extreme privacy."

"For what reason?"

"I shudder to think."

"That's unkind, Eleanor. What has she ever done to you? And she's a
wonderful conservator. The finest in Richmond."

"She's infatuated with you," Eleanor states flatly.

"Why do you say that?"

"Because it's true."

"It isn't true. But even if it were true, why would you care?"

"Because you're my friend, my employer, and someone I care about."

"Maggie's an odd duck," Ann says defensively, "but I think you may
be reading her incorrectly." She feels the sudden heat in her cheeks and
turns away to hide her blush from Eleanor.

"I think she's gay," Eleanor blurts.

"That's none of our business, Eleanor. And it's something I'm not
willing to speculate about or discuss with you."

"Since when?"

"Since when, what?"

"Since when are we not allowed to discuss whether or not someone's straight or gay?"

"Since now."

"Why now?" Eleanor's voice hardens. "If you don't mind my asking, I'd really like to know."

"I consider it an invasion of Maggie's privacy. You haven't formed a relationship with her. In point of fact, you're barely civil to her. You were cold to her the first time you met her. You didn't like her from day one."

"I still don't like her," Eleanor retorts doggedly, "and maybe I'm being too protective of you, as an employee, but I don't like it that you spend time with her. She's bad news."

"She's a fabulous conservator, she gets the work completed in a timely fashion, and her prices are fair." Ann attempts a chuckle. "And she's kind to her rather unkind mother."

"She's indiscreet."

"In what way?"

"The way she looks at you."

"I don't see that."

"Of course you don't. You never see what you don't want to see. Max proves that."

"What happened with Max after I left?"

"He took the roses and walked out."

"What?"

"He took the roses, walked out the door, and handed them to some woman coming out of The Baby Boutique."

"You're kidding!"

"I never kid about Max."

"He should've given them to you." Ann looks at Eleanor curiously. "What did she look like?"

"Who?"

"The woman to whom he gave the roses."

"Blonde, football-helmet haircut, white Bermuda shorts, bosomy. Your typical West End nightmare. They talked a while. The blonde smiled a lot. Then she walked to her car, a dark-green Land Rover. She put the roses in the front seat, got in, and drove off. End of story."

"Ah well," Ann says cavalierly. "Another one bites the dust. I wonder if Max gave her one of his office cards."

"That would be soliciting, wouldn't it?"

"I'm not sure." Ann walks back toward her office. "I'm going to write the children. I think I'll have a cup of coffee after all, if there's any left."

"There is. So, are we finished talking about Maggie Lambert?"

"Definitely. Call Hattie for me, will you? She's been baking oatmeal cookies instead of chocolate chip, and Edwin hates oatmeal."

"How's Edwin doing?"

"He's full of himself," Ann crows. "He took two firsts in swimming—the backstroke and the Australian crawl—and he's met a girl named Lauren from a neighboring camp. Tall, with blonde hair—long blonde hair. And she writes poetry. I get to meet her at Parents' Weekend."

"I'll bet she chased him."

"Not exactly. He participated at a panty raid at her camp but he assured me he only went along to help paddle the canoe."

"Did he paddle back with or without Lauren's panties?"

"He didn't actually say and I didn't ask. I didn't want to keep him on the phone too long. You know how the boys line up to call home for food and money. Oh, will you book me an early morning flight to Kennebunkport for next Thursday? And book a return flight for late Sunday afternoon."

"Sure. What about Max? Should I make reservations for him, too?"

Ann thinks about it. "No. Not this time. Has Max called here, by the way?"

"Nope."

"He will," She says indifferently and shuts her office door.

After Eleanor has brought her coffee and after she has written letters to Edwin and Amory, Ann dials Maggie's number. The line is busy. She blames the much-too-strong coffee for the queasiness in the pit of her stomach. "All this energy with nowhere to expend it and nothing to displace it," she mutters. The perception intensifies the queasiness. She acknowledges that the twist of Maggie's and her relationship has compromised the joy she had anticipated in having Maggie as a close friend. Carefree openness has become a thing of the past.

"Anyone you tell about this will immediately turn away from you," Maggie had warned her that first night, sitting on Ann's tester bed, a cigarette in one hand, the other hand on Ann's thigh, while Ann, exhausted, no longer dulled by alcohol, had listened in abject silence. There was nothing to protest that she hadn't already protested.

She picks up the phone and puts it down without dialing. Maggie can be very long-winded. She's probably talking to that Vitello woman, with Clarissa lurking about, ear to the wall, taking notes. What a formidably knowing person to have for a mother. Sharp-tongued. Clever. A connector of dots. She had told Maggie so, yesterday evening, after dinner at Ann's townhouse.

"She knows, Maggie. Somehow she knows."

"She knows nothing, Ann."

"Why do you deny her knowing?"

"Because, dearest, Zeke makes a point of not knowing what she doesn't want to know."

"She knows you're involved with me."

"That she does know."

"Well, what do you think that means to her?"

"That you're the sun in my universe, and yes, Zeke cares about that because she envisions herself at the center. But that's her dilemma, not mine and certainly not yours. Should I conclude, from your tone of voice and the persistence of your questions, that you don't much like Zeke?"

"I don't dislike her," she had replied, "but I do dislike the way you spoke to her at the studio yesterday morning."

"What did I say?"

"You told her that she was a ninny and that she didn't give a rat's ass about good art."

"Well, she doesn't. She cut down a damn good oil on canvas I gave her because she wanted it in a smaller frame she liked better. Imagine! She took it out of its original frame. She's worse than a ninny! Now, that's enough talk about Zeke. Come back to bed. I'm not finished with you yet." She had motioned to Ann with a crooked index finger, her mouth curved into a naughty valentine.

"No, Maggie," Ann had protested.

"Don't say no when you mean yes or maybe. We're at a place in our relationship where I take no to mean no."

Ann had folded her arms and leaned against the bedroom mantel. Part of her had meant just that—no—no more of this. Let's have a cup of coffee and talk the way we used to. Another part of her, a reluctantly evolving part of her, had wanted to say, "Okay, let's try again, until I get the hang of what you want from me."

"Well?" Maggie had drawled. "What's it going to be?"

"It's going to be maybe."

The intercom buzzer interrupts Ann's reverie. "Yes, Eleanor?"

"There's a delivery for you. You need to sign for it."

"Just sign for me."

"It's listed as a painting, Ann. It's huge and it's from Vienna, Austria."

"From Vienna?" Her pulse quickens. "Sign for it, I think I know what it is."

The painting has already been released from its crate when Ann enters the showroom.

"Who helped you uncrate it?" she asks Eleanor.

"The Artex men. One of them whistled." Eleanor shakes her head in awe. "It's magnificent and the frame is beautiful."

Ann examines the gold-leaf frame, an amazingly wide expanse of exquisitely carved and highly burnished gilded pine. "It's early nineteenth century." She runs an experienced hand down the side of the frame. "And you're right. It's absolutely beautiful."

"And the painting! I love the pose. You're not smiling, but you look content." She gives Ann a nod of enthusiasm. "I'm starting to like this artist."

"You don't even know him."

"I like the way he paints. I like anyone who can capture you on canvas like this." She studies the painting. "I love the riding crop."

"It's the one I used on Max."

"I like it even more."

"We need to figure out where to hang this."

"Why not in your office?"

"What a grand idea. It's the perfect place for it."

"On the wall behind your desk. That crop should let the clients know you mean business," she adds and attempts an evil leer.

"How do you like the cigarette, with its glowing tip?" Ann asks her.

"I like the way you're holding it. It's kind of masculine. Women don't usually hold a cigarette like that." She looks at Ann, then back at the canvas. "It's almost as if he painted you as a ... well ... not a man so much as a ... I'll tell you who ..." She hesitates. "Never mind, I've said too much already."

"For heaven's sake! Finish what you were saying."

Eleanor shrugs. "Maggie Lambert is going to go wild when she sees this painting."

Ann looks at her in alarm. "What do you mean?"

"I mean she's going to be crazy for this painting."

"She might not care for it at all. I imagine she'll view it dispassionately, as she does all of the paintings in the gallery."

"She won't view that riding crop and that cigarette dispassionately. And she won't view the mournful look in your eyes dispassionately. And she definitely won't view the fact that you're dressed up as a boy dispassionately," Eleanor finishes smugly.

"I thought you said I looked content."

"Content, but there's some sadness, too." Eleanor kneels on the floor and examines the bold red flourish of a signature in the left-hand corner of the canvas. "'V. Von Renner.' The V is for Victor, I guess."

"Yes." Ann helps Eleanor to her feet. "I had an idea Victor might do this but I never dreamed he would provide such a priceless frame. It's too much."

"He must really care for you." Eleanor searches Ann's face for confirmation.

"He invited me to visit him and his mother in Portofino."

"When?"

"This summer."

"Are you going to go?"

"I'm not sure."

"Because of this painting?"

Because of Maggie.

"Partly because of the painting," Ann turns away from the intensity of Eleanor's quizzical stare. "Would you call Lloyd and ask him if he can come by and get this painting hung?" She tries to move it closer to the wall. "It weighs a ton. Tell him he'll need a helper."

After the portrait has been hung—not behind the desk, as Eleanor had suggested, but on the opposite wall, facing the desk—Ann is impressed with the room's transformation. The painting, with its massive frame, imparts a baronial connectedness to Victor and to Ireland. It will be as much of an asset to the gallery as to Ann's office.

The thought brings pleasure. She acknowledges a perverse elation at the prospect of showing the portrait to Maggie. It doesn't take long to unearth her motive. She wants a second experience of seeing Maggie at a loss for words—an experience of *Ann's* having rendered Maggie mute.

She decides to call Maggie and ask if she can find the time to stop by the gallery this afternoon. After Eleanor has gone home for the day. She'll tell Maggie she wants her to appraise a newly arrived painting.

An Austrian painting.

Maggie doesn't arrive alone. Ann recognizes Clarissa's honeyed voice. She and Maggie are chatting amiably when Ann enters the main showroom. Clarissa is dressed to the nines in an old-fashioned white pique dress. A black patent leather belt encircles her trim waist. Maggie's outfit is sheer contrast-—faded madras Bermuda shorts and a maroon short-sleeved polo shirt.

"How are you, Clarissa? What a delightful surprise."

"Ann dear, what a marvelous collection you have and so beautifully displayed in this marvelous showroom. No wonder Margaret is taken with your gallery. 'The Ann Cabot Gallery is the finest in Richmond,' she told me on the way over." Clarissa smiles. "I think for once I might have to agree with her."

Ann inclines her head. "Thank you, but you're much too kind. Why don't you continue looking around and I'll pour us some sherry. Or would you prefer a cocktail?"

"Well, it *is* five thirty. Do you have any Scotch?"

"I do."

"And soda?"

"That too."

Clarissa nods. "Just a splash of soda, then. On ice."

Ann walks back to the kitchenette.

Maggie follows.

"Do you mind?" she whispers.

"Of course not. I'm honored."

"Good girl. Now where's that painting you want me to appraise?"

"No, Maggie ... not now."

"Why not?"

"It's not the right time and—"

Maggie eyes her curiously. "And what?"

"I want to show Clarissa around."

"Clarissa is showing herself around as we speak."

Ann remembers that she has left her office door open. The portrait! The last thing in the world she wants is for Clarissa to quiz her about that painting. She turns abruptly to Maggie.

"I wanted you to—" She stops in mid-sentence.

Maggie trails the side of Ann's face lightly, with her index finger. "You wanted me to what?"

"I don't know."

Maggie's smile is tenderly teasing. "Don't you?"

"Here." She hands Maggie Clarissa's Scotch and soda. "Take this to your mother. I'm going to fix a drink for myself."

"Okay."

"I have no beer."

"Not a problem, dearest. I'll be the designated driver." She touches Ann's cheek again. "Relax."

"But Maggie, why did you bring her?"

"Actually, Zeke brought me. She's been dying to see the gallery and she wanted to watch me do the appraisal." She arches an eyebrow. "Are you upset?"

"No. I just wondered why she came. I'm glad she's interested in my gallery."

"Your gallery, your former hubby—the shrink, the kiddies, all of it. She's dying of curiosity," Maggie crows. "Well, let me take this to her." She ambles out of the kitchenette.

Ann pours half a jigger of Scotch, throws back her head, and swallows the burning liquid in its entirety. Her father used to down three full jiggers in a row.

Medicine to quiet the mind and render Constance softer in her pronouncements.

She gasps, wipes her mouth with the back of her hand, and repeats the procedure. "That's Daddy's good little girl," she murmurs. She half fills the jigger a third time, pours it into a julep cup, and splashes milk into the golden-amber liquid. Johnnie Walker Black. Her father's favorite. He had presented her with a fifth on her twenty-first birthday. *"When you drink whiskey, as I know you will,"* he had said, nodding sagely, *"this is what you should drink."*

That was how her father was—a worldly-wise, soft-spoken, and cultured man brought to heel by Ann's mother. And Ann, seeing and mourning, even as a child, the capacity her mother had to override her father's will. But not Ann's will. *"You're worse than your father!"* her mother would snap, and Ann would take the reproach as a badge of honor for defying the enemy. Why had it been that way?

"You were as protective of your father as he was of you," Dr. Greenfield had said when Ann was mourning her father's death. *"He loved you unconditionally and you reciprocated that love. Your mother's love for you and for your father was conditional. When you or your father displeased her, she withheld love."*

Ann looks down at her drink. She doesn't need it. She's already light-headed. She takes a deep swallow anyway and then another. The milk cuts the burn, a trick she learned from Cookie. No ice, only Scotch and milk.

Cookie and her father—the world's finest whiskey connoisseurs.

Maggie and Clarissa are examining the portrait when Ann finally tracks them down.

"Well, here you are," Ann effuses.

Maggie doesn't turn around. "Yes, here we are." Her voice is flat and hard.

"How do you like my office, Clarissa?"

"I like it very much, particularly this splendid portrait of you, which Margaret informs me she hasn't seen until now."

"That's true, she hasn't."

"No, I haven't, have I." Maggie turns around and faces Ann, arms folded. Her eyes flash anger.

"Well, what do you think of it?" Ann attempts.

"I think it's unbelievably good and I'd like to wring your neck. Is this what you rushed me over here to see?"

"Yes."

"Well, Ann Taliaferro Cabot, you're going to be charged a hefty fee for this after-hours consultation."

"How hefty?"

"Twenty-five percent."

"Of what?"

"Of *what*? What do you think of what? Of its value—some appraisers do that."

"What's its value?"

"It's up there." Maggie raises an eyebrow. "Did he provide this frame?"

"Yes."

"That frame alone is worth thousands." Her voice drips ice.

"Are you suggesting, Margaret Lambert, that this visit is going to cost me thousands of dollars?"

"You have no idea, little girl, what this visit is going to cost you."

"Excuse me," Clarissa intervenes, "but am I missing something here?"

"Probably not, Zeke. Finish your drink. We're leaving."

"You just got here," Ann protests. "Surely not so soon."

"Yes," Maggie retorts, "so soon. And don't call me Shirley."

"Who painted this?" Clarissa asks.

"Forget it, Zeke. We're leaving."

"Be quiet, Margaret. I'm talking to Ann."

"An Austrian baron. I met him in Ireland. He paints as a hobby."

"This looks more like a life's work than a hobby," Clarissa says pensively. "The artist has captured a quality of expression in your eyes that reminds me of a marvelous painting in the Metropolitan Museum. It's by Bastien-LePage. I believe it's entitled 'Joan of Arc.'"

"I know that painting well," Ann enthuses. "It's one of my favorites. The first time I saw it I couldn't walk away from it. I was mesmerized. I remember thinking that it wasn't as much about God speaking to Joan as it was about Joan having heard the voice of God."

Clarissa nods. "I understand." Her eyes bore into Ann's. "What a complex woman you are, my dear, and this artist, this—" She peers at the signature, "this V. Von Renner—"

Maggie snorts. "The V is for Victor, Zeke. Victor victorious and I wish you'd pipe the hell down about the man."

Clarissa shrugs annoyance. "As I was saying before Margaret interrupted, this artist obviously saw that quality in you and portrayed it by painting you with a mysterious...well, a mysterious everything—demeanor, costume, pose. I'm curious. Did you commission this painting or was it a gift? Do you mind my asking?"

"Frigging yes she minds!" Maggie yells. "It's none of your damn business. But since you already asked, it was no gift! Ann paid dearly."

Ann shakes her head in disgust. "You should be horsewhipped for talking to your mother so disrespectfully, Maggie, and, in answer to your question, Clarissa, in point of fact, the painting was a gift."

"It was not a gift," Maggie spits out each word. "It was a painting for which the artist exacted personal reimbursement."

Ann is stunned. She looks over at Clarissa, who appears to be intently examining the fabric on the walls, and then turns to Maggie, who is leaning against the desk, arms crossed. "How dare you speak of my private behavior in Clarissa's presence," she says to Maggie in a cold and furious undertone, "but, in point of fact, and for private reasons clearly beyond your repertoire, that was also a gift."

The room is suddenly electric. Maggie eyes Ann up and down, her lips curved in a mocking half smile. "Do you mean that?"

Ann doesn't answer.

"Well do you?"

"Stop badgering her, Margaret," Clarissa intervenes. She drains her glass and hands it to Ann. "Thank you, my dear. It's been a pleasure."

"The pleasure was mine," Ann replies. She can feel Maggie's eyes boring into her back as she follows Clarissa out of the office.

"Are you coming, Margaret?"

"No. I'll be home later. You can drive yourself home. You're not too tight, are you?"

"Of course I'm not too tight but perhaps Ann has other plans." Clarissa stares intently at Ann. "Well?"

"I'll bring her home later," Ann answers.

Clarissa opens her handbag and takes out her key ring. "Is this what you really want, Ann?" she asks. Her astute blue eyes search Ann's face for the answer.

Ann holds the gallery door open for her. "This isn't about what I want," she replies, "this is about what your daughter wants." She smiles, waves a perfunctory goodbye, locks the gallery door, and takes a deep breath before heading back to the kitchenette.

After she has rinsed out Clarissa's glass, she pours a tiny splash of Scotch into her drink, downs it, pours another, turns around, and shrieks aloud. Maggie is standing practically on top of her. "You frightened the hell out of me!" She scowls at Maggie.

"You're easily frightened."

"I think not!"

They glare at each other in silence. Ann's mouth begins to twitch. She wills herself to not smile.

"What the hell are you grinning at?"

"At the sorrow of confrontation."

"Forget it," Maggie snaps. "And I'm not charging a fee for that damn painting."

"What will your mother say?"

"What do you mean?"

"I mean, what will Mommie Dearest, with whom you are amazingly improper, think if you don't charge me for your visit?"

"Forget it, Ann."

"Fine, I'll forget that part. I've already paid dearly by Clarissa's being here to witness that scene, or doesn't losing a round to Clarissa count as payment?"

"What round? You and Zeke aren't in competition."

Ann snorts. "If it looks like competition and feels like competition—"

"Ann," Maggie interrupts, "forget Zeke. I'll never let her come here again."

"Do you have that power?"

"I'll ask her not to and she won't. She wanted to come because she's enthralled with you. She's sometimes like that with—"

"With her competitors for your attention?" Ann interjects. "Not that I give a hot damn. I'm only pointing it out for your benefit. I'm quite familiar with Oedipal triangles. It comes from years of ... of ..." she shrugs, "well, of something I can't recall just now."

"The shrink hubby would be the recollection that's eluding you." Maggie replies sardonically.

"That wasn't what I was going to say."

"Oh yes you were."

"Why would you think that?"

"Because Max still lives and reigns inside your screwed-up little head."

"You can't see inside my head, Margaret."

"I just did."

"Well, I see inside yours now."

"What do you see?"

"The arrogance of a presumptive woman who fancies herself always right."

"I don't fancy anything about myself."

"Then you were thinking about Victor."

"No, I wasn't. But it's amusing that you'd mention Victor just now. I must say it reminds me of the shrink hubby's mention of inappropriate people at inappropriate times. You don't mind my pointing that out to you, do you, dearest?"

"Not at all," Ann retorts, "except that Max did it to put distance between us. I'm not trying to put distance between you and me, Margaret."

"Oh?" Maggie scoffs. "Were you thinking the painting would enhance our relationship? Bring us closer? Have us share secrets, brush out each other's ponytails? I'd have preferred to have never set eyes on that damn painting, Ann. Surely a sensitive soul like you could have figured that one out."

"Is that why you asked me that sensitive question about Victor in front of *your mother*?"

"I don't recall asking you anything about Victor."

Ann's face reddens. "You asked if I meant what I said about that night with Victor being a gift—now do you remember?"

"You do like to lead with your chin, little girl. Yes, Ann, I remember. What about it?"

"Well," Ann persists, "I did mean what I said earlier. Remember?"

"Yes. You said that your one-night stand with baron Victor was also a gift."

"Well?"

"Well, nothing."

"You don't care?"

"No, Ann I don't."

"Why not?"

"Because, dearest, it no longer matters because that was then and this is now and because you weren't in love with him then and you're not in love with him now. Correct?"

Ann shrugs.

Maggie looks at her curiously. "Why, you materialistic little thing."

"That's outrageous."

"It is indeed. But understandable, considering your moneyed upbringing and your moneyed Irish cohorts."

"I mean it's outrageous because it's untrue."

"You didn't love him before you had the painting, but now you have the painting, expensively framed, I might add, and you think you might love him. Fine. You explain."

"What about the quality of Victor's work, his time, his energy? All poured into that portrait. He's in love with me," she adds complacently.

"He's in love with the Ann in that painting," Maggie scoffs. "Would you like to be the Ann in that painting?"

"Aren't I?"

"Not to me, but obviously Victor sees you that way."

"What way?"

"Aloof. Inscrutable. Invulnerable."

"Aren't I like that?"

"With strangers and with those you want to distance yourself from. Victor probably captured your mother more than you, although I give him credit for recognizing those capacities in you. He's certainly astute."

"You're contradicting yourself, Maggie."

"No, I'm not, Ann. I'm pointing out that the aspects of you Victor chose to commit to canvas are not what I would have chosen."

"What would you have chosen?"

"Tender vulnerability."

"You see no tender vulnerability in that painting?"

"Not a drop. Do you?"

"No." Ann breaks into laughter.

"What's funny?"

"I never win with you."

"You never lose with me. You just don't get it yet."

"I must tell you that Eleanor was sure you'd admire this painting."

"I do admire it." Maggie eyes it appraisingly. "I can't tell you how saleable it is."

"Who would buy it?"

"Irony of ironies, my dear. It would particularly appeal to a gay clientele."

"Women?"

"Women and men alike. It has an androgynous quality. You aren't sure if it's a man or a woman."

"What about the hair?"

"Young princes, pages, young men of today grow their hair that length. The costume, the cigarette, and the crop are curiously, maybe even purposefully misleading." Maggie grins. "I wonder if the baron has a penchant for young boys."

"How wicked of you to suggest such a thing."

"I'm not saying it's an appetite he indulges but it's food for thought."

"I really dislike your saying that."

"Then I guess I shouldn't add that the riding crop makes me wonder if he's into bondage."

"Be quiet, Margaret." Ann rinses out the julep cup and turns off the kitchen lights. "What did Clarissa say about the painting before I came in?"

"She said how beautiful you were and how interesting your outfit was. She also noticed you were wearing your crest ring in the portrait. Zeke doesn't miss much. She's big on details like jewelry."

"I would say your mother doesn't miss a trick."

"Actually Zeke misses a lot these days. She used to be very sharp in her younger days."

She's sharp enough now to shred steel, Ann muses. Her parting question, *"Is this what you really want, Ann?"* had absolutely oozed innuendo. She scans Maggie's face coolly. "Have you ever lived apart from Clarissa?"

"Off and on."

"When was the longest time you lived away from home?"

"When I went to college in New York."

"How long was that?"

"Two years."

"What happened after that?"

"I finished my last two years at Westhampton."

"Why?"

"I tired of New York. I preferred living in Richmond."

You mean you preferred living under the all-encompassing wingspan of Mommie Dearest.

She turns off the showroom lights and raises the thermostat. "So," she pursues in a casual tone, "have you lived away from Richmond since then?"

"Not really. A few months here and there."

Sweet Lord! She has no inkling of how tied she is to Clarissa—this "in your face" bold and oh-so-independent woman. At least I had the courage to leave home.

Maggie eyes her suspiciously. "What?"

Her expression is pure innocence. "I was thinking how fortunate Clarissa is to have you for a daughter."

"Whatever."

"Maggie, let's go to my house now. I haven't eaten all day and I'm famished."

"Why don't we eat out?"

"No. Home. Let's spend the evening in."

"How about dropping me off to pick up my car so you won't have to drive me home later?"

Ah, but I'm not going to drive you home later. I'm going to make you my prisoner and then I'm going to wean you away from Clarissa the Hun. She grins at the image of Maggie chained to her poster bed.

"Your grin doesn't answer my question, Ann."

"What question was that?"

"Why don't you take me to get my car so I can leave on my own when I'm ready."

"I don't want to be apart from you just now," Ann murmurs. "And besides, I've been drinking. Really, you should drive." She flashes Maggie a smile of beatific sweetness and flutters her eyelashes.

Maggie returns the smile and reaches for the keychain dangling from Ann's outstretched hand. "I'd like to know what's going on in that secretive head of yours, little girl, but I guess I'll just have to play it as it lays." She holds the gallery door open for Ann.

"Okay, dearest," she drawls. "Your house it is."

Belle and Liza greet Ann and Maggie at the front door. They are overjoyed to see Ann. "My babies," Ann croons.

Belle jumps up and puts her front paws on Maggie's shoulders, after which Liza barks and sniffs Maggie suspiciously.

Maggie backs away. "That Belle is one big dog. I'm relieved that she's friendly ... or is she?"

"Why, Maggie Lambert! You're afraid of her!"

"I'm cautious of her. She's watching me from the corner of her eye. I think she's suspicious of me."

"Only because you're suspicious of her."

"Don't take her side arbitrarily, Ann."

"She's just a baby."

Maggie snorts. "She's bigger than a pony. She looks like the wolf in Little Red Riding Hood."

"Look at her soft black nose."

"The soft black nose is not a problem. What about those crocodile teeth and those bone-crushing jaws?"

"She's my baby lamb," Ann murmurs and kisses Belle's snout. "I'm going to take a shower. Make yourself comfortable. There's beer in the fridge."

"No shower," Maggie orders. "You don't need one."

"Yes, I do need one." Ann retorts and heads to her bedroom, trailing clothes. She doesn't shut the doors behind her and she doesn't glance back to see what Maggie is doing. Her movements are assured—heels kicked off, on tiptoe, head high, shoulders squared. She walks into the bathroom, turns on the shower, pins her hair atop her head, and steps under the steaming spray.

After she has showered and brushed her teeth, she creams every inch of skin—marvelous body cream from Switzerland—softer to the fingertips than silk. Her hair, damp from the shower, gets its ritual fifty strokes after she has toweled it dry. She puts down the hairbrush, pulls her hair back into a loose ponytail, and walks into the bedroom.

Maggie is lying on the bed, both dogs beside her. She looks up at Ann. "Oh my Lord," She murmurs. "You're stark naked. Six years old and trailing baby powder." Her voice drops to a husky whimper. "You're pink from head to toe."

Ann smiles. "I didn't realize you were so close at hand." She turns around and opens the double doors of the closet.

"What are you doing now?" Maggie moans.

"I'm going to get dressed so I can fix dinner for us and Belle and Liza."

"Forget dinner. You're dinner. No clothes."

"What about Belle and Liza?"

"They can wear whatever they damn well please. Come here."

"No," Ann replies. "You come here."

Maggie rises from the bed with alacrity. Liza growls and barks at her. Maggie looks at Ann dubiously. "Is that dog going to be a problem?"

"No." Ann holds out her arms to Maggie.

"I am," she whispers.

Somewhere between that tumbled hazy span of dusk into dawn, Ann gets up to feed Belle and Liza.

They eye her curiously—fishily—and she laughs aloud.

"You don't know what in the world's going on, do you?" she murmurs. "Come here, both of you."

They bound to her joyfully and she settles to the floor and gathers them into her arms. Belle's long tail lashes against Ann's bare thigh as Liza gently nuzzles and then licks Ann's upturned palm. Sudden and rippling sensations of unbearable rapture permeate her consciousness. Hot tears course heedlessly down her face and neck. She tastes the salt of them on her lips and tongue and at the back of her throat.

"We are all one," she whispers.

Ann awakens Maggie with freshly brewed coffee in an oversized English breakfast cup.

Maggie stretches and yawns. "You're up early."

"I've been awake for hours."

"How come?"

"Happiness."

"Are you happy?" She searches Ann's face for the answer.

"Yes." Ann touches Maggie's cheek. "I'm happy," she whispers, "and I'm baking."

"Baking?" Maggie rises up on an elbow and reaches for her. "You look cool as a cucumber to me. How are you baking?"

"Not how but what. I'm baking biscuits."

"Are you baking them from scratch the way Zeke does?"

"Of course from scratch. You've fallen in love with the Pillsbury Doughgirl."

"I've fallen in love with a tigress." Maggie stretches languorously. A slow smile steals across her face.

"Was I a tigress?"

"A tigress … a lamb … a vixen … a Madonna." She sits up and reaches for her coffee cup. "How long do those from-scratch biscuits take?"

"Not to worry. I left Liza in the kitchen. She'll bark twice when they're ready to come out of the oven."

"Where is big bad Belle?"

Ann chuckles. "Either she went out the doggie door and is hiding bones in the garden or she's on the phone in the library, tattling to Eleanor."

"Tattling about us?"

"Tattling about not being given much attention last night and getting served dinner late."

"She's a haughty thing." Maggie reaches for her cigarettes and lights one.

"Are you referring to Belle or Eleanor?"

Maggie exhales slowly. "Eleanor isn't haughty." She pauses in thought. "She's possessive."

"Of what?"

"Of you and anything that involves you."

"That isn't true."

"It's definitely true."

"What makes you think that?"

"I'm an old hand at life, dearest. I know what I see and I call it as I see it. You must be very careful with Eleanor. She's enamored of you, although she most likely doesn't realize it. But believe me when I tell you that our relationship could cause problems for you, if you're not discreet. You must never let Eleanor get the upper hand in her relationship with you and revealing anything about us would give her the upper hand."

"I hate the way you're talking, Maggie. It makes me feel so ... well, duplicitous."

"Our relationship does not conform to current social mores, Ann, and anyone who doesn't conform, no matter how primitive and repressive those mores might be, is fair game for the masses who do conform." Maggie gives a nod of sorrowful acuity. "Don't ever lose sight of that. Shape your demeanor accordingly." Her face breaks into a winsome smile. "Now, why don't you just come over here for a moment. I'm about to do a little demeanor shaping you'll enjoy." She pats the side of the bed.

Ann shakes her head. "Breakfast is ready. Liza just barked twice. And bring your coffee cup with you."

Her voice is cheerful but in her heart she is pondering Maggie's admonishments—cognizant that less than four months ago she had thought so repellant the prospect of a relationship she now cherishes.

George is leaning against the side of his car, arms folded, when Ann and Maggie walk out of Ann's townhouse.

"George! This is a surprise." The color rises in Ann's cheeks.

"Hello Ann." He eyes Maggie up and down.

"Margaret, I'd like for you to meet George Greyson. George, this is Margaret Lambert. She's been advising me on some of the paintings here at the house."

"How do you do." He nods curtly in Maggie's direction but makes no attempt to shake Maggie's outstretched hand.

"How have you been, George, and how are you enduring this dreadful heat?"

"The heat is the least of my endurances."

"I'm driving Maggie back to her studio." Ann attempts a casual smile. "And then I'm off to the gallery. I'm really quite late today. Perhaps we can talk later. I've been meaning to call you since I returned, but I've been so busy."

George's eyes tighten. "Yes, I imagine it's been a hectic three weeks. The three weeks I'm referring to are the three goddamn weeks that have gone by without a word from you since your return to goddamn Richmond." He looks pointedly at Maggie. "How about taking a walk or buffing a nail or something, sweetheart? I'd like to talk to Ann privately."

"George." Ann places a placating hand on his arm. "Please don't be rude to Miss Lambert, and I *have* been meaning to call you."

"The first of what promises to be an ongoing series of lies." He shrugs off her hand. "Would you like to know how many times I've driven by your house or do you just not give a damn?"

"George, please let me call you later."

"You sound like a client with a bad debt. Or should I say a bad conscience? And don't insult my intelligence by saying you'll call later. I've waited too long for your later phone calls."

Ann blushes. "Did you know I'd gone abroad?"

"I make a point of keeping track of your comings and goings." George opens his car door. "I've been keeping track of you for a long time. Too damn long." He settles into his car, slams the door and starts the motor. One of the rear wheels rides up onto the curb as he pulls away.

Maggie stares at Ann. "What the hell was that all about?"

Ann shudders. "He's not to blame. I've treated him badly."

"Why shouldn't you? What a rude person."

"He was upset."

"I could see that he was upset, Ann. He was also threatening."

"He's a trial lawyer. His manner's just an affectation. He's not really like that."

"Oh?" Maggie arches an eyebrow. "What way is he really? And—" She stops alongside Ann's car. "What's he to you?"

"He's an acquaintance."

"His behavior conveys a hell of a lot more than acquaintanceship. He acts like a husband or—" She folds her arms across her chest and looks accusingly at Ann. "A jilted lover."

"Maggie, settle down. He's not a problem."

Maggie opens the car door and gets in. She slams the door shut and waits for Ann to close the driver's door before responding. "Listen, little girl, I'm going to tell you something. If you don't think that man's a problem, then you don't know a problem when you see one. He's been keeping track of you? Why the hell would he do that?"

Ann lowers her window. "Maggie, do you remember me telling you when we first met that I was involved with someone, but that it wasn't a love relationship?"

"Yes, I remember." Maggie stares at Ann. "Him?" She shakes her head in disbelief. "I don't believe it. What in the world would compel you to get involved with a man like that?"

"Well, to begin with, he and my father were friends."

"He's old enough to be your father!" Maggie lights a cigarette, inhales deeply, and takes another long drag. "What else?"

Ann hesitates. "Well, he comes of a good family, Maggie. His great-grandfather was governor of Virginia."

"And that's the basis for his arrogance?" She locks the door and slouches into it, her neck resting against the partially open window.

"Look at me, dearest," she says, "and listen carefully. I make it a point to avoid public scenes about private matters— particularly when those matters concern irate lawyers and their former girlfriends."

Ann counts to ten before replying. "I understand that, Maggie, but what do you expect *me* to do?"

"I expect you to get rid of George."

"He's been a good friend to me," Ann says quietly.

"He's incapable of being a good anything to you. He's a jackass!" Maggie sneers. "Yes, I know—a *landed gentry* jackass—Groton, St. Anthony Hall, Yale post grad—well, my dear, so was my heartbreak of a father." Her voice tightens. "I'm more than familiar with that empty panoply." She holds three fingers in Ann's face. "That makes three."

"Three *what?*"

"Three sorry relationships you need to quit."

"George and who else?"

"George, Victor the painter baron, and the shrink ex-hubby."

"Surely you don't expect me to drop every human involvement I've ever had."

"George is subhuman. The way you touched his arm offended me. The thought of him touching *you* anywhere is sickening." Maggie turns away from Ann, lowers the car window, and tosses what's left of her cigarette into the street.

"And don't call me Shirley," she drawls.

It's midafternoon when Ann finally arrives at the gallery. Eleanor hands her a sheet of paper.

"I've confirmed your reservations for Thursday. You're staying at Hathaway House—the same suite as last year. Your rental car will be waiting for you at the airport and you're flying out of Richmond instead of Norfolk and Max called this morning. He wants you to call him back. It's all on that list. It's been a very busy day, telephone-wise."

"It can only get worse." Ann grimaces. "I had the misfortune of being accosted by George Grayson in front of the townhouse a little while ago. He was as angry and downright rude as I've ever known anyone to be. I had to apologize for his behavior."

Eleanor looks up. "Apologize to whom?"

"To—" Ann's face reddens. "To anyone who happened to be walking by."

"I see." Eleanor shrugs. "I didn't put it on the list, but Mrs. Lambert called a little while ago. She was looking for her daughter Margaret. She asked for your phone number at the house. I told her I wasn't allowed to give it out."

"Thank you, Eleanor," she responds, as neutrally as she can manage, "Maggie might be bringing the Boldini back today. She must have mentioned it to her mother. Did you remember that Belle needs to be examined by Dr. Zuccaro?"

"I've already scheduled an appointment," Eleanor replies. "Where are the dogs now?"

"They're at the house. Flo's doing laundry this afternoon, so I left them there. Between the dogs and her soaps, I'll be lucky to get one set of bed linens pressed." She scans Eleanor's list. "I'm not in the mood to call Max back just now, but I will call Dr. Carter back. I know which watercolor he means. He wants me to convince him that it's worth the asking price."

"I'm sure you'll come up with something," Eleanor replies, pointed and dark of voice.

Ann reaches into her straw satchel, removes a folded tissue and blots her nose and forehead. "I'm going to lie down in my office for a bit. This heat is making me queasy." She tamps down a wave of nausea. "How did Max sound when he called?"

"Like a man used to winning," Eleanor calls out after her.

Ann shuts her office door and kicks off her heels. "Let the ritual pacing begin," she mutters. But she's more exhausted than anxious. She sits down at the desk, feet propped up on its smooth leather surface, her brow furrowed in thought—Eloise at the plaza grown up—Alice in Wonderland grown small. She reaches for the telephone and dials. "Mr. Grayson, please. This is Ann Cabot calling."

The receptionist puts her on hold. The wait seems interminable and just when she's thinking she can't endure another second of waiting, George picks up the line.

"Yes, Ann?"

"George I—" She draws a breath and looks up at Victor's painting. The woman in that portrait would not falter. "George, I don't want you to come to the house again as you did this morning. Please."

"Where is this relationship heading?" he demands in a clipped voice.

"I care for you, George. You've been a good friend. But I can't marry you."

George exhales audibly into the receiver. "After months of silence, this is what you're calling to tell me?"

"Yes."

"Fine. Don't marry me. I can live with that. What I can't live with, Ann, is the way you waltz in and out of our relationship without any regard for my feelings."

She takes a deep breath. "I want to end our relationship, George. It's not only that I can't marry you. I'm stepping away from all of it."

"So that part about caring for me was a load of pure horse manure."

"We both know," she says reflectively, "that friendship with me is not what you want. We should have remained friends but we didn't and now you won't be content with less." She draws a taut breath. "So I'm going to do us both a kindness and end this relationship."

She is surprised at what her words elicit—lightheartedness—not a painful thorn removed, because her heart had never been pierced by love for George, but a burdensome guilt-laden weight lifted because she had not been herself with George. She had been one person pretending to be another.

And, after George slams down the receiver, as she knew he would, she breaks into tears of soft relief.

Edwin walks over to the Volvo station wagon Ann has parked at an oblique angle on the camp's asphalt lot.

"You're way over the line, Mom."

"Did you think your absence would improve my ability to park? Hello, darling." She gives him a big hug and kisses his golden-brown cheek. "What a wonderful color you are." She eyes him approvingly. He looks like an Argentinean polo player. No wonder Lauren forked over her panties. "Is Lauren with you?"

"Not till tomorrow. You'll have to wait till then to meet her. But I have a picture of her in my cabin." His eyes glow with pride. "She's really pretty, Mom, and you should see her hair. It's much longer than yours and it's really blonde. And she's sweet, too."

"It intrigues me that you mention her sweetness only after raving over her incredibly long blonde hair," Ann teases. "What do the boys in your cabin think of Lauren?"

"Tommy's dying of jealousy," Edwin confides. "He's in love with her too but he's being a decent sort. Anyway, Lauren says he's too pubescent."

"Did she use that adjective?"

"Yes. She has a really superior vocabulary. And she's right about Tommy. He's pretty immature."

"What makes you think that?"

"Just some things I know." He gives her an arch look.

Ann turns away to hide her grin. She's seen the same look on Amory's face when she isn't about to give out peer-sensitive information.

"When's your father arriving?"

"Not till Saturday afternoon. How *is* Dad?"

"He's fine, darling."

"And how about the runt—whom I've written three times, by the way."

"Amory's fine, too. Has she written you back?"

"She called to tell me about her arm and the stitches and she's written me twice. Joan, on the other hand, has written me six times and sent a picture of herself in a bikini. She also called me about Amory's arm."

"Did she reverse the charges?"

"She tried, but I couldn't accept. So she hollered through the operator that my only sister Amory had hurt herself desperately and had lost tons of blood and then the operator let her talk and didn't charge for the call." He chuckles. "Don't worry, Mom, I can handle that little twit."

"How does the little twit look in a bikini?"

Edwin's face softens with compassion. "She's a heartbreaker, but in the wrong way. The poor kid looks like a skinny half-drowned rat with a mouthful of shredded tin can slivers. I offered her to Tommy as a consolation prize for not getting Lauren."

"My Son the Judicious. What did Tommy say?"

"He said she might've been a good-looking tomato, but someone had watered her too much." Edwin grins. "I sent her a photo of me."

"You sent *Joan Boatwright* a photo of you?" She stares at him in astonishment. "Why, for heaven's sake?"

"Six letters why. I just couldn't take any more of the kid's begging. Besides which, she made me promise I would when she called about Amory's arm." He groans a laugh. "She tried to make me agree to write 'to Joan with all my love, Edwin' on the back of it."

"And did you?"

"I wrote, 'To Joan, best of luck from your probation officer.'"

"Hmmm, how prophetic." She links her arm in his. "Are we going to your cabin now? I can't wait to see a photograph of your properly watered Lauren-variety tomato."

Ann has two messages awaiting her when she returns to Hathaway House. Once inside her suite of cozy rooms, she kicks off her shoes and strips down to her camisole and tap panties. She lies down on the striped linen sofa in the shuttered sitting room and is asleep in minutes.

The incessant blatting of a tugboat horn awakens her to darkness and the sensation of being lost in unfamiliar surroundings. She keeps her eyes tightly closed and whispers the beloved childhood poem.

> *Dear God, in darkness I approach you*
> *With fear I can't contain*
> *I pray you stay till daylight comes*
> *And I am safe again.*

"*I'm ascared of the dark,*" she had sobbed, and her grandmother had taught her that childhood scrap of prayer-book verse to ward off the three abiding fears of Ann Taliaferro Cabot.

"*Tell me the three things you most fear,*" Dr. Greenfield had asked Ann during one of their final sessions.

"*I have a fear of death. It's my greatest fear.*"

"*What do you fear about death?*"

"*The unknown of it compared to the known of the life I am living—the termination of this physical and mental configuration that houses my spirit—my soul.*"

"*And your second fear?*"

"*A fear of being afraid—of cowardice.*"

"*And your third fear?*"

"*A fear of mediocrity.*"

"*Thank you, Ann.*"

"*A thank you from Dr. Greenfield! Why?*"

"*Your answers were honest and incisive. Everyone fears death, though many deny it. Your second and third fears are aspects of character and personality that most likely came into play to deflect the anxiety of maternal deprivation."*

"If you think my mother deprived me, I've misrepresented her to you, Dr. Greenfield. Mother was aloof but she didn't deprive me of anything."

"To punish one's daughter by withholding affection is a form of deprivation that elicits fear and guilt, Ann, and the earlier it occurs in one's childhood, the more traumatic it is."

She sits up and reaches for the light switch. After her eyes adjust to the brightness, she searches the tiny dial of her wristwatch and gasps at the time. She's been sleeping for two hours, she has yet to return her phone calls, and she's starving. Dinner at camp had been unbelievably bad. Her stomach had revolted at the overcooked Swiss steak, the blob of bone-dry mashed potatoes, and the limp string beans swimming in grease. She had wrapped her fingers around her throat and made a choking gesture.

"Now you know why I wait for Hattie's cookies," Edwin had complained, and the entire table had come to life with horror tales of what had been discovered in the food, including tadpoles, roaches, living mold, staring fish eyes, the remains of a baby mouse— on and on—long past *ad nauseam*. But still Edwin had consumed all of his dinner, most of Ann's Swiss steak, and both of their peach cobblers with vanilla ice cream.

She tries to remember if the kitchen is open after ten. She picks up the phone to ask but her queasiness resurfaces at the thought of anything except a good cup of hot tea with honey. She dials Max's house instead. He answers after the third ring.

"Dr. Cabot."

"Hi Max. Am I calling too late?"

"Of course not. How was your flight and how are your rooms?"

"The flight was fine and the suite's the same as last year. Where are you staying?"

"I'm not sure. Hathaway's booked. The whole town's booked. I'll try to find something when I get in, but if I can't, will you accommodate Edwin and me Saturday night?"

"All right."

"Thanks. We're having dinner at Buckley's. I'd asked Edwin before he left for camp to get us a reservation there and he did."

"Ah yes, Buckley's. My mouth is watering already. Sweet Maine lobster with drawn butter."

"Remember your allergy."

"I haven't had a problem with shellfish for ages."

"Don't worry. I'm a doctor. I know how to treat cardiac arrest. How's our son faring?"

"He's great—taller, more self-assured, and seriously tanned. And he's in love. I haven't met the girlfriend yet but I've seen her picture."

"Is she good-looking?"

"You can decide for yourself on Saturday. She's having dinner with us per Edwin's request."

"I know. He called last week and asked if it was okay."

"He's growing up, Max. Our little boy is growing up."

"You sound sleepy, Ann."

"I have summer sleeping sickness. I do nothing but take naps. I think I'll hang up now so I can sleep some more. It's almost eleven and I need a bath. I'm all dusty from camp."

"I'll see you on Saturday then. Goodnight."

Ann hangs up and walks into the quaint gabled bathroom, turns on the taps, pours several capfuls of Vitabath under the steaming water and adds a handful of sea salt.

She'll call Eleanor in the morning. She can hardly wait to tell her about Joan's bikini photo.

She awakens to the phone ringing.

"Hi Mom."

"Good morning."

"Did I wake you?"

"Actually, you did," she says and tucks the receiver under her chin.

"It's after ten. You never sleep this late at home."

"I know. It must be all the salt sea air. Anyway—" She stretches languidly until her toes reach the ornate brass footboard. "I feel wonderfully rested."

"Tommy met a girl last night. Doug Langtree's sister. She came up with Doug's parents."

"What's she like?"

"Doug with braces and blue eye shadow."

"Hmmm. *Star Wars* meets Estée Lauder."

"Well, the blue took your mind off the braces."

"How?"

"It was electric blue."

"What's her first name?" She glances at the breakfast menu. *Coffee—a large pot, with honey, croissant, cantaloupe, and a side of buttered whole-wheat toast.*

"Do you mind?"

"Do I mind what?"

"I could tell you weren't listening, Mom."

"I'm sorry. I was thinking about food. What might I mind?"

"If I have lunch with Lauren and her parents?"

"Of course I don't mind. Did you think I would?"

"Well, Dad isn't coming until Saturday. It sort of leaves you on your own. "

"I'll find tons to do. Go and have fun. Have you met Lauren's parents yet?"

"Yes. They're in the reception room now. They asked me to have lunch with them."

"What're they like?"

"They're pretty cool. Lauren's dad's a judge and his grandfather ... no, his great-grandfather, was Archbishop of Canterbury during the reign of Queen Victoria."

"What was his name?"

"Archibald Campbell something," Edwin replies.

"Is Lauren an only child?"

"Yes, and so are her parents."

"You certainly know a lot about Lauren's family."

"From her mother. She wanted to know all about you and Amory and Dad and about your art gallery. And about Harry and Cookie—Sir Horace and Lady Constance Fairfield. She's impressed that we're related to royalty."

"Harry and Cookie aren't royalty, darling."

"Well, they're titled, which evened out the Lord Baron what's-his-name, Archbishop of Canterbury, great-grandfather pedigree," Edwin says blandly. "So Mom, are you going to be all right on your own this afternoon?"

"Of course. I'll see you this evening. Have fun." She disconnects, dials room service and places her breakfast order, and then dials the gallery. "Hi Eleanor. How are things in Richmond?'

Eleanor clears her throat. "I have several things to tell you, some good and some not so good. What do you want first?"

"The good."

"Amory called. She got your care package and loved the polo shorts and baseball cap. She'll call her dad and Edwin at Hathaway House around eleven on Sunday. She sounds all cheery and in charge. And no more sling—her arm's fine. The second thing is I sold the matador painting for three thousand. A Baltimore dealer bought it. I gave him fifteen percent. He asked for twenty. I told him I couldn't get in touch with you to okay the sale and that you might decline the offer because you really loved the painting but that I'd do fifteen on my own. He said 'Let's do it.'" Eleanor draws a breath. "And you got a letter from the baron yesterday—sealed with a crested blob of dark-green wax and postmarked Italy—and that's it for the good."

"What's the bad?"

"Hattie called to remind you she leaves for her trip next Friday. She froze plenty of cookie dough and you can bake the cookies and mail them when you get back. She left you enough for three batches—and now for the really bad news. Belle's pregnant."

"Oh no!" Ann's nausea resurfaces. "And we have no idea who the father is."

"Dr. Zuccaro said Belle could be spayed." Eleanor relates the information in a dubious voice. "But it has to be done immediately if you want to go that route."

"No," Ann moans, "it would be easier, but no. We'll just have to see it through. Does Dr. Zuccaro foresee any problems?"

"He thinks Belle will do fine. The ultrasound detected three heartbeats and he says Belle's built for easy breeding."

"Obviously! When does Dr. Zuccaro think she'll deliver?"

"He's not positive, late July or early August."

Ann computes. "They'll be born under the sign of Leo—Leo's of uncertain origin. My virginal Scottish lamb raped by—" She groans. "How can this possibly turn out well? Come on, Eleanor, think of something positive to say."

"Belle will be fine," Eleanor says in a calm voice, "and you'll have folks lined up for the pups because Belle's beautiful. Every time I walk her, she gets raved over. Her beauty will make up for the father's shortcomings."

Ann gasps. "Please don't suggest 'shortcomings.' It makes me think of a Chihuahua."

"Anatomically impossible."

"Not necessarily."

"Yes, necessarily."

Ann hears a knock on the sitting room door. "Well, my breakfast, for which I now have no appetite, is here. I'll figure things out when I get home. I can't wait to inform Max about Belle's pregnancy. He was staying at the house the night Belle got out. He probably left the driveway gates open for just a few minutes because he was going right back to the hospital and figured it would be okay. He's done that before. He was so positive Belle wasn't in heat and hadn't gotten out that he didn't even bother calling Dr. Zucarro—who would have suggested an immediate cortisone shot to terminate the pregnancy."

"Maybe you should have Dr. Zuccaro give Max the vet bill."

"No," Ann replies, deadly earnest of voice, "Max gets the babies—all three of whatever mystery breed and astrological sign they turn out to be."

Ann spends the afternoon browsing the shops on Western Avenue. She finds a sweater for Amory at Green Tomato and madras bathing trunks for Edwin in one of the hotel gift shops. She orders an arrangement of white daisies in a white wicker basket from the Kennebunkport florist shop and heads back to Hathaway House for afternoon tea in her sitting room. And then she calls Maggie.

"Well, I'm going to be a grandmother," she announces.

"It can't be Amory and it better not be Edwin."

"Belle's pregnant."

"Big Bad Belle? I thought the cardiologist-turned-shrink hubby checked her over and said no."

"Are you ever going to call him Max?"

"No, Ann, I'm not. You do it enough. What are you going to do about Belle?"

"I'm going to see it through with Belle, of course. She has a marvelous vet."

"Is it too late for an abortion?"

"She'd have to be spayed at this point," Ann replies, "and I'm not willing to have Belle's pups destroyed."

"Why subject that dog to a litter she probably never wanted to begin with?" Maggie takes a long drag, exhales, and waits for Ann to respond.

"Belle's still too young to be spayed. I don't know how she'd respond to having her pups aborted."

"She's a dog, Ann. Dogs don't get morally hung up about abortion."

"Dogs are intelligent and highly sensate creatures, Maggie." She collects her thoughts before continuing. "Belle knows she's pregnant—her behavior has been quite different lately—she would surely mourn the loss of her pups."

"What you're suggesting is as fatuous as Zeke's reading Jane Austen novels to her birds and swearing that they chirp at the sad parts," Maggie scoffs.

Ann laughs with delight. "How perfectly darling and how dear of Clarissa to swear to it. Read *Music for Chameleons* by Truman Capote—it's a short story about chameleons with a penchant for classical piano." She takes a final swallow of tepid tea and returns the cup to its saucer. "I'd like to help with your enlightenment about such matters but Edwin will be here long before I can persuade you to Clarissa's and my point of view." She pauses in anticipation of a sardonic quip from Maggie, but no quip ensues. "Is something wrong?" she finally asks.

"Not at all."

"Good, because I bring tidings of great joy. Hattie's taking her two weeks' vacation and I'll be staying at the river house while she's gone. You are hereby invited to pack a hobo stick, get in your car, and join me for two weeks of totally private time together. We can fish for our supper, paddle about in Edwin's canoe, loll about in hammocks, have afternoon tea in the greenhouse, sunbathe naked in the secret garden, eat, drink, and be merry," soft of voice—totally expectant of Maggie's snort of pleasure. "How does that sound?"

"It sounds idyllic but I couldn't possibly manage it," Maggie answers.

"Apart from being merry, what couldn't you manage?" Ann teases.

"Two weeks in Hampton," Maggie replies.

Ann emits a slow sigh. "You don't sound at all enthusiastic. I thought you'd be thrilled. Is something wrong?"

"Nothing's wrong, I am thrilled and I will come down. I just can't stay as long as you're suggesting."

"Well, how long can you stay?"

"One night, maybe two. But definitely not two nights in a row."

"Why *definitely* not?"

"Because I have commitments," she replies, cool and patient of voice.

"Maggie, please tell me what's wrong."

"Ann, dearest, and this is the last time I'm going to say it—nothing's wrong."

The clutch of fear is sudden and harsh.

And do you have a fourth fear, Ann?

A fear of diving too deep—bottoming too quickly—surfacing too late.

"Surely you can stay longer than one night at a time," she suggests, her voice artificially casual. "It's summertime. Everyone deserves a summer vacation."

"I know, Ann, and it sounds lovely, but I can't be away for nights in a row. Now let's change the subject. How's Edwin?"

"I don't want to talk about Edwin, Maggie. I don't understand why you're so adamant about this. We haven't spent an entire night together in ages ..." She thinks back. "Since the night after Clarissa came to the gallery." She places her hand over the mouthpiece, breathes deeply to fight the sudden wave of nausea that assails her, and then continues in a quiet voice. "Is it because you don't want to be away from Clarissa in case she needs you? Is it because Clarissa doesn't like being alone at night?"

"No," Maggie retorts in a clipped voice, "Zeke can take care of herself. She and I lead totally separate lives."

"Well, what is it then?"

"Don't do this, dearest."

"Don't do what?"

"Don't force me to defend myself."

"Do you see my wanting us to have uninterrupted time together as an attack of you?"

"We have time together in Richmond, Ann."

"The Richmond house has no privacy, no property to speak of, no river, and you rarely stay the night. Trust me. You'll love it there."

"What about the shrink hubby? The thought of crossing paths with him puts me in mind of the Richmond encounter with George, the former governor's whatever."

"Max has his own place. The river house is entirely my own. And Max will be vacationing with his brothers in Mexico next week and the following week also. You and Max will not cross paths in Hampton. Please say yes. I want us to have this time together. You can bring down one of your canvases and work there if you like. I'll turn the sunroom into a studio for you. It gets wonderful light most of the day."

"Forget it, Ann, it's not going to happen."

"Why not?" Ann protests.

"Because I don't want to."

"But why don't you want to?"

"Because, dearest," Maggie answers, quiet and final of tone, "it isn't who I am and it isn't who I choose to be."

A second wave of nausea washes over Ann as she struggles to assimilate what Maggie is telling her, and when comprehension dawns, the blood rushes to her cheeks in a stinging blush. It's *she* who is *Maggie's* plaything. Cookie had it entirely—she flinches—agonizingly backwards. She draws a ragged breath before speaking. "We'll have to discuss this another time. I hear Edwin at the door. I'll call you when I get back."

She disconnects the line and lies down on the sitting room sofa, heedless of her freshly pressed linen slacks and jacket. She had been so looking forward to the parents' campfire with Edwin, but all she wants to do now is climb into bed and sleep off her conversation with Maggie.

Ann is quiet during dinner but Lauren's ceaseless chatter is more than adequate to the occasion. She is a self-assured natural blonde beauty with whom Edwin is clearly smitten.

Max catches Ann's eye and winks.

He's pleased with Edwin tonight. The perception lifts her spirits.

After dessert and coffee, both of which Ann declines, they walk to the oceanfront. Max turns to her. "Why don't you head back to Hathaway and I'll stay with these two and play duenna. You look tired." He checks out Edwin and Lauren, several paces behind, hand in hand, sweaters tied around their waists in anticipation of the cool Maine night. "They're so wrapped up in each other they'll never even notice."

Ann nods gratitude. "Last night's campfire was really everlasting. I didn't get to bed until past midnight." She doesn't add that she had stayed awake well into the early hours of the morning reliving her conversation with Maggie, pacing the parameters of the sitting room over and over, hands clenched behind her back, mind and heart doing battle.

Max takes her gently by the shoulders and looks into her eyes. "You're a million miles away tonight. What's wrong, Ann?"

"I was thinking about Belle," she replies. *Great. Now I can add guilt-inducing habitual liar to my list of sins.* She gives a shudder of self-mockery.

"Belle will be fine." Max looks at her closely. "And I don't believe—" He pauses.

"What?" she snaps. "You don't believe what?" She adds bad-tempered to the list. "Forgive me. I didn't mean to snap at you. I'm toxic this evening."

"You're not toxic. Just preoccupied and—" His eyes soften. "Perhaps a little sad. Maybe you're feeling the loss of Edwin. We'll talk when I get back to the hotel. Edwin has plans to stay at the Colony Hotel with Lauren and her parents. He says they have accommodations that could house the population of Guam."

She stares at him. "Does Edwin plan to stay there all night?"

"I think so."

"Well, I don't think so. I don't think so at all. It wouldn't be proper. What would Lauren's parents think?"

"It was their suggestion," Max replies. "They were chatting away with Edwin when I stopped by his cabin. I invited them for brunch on Sunday. They seem pretty conservative to me. I can't imagine Lauren's mother being offhand about her precious daughter in any way."

She shakes her head. "I don't like it, Max."

"Then it's a no. Edwin will be disappointed, but he'll get over it."

"I want him back by eleven thirty. My mother would never have allowed such a thing." She winces at the anger in her voice. "Never," she whispers.

Max returns to find Ann pale, clammy, and nauseated.

"It's from the lobster. You're going to have to vomit it up. Let's get you into the bathroom."

"No ... not yet," She wails. "It might pass."

"Come on, Ann. Let's get it over with."

"I don't want to. It may pass. I shouldn't have had so much wine with dinner."

Max shakes his head. "You shouldn't have eaten that entire lobster, including the coral. You're allergic to lobster. There's no question of it now."

"I'm not allergic to lobster. I've eaten it since I was a child."

"Come on, honey. I'll put a finger down your throat and then you'll feel better. It's either that or a stomach pump in the emergency room." He places his hands under her armpits and propels her into the bathroom.

When they finally emerge from the horror of that ordeal, she is spent and trembling. Max settles her on the sitting room sofa and covers her with a thin cotton blanket.

"I'm going to fill the tub with warm water. It will open your pores and help those toxins to escape. Then maybe a cup of hot tea."

"Not a tub, Max, I'm too weak. Maybe a shower."

"No, a bath. With a couple of handfuls of sea salt, which I noticed you've brought along."

Her mind balks at the idea of Max bathing her.

What difference does it make? What difference does anything make in the long run?

"What time is it now?" she calls out in a raspy voice.

"It's a little after ten," Max answers from the bathroom. "Stop thinking about Edwin. I gave him a stroke-of-twelve-curfew."

But she isn't thinking about Edwin. She's thinking about what Maggie is doing at this moment and about what Maggie would say about what went on in that bathroom. What Maggie would say about Max removing Ann's camisole, bending her over the toilet bowl—gently wiping her face and neck with the hand towel he had soaked in hot water scented with Vitabath. And now he was going to bathe her unless she asked him not to, which she wasn't going to do because what difference could it possibly make in the long run since there wasn't going to be a long run. Tears fill her eyes and roll into her already-damp hairline and down the sides of her face.

Max helps her to her feet. "Come on, your bath's ready. You don't realize how much better you're going to feel. Come on, honey, don't cry, Daddy's taking care of you. I've already called in a prescription. You'll be in bed sleeping peacefully before Edwin gets back. I'll wait up for him. Don't cry."

She awakens to darkness mitigated by a flickering pinpoint of light beyond a partially opened door.

The captain lies beside her, his face tender in sleep. She tries to rise but cannot. He is lying on top of the covers—she, under layers snugly tucked between mattress and box spring. Her body feels heavy and lethargic of limb, resistant to the mental press to be up and about.

"I must get up," she whispers. "Please, sir, let me up."

He awakens and sits up. "What's wrong? Are you sick?"

"No. Not sick but all bound up. I need to … I need to get up."

"Why do you need to get up?"

"I don't know why," she answers forlornly. She eyes the dim outlines of his clothing. "Why are you in bed with your uniform on?"

"I must have fallen asleep with my jacket on. Why do you call it a uniform?"

"Aren't you wearing your uniform?"

"I'm wearing what I always wear."

"Well it scratches me."

"No, it doesn't. You're wearing one of your long-sleeved granny gowns. But I'll take it off."

"Yes. Take it off."

He removes his jacket. "There, is that better?"

"Take off the shirt, too."

She watches as he unbuttons the shirt—button after button—his bare flesh emanating the lingering, joyously familiar scent of his aftershave.

"How's that?"

She sits up, brushes the covers aside, and leans back, her buttocks atop the heels of her feet, the palms of her hands resting on her thighs.

"Take everything off."

"I'm not sure I want to do that and I'm not sure it's what you want either."

She remembers then that all officers are taught to resist capture. "Hurry," she whispers, "it may have already happened. It may already be—" She counts on her fingers. "Too late."

"Too late for what?"

She knows the answer but it slips beneath the veil of conscious thought. "No more questions." She slips off her nightgown and straddles his body, opens his lips with gentle fingers, and takes his mouth with hers until he is beyond resistance.

"Sweet Lord," he pleads. "Sweet Lord."

She presses her body against his. "You're lost, sir," she whispers, "totally and entirely lost. Allow me to show you the way home." And then she angles a hip and takes him in.

Ann is standing outside the terminal when Eleanor pulls up.

"You're late."

"And a good morning to you," Eleanor retorts.

After the porter has put her luggage in the back of the wagon and Eleanor has switched places, Ann eases in behind the wheel and turns the key in the ignition.

"Why were you so late?"

"I wasn't that late, Ann, but I'm sorry."

"Thank you for apologizing."

"What's wrong?" Eleanor's voice rises in alarm. "Is Edwin okay?"

"He's fine. He's infatuated with a lovely adolescent named Lauren. But the mother—the mother was exhausting."

"Where'd you meet the mother?"

"I more than met her. We all had brunch together at Hathaway House."

Eleanor emits a low whistle. "I guess you didn't care for Lauren's mother."

"In point of fact, I found her really annoying—a nosy, casually overbearing older version of Lauren." She sighs. "What's wrong with me? How can I be so vicious about a perfectly respectable person?"

"It's called Mother Hen Syndrome, and you become immune after the third girlfriend. How was Max?"

"He was kind." Her voice softens. "And he was wonderful with Edwin."

"Was he kind to you?"

"Very kind. He had to play doctor and he handled the role beautifully. I had the experience of dinner passing through my lips and throat twice. Max's finger participated in one of the—" She makes a choking sound.

"You ate lobster, didn't you?"

"I think it was the wine. I requested and Max ordered a bottle of truly superior Châteauneuf-du-Pape. There must be some health reason why white wines are recommended with seafood."

"If you ate lobster, it was the lobster."

"I wish you'd stop saying that, Eleanor. I should know what I was sick from."

"Yep. You should and do and it wasn't the wine."

"Oh be quiet."

"I hope it didn't ruin your night with Max and Edwin."

"I don't exactly know what I did—I mean what *it* did." She scowls. "I'm leaving this afternoon for Hampton. I don't want to stay in Richmond. I'm still sick. Can you manage the gallery on your own or do you need Brandon to help you out? She's dying for the work and the clients like her."

"I don't think I'll need her, but I'll call her if I do." Eleanor glances over at Ann. "Where *is* Max, by the way? I figured he'd fly back with you."

"He's probably in Boston as we speak. It's his annual 'two weeks with the brothers' vacation. They're flying out of Boston to Mazatlán. Wyatt's into surfing these days."

Eleanor nods approval. "That's nice. Max always loves those vacations."

Ann parks in front of the gallery and lets Eleanor out. "Don't forget to book my flight for Amory. The dates are circled on the calendar."

She spies Belle and Liza at the window, ears up, tails wagging. Eleanor walks them out, opens the rear door of the wagon, and they bound in. Liza barks excitedly and Belle pokes her head over the driver's seat and licks the side of Ann's face. Ann melts. "You naughty hussy!" A wave of anxiety washes over her. "What are we going to do?" she whispers.

Eleanor shuts the tailgate, walks over to the driver's window, and hands Ann the dogs' leashes, a plastic container of marrowbones, and a stack of gallery mail and auction catalogues. "What are we going to do about what?" she asks.

"I'm babbling, Eleanor. A conversational tactic I picked up from Lauren's mother." She checks the rearview mirror, waves a cheery goodbye, and pulls slowly away from the curb.

She doesn't call Maggie until she has settled in Hampton—walked through the ample, comfortable rooms of the tucked-away river house, wended the familiar path to the river's edge—where the moon sends silver to the rocks, where Belle and Liza clamber down the sloping seawall to chase a scuttling crab and flip a desiccated fish back onto the grass. She physically restrains Liza from wallowing in its horrendous stench, picks her up, and carries her down to the greenhouse, with Belle following at a reluctant pace.

Caught between longing and anger, she delays the call and diverts the energy of her anger into baking cookies, cutting a basketful of lilies, camellias, and gardenias and arranging them in vases. She cooks a pot of brown rice and ground lamb for Belle and Liza and tosses an elaborate salad for her dinner. The note from Victor, on the block front secretary in the upstairs sitting room, still awaits her reply. *What to do about Portofino? What to do about Maggie?*

She opens the sunroom door and whistles for Belle and Liza. They amble listlessly into the living room and sprawl onto the cool marble hearth. Her dinner salad sits uneasily—a wave of nausea that elicits an internal vow to never consume shellfish of any sort again. She walks over to the desk, flips through the pages of her small, leather-bound directory, locates the number, and dials resolutely.

He answers after the second ring. "Dr. Greenfield."

"It's Ann Cabot, Dr. Greenfield. Am I calling too late?"

"Not at all, but what a surprise! How are you?"

"I'm fine. How are you?"

"Things are going well for me."

"I'd like to make an appointment to see you at your earliest convenience. Perhaps a double session." She manages a chuckle. "It'll take that long to fill you in on what's been happening."

"It will have to be an evening session. I'm booked solid this week. How about Wednesday at seven?"

"Wednesday at seven is good."

"I'll see you Wednesday, then. Goodnight, Ann."

She disconnects the line and dials Maggie's number. She hangs up after the sixth ring. Maggie must not be home. Or perhaps she's home but not taking the call. Perhaps she and Clarissa are at the theatre or dining out. Perhaps Maggie has just stabbed Clarissa in the heart for prying open Maggie's strongbox filled with old love letters and is busily chucking Clarissa's dismembered body parts down the loft's ancient laundry chute. Or perhaps she has just been served a superb dinner at the house of that maladjusted pediatric former lover of hers and they've vacated the dinner table and are enjoying dessert elsewhere.

At the first stab of jealousy, her heart recoils and the thought flashes through her mind that captains are trained to resist capture.

The telephone awakens Ann. She looks at the clock on the nightstand. It's ten thirty.

"Good morning, Ann. How are you today? Feeling any better?"

"Hi Eleanor. I do feel better." But she doesn't feel at all better. Her body is thick and sluggish from too much sleep and her spirit is low and edgy from sheer unhappiness. *Less than two days before Dr. Greenfield. Thank God.*

"Ann? Are you there?"

"I'm sorry, Eleanor. I'm so preoccupied these days. I'm sure it's driving you insane."

Eleanor takes the ball and runs with it. "It's really irritating. I feel like I hardly know you anymore. I hate the way you've been treating me. I've been a darn good employee as well as a good friend and all you do is ignore me and—" Her voice darkens. "Keep secrets from me."

She's going to tell me off and then she's going to cry and apologize for telling me off. But not today, Eleanor. Not today.

"Eleanor, listen to me." Ann's voice hardens. "And listen carefully, dearest. I know you're peeved that I've been so distant lately and haven't made time to sit down and chat, as we usually do. Possibly you're hurt and think I don't care. But please don't be hurt and I do care. We're friends as we've always been and always will be. Our relationship is good and will continue to be good unless you try to get involved in my private life, as you occasionally do. It's for me to decide what I want to share with you, but you and I are fine." She draws a shallow breath. "However, even if we weren't fine, this is not a good time for us to talk it through. Do you understand?"

Eleanor doesn't answer.

"Well?" Ann presses.

"Yes."

"Yes what?"

"Yes, o great ruler of the universe."

"It's not the response I was hoping for, but I'll accept it gratefully. So, what are you calling about?"

"To let you know I'm thinking about quitting the gallery."

"Fine," Ann retorts indifferently, "call Brandon. Tell her she's hired full time if she wants the job. If she says yes, have a set of keys made for her. Are you giving me two weeks' notice or are you walking off the job today?"

"Is that all I mean to you? You are one cold woman."

"It would seem that you're one cold woman, too."

Eleanor bursts into tears. "I wasn't really going to quit," she sobs. "I was only kidding."

"Well," Ann responds, unrepentant of voice, "if you aren't going to quit, please move on to the real reason for this phone call."

"Ann, I'm saying this as a friend, not someone who works for you." Eleanor draws a harsh breath. "Sometimes you can be a twenty-four carat bitch."

"Yes, I can be. I use it as a defense against self-serving anger camouflaged as unfairly treated victim."

"I'm starting to feel sorry for Max."

"We all feel sorry for Max. What's your point?"

"I'm sorry I said that, Ann. Do you forgive me?"

"Yes, Eleanor. I forgive you for all of this, but I'd appreciate your moving on to the real reason for this phone call. Clear your mind, take a deep breath, count to ten, and tell me why you're calling, and please, just the facts, ma'am."

"Max called the gallery from Boston. He said he'd been trying the townhouse but couldn't get an answer."

"Did he say why he was calling?"

"He said he wanted to talk to you before he left for Mexico. I told him that Cookie had called you from New York but I didn't know if you and she had gone off somewhere or not. I figured I'd better check with you before I told him you were at the river house."

"That was prudent, but *did* Cookie call?"

"Yes. She's at the St. Regis. You're to call her. Oh, and Max said he'd call you when he got back from Mexico."

"Anything else?"

"Max was nice, Ann. He told me about Edwin and the trip to camp like we were old friends."

Oh yes. And when Max is nice like that you take it in hook, line, and sinker and I become the villain.

"Max turns niceness on and off like tap water. Any other calls?"

"Maggie Lambert called," Eleanor replies in a flat voice. "She wanted to know where you were."

"What did you tell her?"

"I said I thought you might be in New York."

"For heaven's sake, Eleanor! What exactly did you tell her?"

"I told her your cousin Cookie, Lady Fairfield to her, was in New York and that she wanted you to drop everything and fly up to the Big Apple to be with her." Eleanor coughs and then clears her throat nervously. "I hope you won't fire me for doing it because I really do want to keep on working here but that woman's attitude drives me up the wall. Why the heck is she so much in my face these days is what I'd like to know."

"She's in your face these days because she's an art conservator—a good art conservator. As for her presence in my life, which is what you're really harping about, hers is, quite frankly, a friendship I wish to maintain and it's not your concern. So, if Maggie calls back, please tell her that I tried to reach her and couldn't get her but that she can reach me in Hampton. I'm going to hang up now because I'm feeling queasy again. Be happy and please stop worrying yourself to death about things that don't really concern you. Goodbye."

She disconnects the line and leaves the receiver off the hook. If the world blows up and no one can get to her because the line rings busy, so be it. If Cookie can't reach her and is reduced to dining at La Grenouille solo, so be it. All she wants to do is sleep.

Sleep—sleep—and more sleep.

The pure oblivion of an infant's dreamless sleep.

Dr. Greenfield's office is exactly as Ann remembers it. She sits down in her favorite chair, a large wingback covered in tufted black leather. He sits down at his desk, a modern chrome-and-glass affair, leans back in his black leather desk chair, adjusts his horn-rimmed glasses, and looks at her appraisingly.

"You look wonderful, Ann."

"Thank you." She gives a faint smile and clears her throat. She knows he's waiting for her to begin, but she's suddenly at a loss for words. She clears her throat again.

He scans her face. "You're anxious."

"Yes."

"Why?"

"Because I have something to tell you that's going to shock you."

"Hmm. You may surprise me, but I don't think you'll shock me."

"I'm involved in an intimate relationship with a woman." Her color rises. "So—are you shocked or surprised?"

Dr. Greenfield laces his fingers together. "I would say that you have surprised me, because I hadn't thought of that possibility for you."

"What possibilities had you thought of?"

"I thought it possible that you were considering marrying again and I thought it possible that you and Max might have reconciled."

"I recently terminated my relationship with George Grayson and Max and I ... well." She shakes her head. "I don't think Max and I will ever remarry."

"Why is that?"

She thinks about it. "I started to say because of the affairs but it's more than that. It's because I don't feel safe enough with Max to be open and, without that openness..." She sighs. "What's the point of being married? No, it wasn't only the affairs—although they were akin to wild beasts raging in the corridors of my mind and heart—and for quite a while, too—particularly with Faye Graham." She flexes her hands, places her elbows on the arms of the chair, and joins her fingers in steepled prayer.

"I've often wondered why Max became involved with Faye. I'm sure he desired her, because Faye exuded desirability, but I think Max derived a dark secondary pleasure from observing Faye in a double bind because of her relationship with me." Ann nods sagely. "And that same dark pleasure may have been what impelled him to tell me about their affair."

Dr. Greenfield considers her perspective. "Max may have been concerned that you'd hear it from someone else. Or he might have been trying to ease his conscience by making a clean breast of it. It might have been a way to end an affair he had tired of. It may have been for all of those reasons. Motivation is seldom single-pointed."

"I think Max wanted me to find out, and when I didn't find out, he told me. He told me on New Year's Day—five hours before a party to which we'd invited more than two hundred guests—a party to which Faye and Leonard had been invited but didn't attend because they went on a last-minute cruise to Bermuda. I went through the motions of hostess like someone suffering from shell shock, but Max was the perfect lord of the manor, and after the last guest had departed, he said he thought it was quite the best gathering we'd ever had."

"What about the affair with his former therapist? If I'm remembering correctly, you became aware of that through pure chance."

"Not pure chance at all. That open journal with the photographs and love letters was on Max's desk for anyone to see, including his secretary. He knew I was coming to the office to meet him for lunch. I think he left it there intentionally rather than locked away in his file cabinet. Max is a stickler about patient privacy. He told his secretary to have me wait in his office. He *wanted* me to see that journal."

"Why would Max want that?"

"Because he had determined to use my knowing as a catalyst for ending the affair. He egotistically assumed I wouldn't be brokenhearted, as I'd been with Faye, because he had not bonded with this woman. He acknowledged that when I told him I wanted a divorce. He also informed me that this woman, a friend and colleague, couldn't sue him because she had been *his* therapist at one time. Oh, Max told me many things that I nurtured to fortify my determination to divorce him." She looks up in surprise. "I realize now why I was so determined to end my marriage to Max. It was because he continuously deceived me by fostering the illusion that he could keep nothing from me, whereas, in point of fact, he was a man of many secrets—many pretensions. He was precisely as my cousin Cookie had pegged him—one person pretending to be another." She leans back into her chair. "Maggie, that's the name of the woman I'm involved with, is unreal in the same way. It's a hard trait for me to ignore—probably because my mother was that way also."

"Give me another word for unreal."

"Inaccessible."

"I have another question for you, Ann."

"Yes?"

"I know we've discussed the impact your mother's death had on you, but I'd like to hear your thoughts about it now."

"Well, I was twenty-four when mother died. I'd been married less than two years and I was in my sixth month of pregnancy with Edwin. Mother was fine and then she had a sudden and totally unexpected heart attack and died a few days later. I took her death hard—even harder than my father's death. In retrospect, I think it was because my father and I had no unresolved feelings between us. I mourned him terribly but there's ... well, there's less devastation in loss that isn't clouded by regret. With Mother, I regretted so many things—that we had never really connected and that there had always been an unspoken anger between us—anger in her because she felt diminished by having a daughter like me and anger in me because I knew she felt that way."

"What kind of a daughter would she not have felt diminished by?"

Ann considers the question for several moments before replying. "A daughter like Cookie. Someone who was confident, unflinchingly bold but smooth as silk and eternally unruffled. I affected boldness but it wasn't who I was. I didn't really have the temperament for boldness." She exhales a sigh of resignation. "I still don't."

"Would your mother have approved of Maggie?"

"Hmm. That's an intriguing question and one that I've asked myself. Why do *you* ask?"

"I ask because I see your relationship with this woman as I think you see it—alien to your inherent sexual orientation. I'm going out on a limb in saying this, but I've known you for many years and my instincts tell me that Maggie is in your life as a mother figure and not as a change in sexual orientation."

She clears her throat. "Maggie and I have a physical relationship."

He sits back in his chair, hands behind his head. "Consider the possibility that Maggie has taken on the role of your mother in a re-enactment with a twist of the Oedipal struggle—a triangle from which you emerge victorious and pretty much guilt free."

Ann shakes her head. "Don't you think that's just a little *too* pat?"

"The underpinnings of relationships are far more complicated to sort through than they are to identify."

"But Maggie isn't at all like my mother," she protests. "Mother's demeanor was invariably genteel. Maggie's demeanor is aggressive, brazen, and often rude."

"Demeanor is what a person affects. A person's character can be difficult to discern when a demeanor of long habit is in play," Dr. Greenfield states.

Ann reflects. "In which case, I don't really know what Maggie's attributes of character, bottom line, are. She generally insists on things her way and there's a hard edge to her manner that can be intimidating. I had a taste of that aspect of Maggie the first time we met. Anyone with a drop of self-protectiveness would have run like Peter Rabbit— hightailed it back to his mother and baby sisters. But for me ..." she nods as comprehension dawns, "For me, Maggie's aura was the burrow. I felt with Maggie as I felt in my mother's presence—a subtle but continuous undercurrent of anxiety to not earn her disapproval—which might then earn me her love." She pauses in thought. "But that familiar tension was only part of what I found compelling in Maggie."

"What else compelled you?"

"Her capacity... and perhaps her need to believe I was perfect. I soaked up her admiration like a sponge. I may have disliked the impetus behind Maggie's pursuit, but I liked it that she was enamored. I confided those perceptions to Maggie, at the beginning of our relationship, and it felt as if a genuine kinship had begun between us. But then, one night, after dinner at my house, she laid it on the line. Literally laid it on the line. She said she was obsessed beyond endurance—weary beyond endurance—with wanting to express her love physically but not being permitted that freedom and that if I denied her again she was going to quit our relationship completely. I declined, of course, but ..." She stands up and begins to pace the room and then returns to her chair, stands behind it for a few moments and then sits down. "But when Maggie started to leave," she says quietly, "I could not bear the aloneness ... the sheer aloneness of her not being there ... and so—" Her jaw tightens. " I asked her to stay and I did as she asked."

"Did you feel guilty afterward?"

"I don't think so—at least not consciously, partly because the experience wasn't pleasant, but mainly because I'd had a sort of epiphany about homosexuality one afternoon when I was driving back from Richmond. I can remember it and still feel it, but it's impossible to put into words. It's like flying in one's dreams. You try to articulate the sheer delight of being purely airborne—of soaring without fear—without effort—without end—but the entirety of the experience is ineffable. I can only say that, in the car, at that moment, I came to see homosexuality non-judgmentally—as an aspect of libido beyond the pale of good and evil, and with that insight came freedom of choice rather than blind adherence to a code of social mores that excluded homosexuality de facto. My mother would never have applauded such a perception and probably my father wouldn't have either." Her face grows hard in memory. "I was reared in an environment that fostered subtle levels and patinas of cool exclusivity. It was my mother's eleventh commandment and it was a commandment I obeyed without question. But, when exclusion fell away in the car that afternoon, the sensation was utterly joyous—utterly liberating."

Dr. Greenfield nods. "Yes, being nonjudgmental is one of the more liberating aspects of my profession." He regards Ann closely, assesses her composure, and then glances at his watch. "I think this is a good place to stop for now. Would you like to schedule another appointment?"

"This was quite an intense session," she says. "I may be going out of town next week. May I schedule when I return?"

"Of course."

She exits the office and walks to her car, deep in thought.

Ann is almost asleep when Maggie phones. She fumbles for the receiver without turning on the light. "Yes?"

"Where the hell have you been?"

"I don't know what you mean."

"I mean what I asked. Where the hell have you been for the past week?"

"Well, let me recount my past week's itinerary for you, some of which you already know. I went to and came back from Edwin's camp in Kennebunkport, Maine. I flew back to Richmond, met with Eleanor, picked up Belle and Liza, drove to the townhouse, packed a few things there, ran some errands, emptied the fridge of perishables, cancelled the newspaper, set the timer for the sprinkler system, got the dogs back into the car, and then headed down to Hampton. I think that about covers all the bases except I neglected to mention that I called you but you either weren't home or weren't taking any calls. Does that answer your snarly question?"

"Camp with Edwin and the ex."

"Excuse me?"

"You said camp with Edwin. You left out the shrink former hubby, or did he not make it to the Kennebunkport family roundup?"

"He made it."

"And?"

"And it was good that he made it because I became violently ill. Max thought it was a lobster reaction, which, in retrospect, probably wasn't a wise dinner choice for me. Also I drank two glasses of Châteauneuf-du-Pape, a full-bodied red, which was another bad choice. A Riesling would have been more suitable. And," she teases, hoping to lighten Maggie's mood, "I forgot to thank that precious little creature, with its beady eyes and hair-like antennae or whatever those things are on both sides of its head, for sacrificing its life so that I might feast upon its succulent flesh. That omission might have had something to do with the grief that dinner caused me."

"Did you have to go to the hospital?"

"No. I forfeited everything in my hotel suite."

"Everything? What did you forfeit besides dinner?"

"Maggie, dearest, if you want to know if I slept with Max, why don't you just come right out and ask me?"

"Why don't you just come right out and tell me where the man was during all of that?"

"He was by my side, Maggie, inducing me to vomit, and he gave me a shot to alleviate the nausea and help me sleep. I was frankly glad to have him there. I was that sick. But before we go on with this interrogation, which is quite beneath you, I have a question for you."

"What's your question?"

"Did you spend an evening with Jane Vitello recently?"

"Why in the world would you ask that?"

"Because I dreamed that you did. I dreamed that you and she were having dinner together."

"Jane and I did have dinner together. I'm going to tell her that you dreamed it. She's fascinated with anything that even hints of the occult."

"Ooh, do tell her," Ann gushes. "Tell her I have my inner eye on her. That ought to straighten her teeth."

"They're already straight. Jane has marvelous teeth and a marvelous smile."

"How nice! That should compensate for Jane's lack of virtue, fidelity-wise. Right, dearest?"

"Do you want me to come down tomorrow?"

She is taken aback by the abruptness of the question. "Well, yes. Of course I do. You know I do."

"Why didn't you call me?" Maggie hisses. "That hateful bitch, that damn Eleanor the evasive, I can never get a thing out of her where you're concerned. She implied that you and Dr. Cabot were unclear about your travel plans, not your plans separately, but the two of you together. I was so angry I wanted to drive to the gallery and demolish the showroom barehanded. Eleanor, I intended to draw and quarter, after which I intended to burn her at the stake for being the witch that she is."

Ann makes a mental note to shake Eleanor until her teeth rattle before handing her over to Maggie to finish off. *No wonder she threatened to quit the gallery!*

She exhales an audible sigh. "Max was very decent this trip, Maggie. He was attentive to Edwin, for which I was everlastingly grateful. He and Edwin don't always see eye to eye and Edwin cares about his father's approval. And Max was really helpful when I got sick. He went to the pharmacy and got me a shot of Demerol, which eased those gut-wrenching pains that are as sharp as labor pains." A quiver of anxiety assails her but she continues without pause. "Max and Edwin both stayed the night. Max left the next afternoon for Boston and from there to Mexico. I drove Edwin back to camp, dropped my rental car off at the airport, and flew home. End of story." Her voice softens. "Come down tomorrow. I want to see you."

"Okay."

"Good. I'll call you in the morning with directions. I'm so sleepy that if I give them to you now, you'll miss the exit and end up stranded in the Norfolk tunnel. Goodnight."

She returns the receiver to its cradle, turns on her side, and is asleep in seconds.

Ann is standing on the front lawn with Belle and Liza when Maggie's van pulls up to the driveway. She clicks the gates open, waves Maggie in, clicks the gates closed, and walks over. "Gosh, but I'm glad to see you."

Maggie eyes the dogs suspiciously. "Liza's tail is wagging but Belle's isn't. What does that mean?"

"It means the troops are divided. Liza is happier to see you than Belle is not. Don't worry, Liza's bites always require stitches but Belle's bites barely pierce the skin. How was the drive down?"

"Lots of cars with beach gear hanging from sunroofs and snot-nosed, bathing-suited kids hanging from tailgates. Is it okay to park here?"

"It's fine."

"I won't be blocking anyone?"

"No one. We have the place entirely to ourselves." She notes the zippered and tastefully MDL-monogrammed canvas tote. "What does the 'D' stand for?"

"It stands for 'Don't ask.'"

They enter the house's cool and spacious center hall. Maggie draws a breath at the broad vista of sparkling blue water that can be seen through the wide archway that leads into the awning-shaded sunroom.

"What a breathtaking view of the river and what a marvelous property. I can't believe the girth of that tree! It must be at least a hundred years old. I believe it's the most imposing magnolia I've ever seen."

"It's over two hundred years old and reputed to be the finest magnolia in Hampton," Ann boasts. She reaches for Maggie's bag. "Let me carry that upstairs for you."

"Not just yet. First I want to know where the former shrink hubby slept during 'The Cabots Do Kennebunkport' adventure."

"For heaven's sake, Maggie. Why do you care? I already told you I was sick."

"Yes, you told me that. Now I want you to tell me where Max slept."

Ann manages a shrug. "I don't actually know where Max slept. The suite had a sitting room and two bedrooms. He probably stayed up most of the night. The last I clearly remember he was sitting on the side of the bed after he'd given me the shot." She bites her tongue but it's too late.

Maggie arches a brow. "What part of your body?"

"My left buttock."

"That's disgusting."

"It was professional. He was gone when I awakened the following morning." She doesn't mention the note he left on the night table, on top of her compactly folded nightgown.

Ann, darling—

You were sleeping so peacefully I hadn't the heart to awaken you.

I'll be back in time for Amory's phone call.

 Max.

"He might have slept in the wingchair next to the bed," she reflects, thin of tone, steady of timbre. "He's used to sleeping in chairs. He's done it many times with patients who were in crisis. He's a physician, after all." She looks across the sunroom at Maggie, whose eyes are riveted on Ann's face. "I wish you'd stop this ridiculous line of questioning. It has nothing to do with you and me."

Maggie sprawls on the wicker sofa and slouches into its down-filled cushions. "It has everything to do with you and me. The man lurks in the shadows like that badly-in-need-of-a-hair-stylist, *Magnum, P.I.* detective Zeke fancies."

"Max is the father of my children. I would always—" Ann hesitates.

"Always what?" Maggie sits up. "Finish what you started to say."

"I don't know what I was going to say. Perhaps I was going to say that there's always going to be a relationship between Max and me because of the children. Surely you realize that?"

"Don't call me Shirley and of course I do. I'm the product of divorced parents myself. But you two have a way of hanging on to each other that's infuriating." She reaches into a straw creel of a handbag and extracts her cigarette case. "He had his chance and he botched it. Miserably, I might add. Both of you use the children as an excuse to spend time together far beyond the normal parameters of divorce."

"Oh?" Ann scoffs. "If we're going to clarify parameters, let's include your intimate little rendezvous with Jane Vitello a few nights ago, shall we? Your highly accomplished pediatric MD former perfect fit Jane. You remember, Jane with the wonderfully straight teeth and marvelous smile. Or do you not call that hanging on? Hanging on with no shared children to justify the ongoing telephone conversations, late-night supper trysts, and whatever else may occur between the two of you." She sits down on the sofa across from Maggie, arms folded.

"Is that what you think?" Maggie lights a cigarette and exhales. "What should I use for an ashtray?" she drawls.

"An ashtray," Ann drawls back and points to the shallow Imari bowl on the circular oak coffee table.

"You're not bad." Maggie purses her lips appraisingly. "Not bad at all. In fact, your counterattack was good. Perfect timing with a nicely clipped delivery." She slouches back into the cushions. "But you're off the wall because I'm no longer involved with Jane. You, on the other hand, remain intimately connected to Max. You're in love with the possibility of him. I may not have known it before, but I know it now. I know because of the way you get when you talk about him." She takes another long drag from her cigarette and exhales slowly. "As far as Jane is concerned, I cared about her once—thought she might have been perfect once, but she wasn't and I no longer care." She stubs out her cigarette and lights another. "You wanted Max to be your mate—I understand that. But he wasn't and he still isn't. And he isn't in ways that go against the grain of you – maybe not as you were when you married him but certainly as you are now." She gets up from the sofa and brushes a few stray ashes from her madras wraparound skirt. "So," she continues, in a neutral voice, "show me where I'm to spend the night in this marvelous house. And fix me a hamburger. I'm famished."

"But I have some things I'd like to say," Ann protests.

"No," Maggie says, ever so gently, "we've said everything that needs to be said about this. We don't need to discuss it again. It's either going to be behind us or between us. And that's the catch." She places her middle finger under Ann's chin and tilts Ann's face up to hers.

Ann gazes into Maggie's eyes. "What's the catch?" she asks.

"You can't have it both ways, because I won't allow it," Maggie replies.

She awakens to waves of nausea. She slides out from under the covers and pads on tiptoe from the bedroom, shutting the door behind her. She reaches Amory's bathroom just in time.

After the ordeal is over, she splashes water on her face and rinses her mouth with peroxide and sea salt. She can still taste the coffee ice cream banana splits she and Maggie had contrived before going to bed. They had devoured the rich concoctions greedily, sitting cross-legged on the sunroom sofas, clad in T-shirts and shorts, silently observing a mother raccoon and her two babies patiently explore, with delicately mobile fingers, the thick ivy beneath the old magnolia. *Searching for turtle eggs,* Maggie had suggested. *Duck eggs,* Ann had whispered.

She brushes her teeth with toothpaste to get rid of the lingering sour taste and turns on Amory's shower—a bishop's shower with pierced copper pipes that form a spiral from top to bottom. It was the reason Amory had elected to keep the nursery for her bedroom instead of moving into one of the larger rooms as Ann had suggested. But it hadn't mattered, because she had known by then that there would be no more babies for her and Max.

She steps out of the shower and towels herself dry with one of her grandmother's monogrammed linen bath sheets, turns off the bathroom light, and tiptoes into the hallway. And then the nausea returns in steady waves. A shock of fear runs through her and she breaks into a sweat that turns her body cold and then hot. She feels as if she has fallen into a bottomless well. A well whose oxygen supply decreases with every ragged breath she takes. She drops to her knees and crawls slowly back to Amory's bathroom and lies down on the floor. The tiles are hard and cool against her bare flesh.

What's wrong with me? What in God's name is wrong with me? Do I have an illness? Am I going to die?

She struggles to her feet, turns on the bathroom light, and looks at her reflection in the mirror above the old-fashioned pedestal sink. A few broken capillaries from the vomiting, but the whites of her eyes are clear and her skin is unblemished. She sticks out her tongue—an uncoated healthy pink. Her gaze travels downward to her breasts, pale against the tan of her shoulders and belly—pale from where the sun hasn't been. She presses the palms of her hands into their full soft centers and winces. Firm, a bit fuller and—she presses again—abnormally tender. She computes on the fingers of both hands and then stops because counting backwards isn't required for her to know what's happening inside her body.

She's in the kitchen preparing breakfast when Max telephones.

"How are you?"

"I'm fine." She shuts the swinging door that separates the kitchen from the butler's pantry. "Where are you calling from?"

"I'm back in Boston. The Mazatlán expedition was a disaster. Wyatt's sick. He has dysentery."

"Wyatt always gets sick in third-world countries. It's a form of snobbery. How did Hilton fare?"

"Hilton fared better. He hooked up with a sexy little redhead at the airport. He'll stay until the day of her return flight, I imagine."

"Why didn't you stay?"

"I was missing you."

"You won't be missing me for long."

"Does that mean you're thinking about flying up here? Dad would be thrilled. He asked before I left for Mexico when you were bringing the children for a visit."

"I'm not up to a trip to Boston just now. I'm not even sure I'll make it to Amory's camp."

"Why not?"

"Because I'm—" She hesitates. "Because I'm pregnant."

"You're pregnant?"

"Yes."

"Well, it's certainly possible. But—"

"But what?"

"It's too soon, Ann. Too soon to know." Max exhales into the receiver. "You did mention something that night ... let me think a minute ... about the time being wrong or too late but then you said —" He exhales again and pauses. "You said so many odd things I figured, well, I wondered if you were hallucinating from the shot. Tell me why you think you're pregnant."

"You're a doctor. You figure it out."

"Are you sure?"

"I haven't had a urine test but I'm sure."

"Well, I hope it's true. And I trust your instincts. You knew right away with Edwin. Remember? You knew practically the second you conceived. I kept teasing you about desire clouding reality, but you just knew." He chuckles. "Now we know what happened with Belle."

"What do you mean?"

"Belle was in heat the night she ran off. She was ripe to conceive. Perhaps you were ripe to conceive in Kennebunkport. You were certainly ripe for something. You were, well, frankly, no adequate words come to mind. You practically raped me. Not that I minded. Sweet Lord, I anything but minded. But I've thought a lot about that night ... the way you were. It might have been the Demerol, or it might've been you, Ann, the way you've always wanted to be. The way I've always wanted you to be with me." His voice softens. "Listen, honey, I'm going to spend some time with Dad and then I'm coming home. In the meantime, I want you to call Bert Phillips and schedule an appointment. And don't worry about Amory. We can drive to camp together. That way you won't have to fly."

"No, Max, I—"

He interrupts. "There are no accidents, Ann. This happened for a reason. Just as Belle's getting pregnant happened for a reason. And we don't always get to know the reasons. If it's true that you're expecting a child, it's ... well, it's wonderful news. It will change things between us."

Ann's throat tightens. "Oh, it will most definitely change things. I'd bet the farm on that." She hears Maggie coming down the back staircase. "I have to go," she murmurs. "We'll talk when you get back." She disconnects the line before Max has a chance to say anything more and has the receiver in its cradle seconds before Maggie ambles into the kitchen.

"It's about time you woke up. I've made your favorite breakfast— French toast and bacon."

After Maggie and Ann have finished breakfast, they head for the sunroom to read the paper and to partake of the glorious morning view of the Hampton River. Maggie lights a cigarette and motions for Ann to join her, but she declines. She has eaten little of the rich breakfast and has replaced her ritual morning coffee with a cup of green tea liberally laced with honey.

Maggie eyes her quizzically. "Are you hoarding your big three for a special event?"

"I've decided to quit."

"Quit? You barely partake! How come?"

"I quit from time to time. It's not a big deal. So," she says, looking over at Maggie, "what shall we do today? Want to drive to Virginia Beach and play in the surf?"

"I don't think so, dearest. I have to get on the road by two at the latest. I'm hoping to make it back to Richmond before rush-hour traffic."

The sting of disappointment is followed by a stab of cold fury. Ann counts to ten before speaking. "You just got here. Why do you have to leave so soon?"

"Because I have work to do."

"Such as?"

Maggie's brows draw together. "Do I really need to answer that?"

"No, you don't. Your expression says it all."

"Mental TV," Maggie banters, "I think it and you watch it on my face." She smiles at Ann. "Let's go upstairs and rearrange your bedroom. You were up at the crack of dawn. I didn't have a chance to say good morning."

"I don't think so." Ann snaps. "I might as well get this over with now. You've made it easier for me by clarifying what it means to be Margaret Lambert's perfect fit. It means being available when Margaret feels like rearranging the bedroom."

"Stop it, Ann."

"I wouldn't think you'd want to show your hand so soon, Maggie."

Maggie extinguishes her cigarette and walks over to where Ann is sitting. She leans over and tilts Ann's face up to hers. "What exactly is it that you want from me?"

Ann's eyes tighten. "What I want is what you threatened to take away from me if I didn't accede to your demands. Do you remember our first time or would you like me to refresh your memory?"

"Ann," Maggie straightens up, "I'm going to leave if you don't settle down. You're trying to provoke a fight and I've informed you on numerous occasions that I make it a point not to fight."

"You're going to leave whether I settle down or not and what you make it a point to not do," Ann hisses, "is to remove your foot for more than one brief 'no questions asked' night from home base where you reside with Mommie Dearest."

"You've got gall, little girl. Take a gander at your own foot—directly beneath Max's, divorce notwithstanding."

"What I've *got, notwithstanding,* is a divorce from Max and my own residence. You're still attached to your mother by your atypical Sterling Rucker navel and—" She looks at Maggie with discernment. "It isn't because Clarissa can't manage without you, it's because you can't manage without Clarissa. Face it, Maggie, what you really care about is Clarissa's attention and, for now anyway, I and my tortoise-framed photograph on your nightstand are what earn you that attention."

"How dare you speak to me like that – and you couldn't be more wrong."

"I'm right and how cowardly, not to mention dishonest, of you to deny it."

Maggie walks to the sunroom archway. "Well, dearest, you've implied that I'm obsessed with my mother and now you're implying that I'm a coward and a liar. Is there anything more you want to add before I pack the hell up and head to Richmond?"

"Yes," Ann whispers, "what you said to me not very long ago. You have no idea what an absence I'm going to be in *your* life. Margaret 'Don't ask' Lambert. And, just for the record—it never was about the sex—but then, it never really is."

She does not ignore the swell of fear that sounds in the wake of her tirade and she senses that, if she presses on in this vein, her relationship with Maggie will most certainly be terminated—at least temporarily—but she tightens her jaw and continues speaking. "And yes, Clarissa fosters this codependency by monitoring her fifty-two-year-old daughter's nightly whereabouts like a bloodhound—what business is it of hers where you stay and with whom and for how long? My God, she's even called Eleanor to find out where you were, when, in point of fact, she knew exactly where you were." She laughs, a dry, bitter laugh. "Hurry home now, little fledgling—you mustn't keep Clarissa and the rest of her flock of feathered Jane Austen devotees waiting."

"Why don't you just shut the hell up," Maggie hisses, "before you go too far for me to ever return to you."

Ann looks Maggie up and down with cool disdain. "Are you suggesting it's possible for you to leave *me*—the person for whom you've searched your entire life?" Her face twists. "I turned myself inside out for you, Maggie. I stepped beyond the security of what I knew and trusted so that you could have what you implied you couldn't be complete without. And now you have me, but you're still not complete, are you, dearest, because your search is a charade that adheres to your mother's rules—one of those rules being that you are never to spend two nights in a row with me. Oh yes, I do understand, Maggie." She squares her shoulders, lifts her chin and arches a mocking eyebrow—a pose she learned at Constance's dressing table mirror. "I didn't before but I do now."

She gets up from the sofa, turns slowly on a steady heel, and walks calmly to the French doors leading to the terrace. Belle and Liza follow. "I'm taking Belle and Liza for a walk," she announces placidly and opens both doors. The dogs bound toward a section of mossy lawn upon which a flock of mallards is roosting. Ann turns back around and faces Maggie. "Are you coming?" she asks.

Maggie removes a cigarette from the pack and lights it. She smokes in silence—reflectively—her gaze directed nowhere in particular. "I'm leaving, Ann. Sooner than I had hoped or expected but," her eyes connect with Ann's, "I will be leaving."

"In which case, be sure to close the gates after you pull out of the driveway, and leave the remote control in the mailbox," Ann replies and steps outside.

The midmorning air has the slightly briny scent of low tide. She shuts the sunroom doors and follows Belle and Liza down to the seawall, where the mallards are now cautiously gathered—poised for flight.

It's only after she has called Bert Phillips to arrange a pregnancy test, called Victor to confirm her flight to Portofino, and called Cookie to decline her invitation to partake of the Big Apple, that Ann allows herself to acknowledge the misery of what she has elicited in Maggie.

She had taken the dogs for a long walk—beyond her seawall and onto the seawalls of neighboring properties, stopping to chat with acquaintances and admire the bounty of their gardens—mindful of the slim possibility that when she returned she would find Maggie on the porch, reading the morning paper, a cigarette dangling from the corner of her mouth. But when she turned the corner of seawall and scanned the long driveway, Maggie's van was gone, the gates were closed, and the remote control was on top of the mailbox.

She had spent the rest of the afternoon and evening within earshot of the telephone, hoping that Maggie would call, but Maggie had not called.

In bed, long past midnight, disheartened and miserable, she replays the bitter fight she initiated and holds herself responsible.

Why had she fought with Maggie? Was pride what had impelled that tirade of abuse?

Surely pride had been a large part of what had driven her to divorce Max. And rage at not being first. But wasn't that as it should be in marriage? *"A man shall leave his mother and a woman leave her home." Her heartbeat quickens. "The two shall be one flesh"—automatic at the beginning of love—but no lifetime warranty.* She draws a ragged breath. "Too hard, Ann," she whispers, "too hard."

She gets out of bed and walks through the sitting room, stops to pet Belle and Liza, snoring peacefully away. They barely acknowledge her presence. How curious that dogs who began their evolution by sleeping during the day—hunting in packs at night—now kept the hours of their owners. And herself? Whose hours was she now keeping?

She turns on the kitchen light. She'll have a cup of warm milk laced with honey. But what she really wants is a cigarette. What she really wants—her eyes mist. Surely Maggie won't want to leave things like this —to leave *Ann* like this. Surely Maggie will call or drive down and say *whatever* it takes to make things right. Perhaps she should call Maggie and elicit that *whatever*.

But—she swipes at her cheeks with the sleeve of her T-shirt and tightens her jaw in resolve—she should not and will not make that call because she already knows what Maggie would say.

She'd say, "*But I've already left you, little girl, and don't call me Shirley.*"

Ann is on the phone with Amory when the call comes from Bert Phillips' office. "All right, lamb," she concludes. "Your father and I will see you next weekend."

"Bye, Mommy. I love you," Amory sings out. She's happy—happy at camp and happy to have her parents coming to camp together for Parents' Weekend.

Ann switches over to call waiting.

"Good morning, Mrs. Cabot. Please hold for Dr. Phillips."

He takes forever and Ann's pulse races furiously while she waits. Finally, he clicks on. "Well, Ann," he booms, "as my daddy used to tell his pregnant ladies, the rabbit died."

"Are you sure?"

"The urine tested positive, honey. I hope you're pleased. Max sure is."

"You've already told Max?"

"He called this morning. He was thrilled. Are you?"

"I am. I didn't plan it, but I truly am." She feels an adrenaline rush of pure joy. Another baby! Her third child!

"Now listen, Ann. I want you to come in. I don't anticipate any problems but I want to check you over. I'll give you back to Sylvia and she'll schedule you."

"I'm going to be out of town for a while, Bert. I'll call your office when I return and schedule then."

"Where are you off to?"

"Portofino," she replies. "Il bellissimo Portofino sulla Riviera dei Fioiri."

She's packing evening gowns between sheets of blue tissue when she hears footsteps in the downstairs hallway.

"Where are you, Ann?"

"Max? What in the world are you doing here?"

"Are you coming down or should I come up?"

She glances at the array of discarded items of clothing next to her grandmother's tidily packed train case and matching portmanteau. "I'll be down in a minute." She shuts her bedroom door and walks downstairs, tucking her hair behind her ears on the way. "Well, this is a surprise," she says in a low voice.

Max reaches from behind his back and brings forward a mass of long-stemmed white tulips wrapped in a swath of pink tissue paper tied with a huge gold bow.

"They're beautiful, Max. And such prodigious bounty."

"Three dozen," he states proudly. "Dick found them for me and he said it wasn't easy this time of year. I called him from Boston. I didn't tell him why, although the nosy bugger tried like hell to pry it out of me."

"Pry what out of you?"

He smiles. "Our baby."

Ann lays the tulips on the baby grand and draws a breath before turning around to face him. He eyes her curiously.

"The baby isn't yours, Max."

He is shocked by her pronouncement. He shakes his head as if to clear it. "What are you telling me?"

"I'm telling you that you're not the father of the child I'm carrying. I'm not in love with the father. As a matter of fact, I only made love with him one time. But it happened. It just happened. I was already pregnant in Maine but I didn't realize it."

"Is George the father?" He asks hoarsely.

"No. I haven't been involved with George for a long time. That's why I went off the pill and that's what I attributed my irregularity to." She draws a breath. "Getting off the pill, I mean." She attempts a chuckle. "Amory would take me to task for saying 'I mean.'"

"Who is the father? Please, Ann, I want to know."

"He's a friend of Harry and Cookie's. Someone I met in Ireland."

"The man who painted your portrait? The baron?"

"Yes."

"Good Lord. Does he have other children?"

"No."

"Have you told him?"

"No."

"Are you going to tell him?"

"I think I must tell him. Don't you?"

"Not necessarily," He says reflectively. "It depends on what you want."

"What *I want*? What does that mean?"

He rubs his forehead with his index finger. "Hmm. Good question." He walks over to his habitual wingchair and settles heavily into it, brows drawn together in thought. "I think we should consider remarrying. It isn't a perfect solution because we have difficulty living together. Maybe we shouldn't live together all the time. I could still keep my place—at least for a while. But we could honor our marriage vows. We're divorced in the state of Virginia but not in the eyes of God. I think we both realize Edwin and Amory would be happier. And I think we'd be happier, too." His eyes capture hers. "That's actually what I came home to tell you."

"What about the fact that I'm pregnant with another man's child?" She asks quietly.

"Ironically, that makes it even more vital for us to commit to one another. Someone has to be this child's father. The biological implications have little to do with the actuality of child rearing. I don't think you'll want to raise the children with different fathers because siblings need a continuity of beliefs, values, lifestyles, and role models. And this man might want to share legal custody. That would greatly complicate things."

"Well, Max, you've covered everything except what I most care about."

"I was hoping it was us. What do you most care about?"

"I can't live with jealousy being a continuous part of my consciousness. I don't struggle with it anymore because we're no longer sworn to each other, but remarrying you would change that."

His jaw tightens. "I would think that after George and the baron you'd understand that sexual involvements can happen to the best of us."

"Max—" Ann paces the living room in thought. She sits on the fireplace bench and looks into his eyes. "I don't want to hurt you, but surely you understand that I no longer trust you to be faithful. The difference is that—" She mentally recounts and blanches—*George. Victor. Maggie, Max*—"I have to think this through," she says tonelessly.

"Ann, listen to me. We can work this out."

She considers his statement. "Perhaps we could," she finally concedes, "but I wonder if it's ever really possible to want another's child as one wants one's own."

He looks up. "It interests me that you would say 'want' instead of 'love.'"

She turns her face away from his.

I say it because Maggie loved me but didn't want me.

I say it because you wanted me but didn't love me.

She stands up. "I have to go. I have a million chores to take care of." She walks to the doorway and pauses. "I have another question. What about the Faye Grahams of this world?"

He considers the question. "My indiscretions would be a thing of the past." He regards her cannily. "And so would your indiscretions be—although I suspect you've already managed to justify George and Victor and—" He shrugs. "Perhaps some others, because they were post-divorce."

He gets up from his chair and precedes Ann into the hallway. "I have to leave too, but I want you to think about everything I've said. Think about it, but let's not decide anything until after we get back from Amory's camp."

He opens the front door and steps outside. "Just look at the white gold of the sun on the sparkling blue of the river. It's so beautiful here. Don't forget to put the tulips in water, and you look beautiful, too, by the way. Beautiful and glowing with child."

He shuts the front door firmly behind him.

"You can fly out of New York, darling. I have a limo with an absolutely brilliant driver. He'll get you to the airport in thirty minutes tops."

"I can't, Cookie. I promised Victor I'd be in Portofino tomorrow. He's meeting my plane."

"Well, only because it's Victor. Otherwise I'd throw a pout. I'm bored to tears without you here."

"I've already been informed that your incoming calls are keeping the switchboard lit up like a Christmas tree and that you've had a parade of nonstop visitors. You were at Elaine's last night and Lutèce the night before. I'll call you when I get back."

"All right, lamb, but I want lots of juicy tidbits. I can't wait to hear what you think of Victor's mother, not to mention that gorgeous villa of hers. I have to hang up now. Nan's meeting me downstairs for après-dinner cocktails. She said to tell you 'Ciao, darling.'"

"Nan must be sleeping with an Italian these days," Ann retorts drily.

"Aren't we in a hateful little mood! In point of fact, one strives to be egalitarian with one's terms of endearment. You Americans seem to thrive on it. So, with that said, buenas noches, cara mia." She clicks off.

Ann sinks gratefully into the pillows. Her luggage is packed and waiting in the hallway. She's already pulled out what she'll wear on the flight and arranged a purse with passport, hankie, lipstick, hairbrush, a collapsible drinking cup, and five one-hundred dollar bills tucked into a hidden pocket. Eleanor has agreed to keep Belle and Liza and she's driving Ann to the airport. Her flight leaves Richmond tomorrow evening. The only thing left to do is to get a good night's sleep so she'll arrive in Genoa looking rested, because Victor will be meeting her flight and portrait artists notice things like smudges under the eyes from sheer exhaustion.

But she can't sleep. Her thoughts are full of seeing Victor and whether or not she's going to tell him she's pregnant with his child. She has a notion that if she tells him, he'll suggest marriage. A notion that seems implausible, given that they barely know each other. Would Victor marry a woman he barely knows? Would that explain his previous short-lived marriages? And what about her? Could she marry a man she barely knows?

And ... if she were to marry Victor ... where would that leave her and Max?

Where would it leave her and Maggie?

The jolt of finality is followed by a flicker of hope. She had avoided telling Maggie she was pregnant, but if Maggie hadn't left, Ann would surely have told her.

Her heartbeat quickens.

Why not call and tell her now? It doesn't mean anything you said was untrue. It means Maggie has a right to know and it might soften her anger toward you. It means you have a reason—an important reason for calling her. It means you're not too proud to call her just because ... just because ... don't worry about justifying it ... just pick up the phone and make the call. It's a bit late but she'll answer the phone because she always answers the phone.

She picks up the telephone, hesitates, and then dials resolutely and waits for Maggie to answer

She disconnects after the eleventh ring.

Villa Blanca is as quietly elegant as Victor had portrayed it to Ann that first afternoon in Cookie's costume room. Stucco walls bleached white by sun and salt sea air, a riotous profusion of trees, tall shrubbery, trailing flowering vines, potted plants in fullest bloom, and, inside the main house, high ceilings with elaborate crown molding and floors of gold-veined black marble. Most of the furniture, eighteenth-century French and Italian, is slipcovered in cobalt and cream linen toile.

"For the summer only," Victor's mother had explained when Ann admired the fabric. "In November the covers come off and everything is coral and forest green silk."

Victor's mother—a tall, cool blonde, pencil slim, impeccably coiffed and with perfect features rendered unforgettable by the largest delft-blue eyes imaginable. She had greeted Ann warmly, kissed her on both cheeks. "Welcome to Villa Blanca. You must call me Mercedes. Now, come have a cocktail and then off to your rooms. I'm sure you're longing for a rest before dinner."

Ann, exhausted from traveling as well as the previous night's sleeplessness, had nodded mute acquiescence, said she would prefer hot tea laced with honey, and followed her hostess onto a wide granite terrace that spanned the villa and overlooked a vibrant rippling turquoise of endless sea.

This is her fourth day in Portofino. She and Victor had lunched on the handsome view-laden balcony of the Hotel Splendido and then whiled away the remainder of the afternoon wandering the narrow cobbled streets of the quaintly chic coastal village. It's now half past ten in the evening and she's sleepy. The superb supper she has eaten sits uneasily. Tonight they have dined alone—she, Victor and Mercedes—in contrast to the formal dinner parties for twelve the previous two nights—and the three of them are relaxing on the terrace, sipping tisanes. Mercedes rises majestically from her chair and turns to Ann.

"Good night, my dears," she says fondly. "Don't stay up too late. You've had a long day and there's tomorrow's masked ball to come."

Victor excuses himself and walks into the villa's wide central hallway with his mother, leaving Ann to enjoy the view. She walks over to the broad granite balustrade that encloses the terrace and gazes up at the canopy of midnight blue and then across and beyond the stepped hillside to the gently undulating expanse of sea. Portofino, she acknowledges, transcends the merely beautiful with a majesty that is ever-changing. Tonight it is still, sweet-scented—intermittently lit by stars that twinkle in an entirely clear sky. The random streetlights and windows of the winding hillside village twinkle. The bobbing lights on the distant fishing boats twinkle. It's as if she were standing atop a vastly sprawled Christmas tree.

She searches overhead and chooses a particularly shimmery star to the left of her. "Star light, star bright, grant me the wish I wish tonight," she whispers, closes her eyes, and most fervently wishes.

She opens her eyes, looks up, and gasps in amazement. Her fiery little star has come alive. It pulsates briefly and then hurtles across and beyond the vast horizon.

She trembles with elation. She has wished upon a falling star.

Her wish will be granted.

AUGUST 1987

This beast that rends me in the sight of all,
This love, this longing, this oblivious thing
That has me under as the last leaves fall,
Will glut, will sicken, will be gone by spring.
The wound will heal, the fever will abate.
The knotted hurt will slacken in the breast.
I shall forget before the flickers mate,
Your look that is today my east and west.
Unscathed however, from a claw so deep,
Though I shall love again, I shall not go
Beyond my body – waking while I sleep,
Sharp to the kiss, cold to the hand as snow.
The scar of this encounter, like a sword,
Will lie between me and my troubled lord.

— EDNA ST. VINCENT MILLAY

She's waiting at the office door when Dr. Greenfield pulls in.

"Why Ann! You're early." He glances at his watch. "Ten minutes early."

"I have dilemmas that need resolving."

He unlocks the door. The lamps are lit and the office is cool. "So, what do we need to resolve?"

Ann scrunches into the lap of her chair. "You'd better sit down for this one. I'm sure it's going to take you by surprise."

He sits down. "I'm ready."

"I'm expecting a baby."

"Well, now. That *is* a surprise. Congratulations, Ann! When is the baby due?"

"By my calculations, which are accurate down to the actual hour of conception," she says, arching a brow, "the due date is February 29, 1988. Wouldn't that be exciting! A leap year's day baby!"

"Exciting and rare. Am I going to be told who the father is?"

"Yes," she smiles, "but in a roundabout way, because that's how it happened." She leans back in her chair. "His name is Victor and he's Austrian. I met him for the first time during my trip to Ireland three months ago. He painted my portrait, a strange but marvelous painting of me in an elaborate black-velvet Lord Fauntleroy suit, holding an ivory riding crop in one hand and an unfiltered cigarette in the other. The portrait required many sittings and during those lengthy sessions, Victor and I dwelled as if...as if in a cocoon...and formed a...a tenuous intimacy that culminated in our making love in the wee hours of the final morning of my stay in Ireland."

She pauses in memory. "It was an oddity because Victor and I had never even kissed before that night. I wasn't drawn to him and I certainly didn't love him."

She leans forward, elbows on the desk, and cups her face with both hands. "I don't know … perhaps it was purely karmic. Maybe Victor and I were brought together and ended up making love for the sole purpose of bringing a child into the world."

Twice she had come close to telling him she was carrying his child. The first time they were playing in the cool sapphire waters of the sea. He had submerged his head and shoulders in the waves and then arisen like an unbearded Neptune—his hair a spiked trident trailing droplets of water. She had caught an expression on his face that his mother must have seen many times—a carefree child reveling in the pleasurable aspects of his existence.

"My father used to play monster with me here—Mama fretting on the shore. 'Don't go out too far, Gustav! He's just a little boy!' Sometimes we would go out on Papa's yacht and drop anchor. Papa loved the sea."

"I'll tell him now," she thought. But she had let the moment pass.

Ann looks down at her hands, now tightly clasped in her lap. "I struck Max in the face with that same riding crop and on the same night I arrived home from Ireland—no, it was early the next morning. I awakened and Max was standing over me. We began to ... I don't know. Perhaps we were going to make love, which would have been yet another dilemma because then I wouldn't have known for certain who the father was. Interesting, isn't it?"

"Interesting in what way?"

"In several ways. When I was telling you about having made love with Victor and about his portrait of me looking like a young aristocrat ... well ... I was totally caught up in the dilemma of Maggie at the time but, in retrospect, Victor's choice of costume and pose was curious and—" She pauses to gather her thoughts. "It has occurred to me that Victor, who's a baron, might presciently have painted a portrait of his own son. It's an unsubstantiated stretch." She gives a knowing nod. "But visits to India have taught me to consider seemingly coincidental events in that light."

Dr. Greenfield weighs Ann's words. "It's tempting to explore that realm of possibility. E.M. Forster toys with the notion in *A Passage to India* by implying that there are no accidents or coincidences. All that occurs is determined by that which precedes it."

"Yes," Ann affirms, "that's exactly what I meant." She leans back in her chair, laces her fingers together. "Lots of karmic debts to connect—"

An intake of breath. "I meant to say 'dots to connect,' but instead I said 'debts,' which is telling because karmic debts are obligations that shape the events of one's life." She nods sagely. "Slips of tongue are so revealing. Anyway, I was going to say that I connect dots between Victor's riding crop and my viciously striking Max in the face with that crop. Max snatched it from me and broke it in half. Then he threw it at me. I connect dots to that, too. It has sexual connotations, I suspect. I'm just not sure what they are."

"Well, a riding crop by its very nature is phallic. Some crops were actually made from the penises of bulls. Did you know that?"

She nods. "Actually, I've held one. My grandfather kept it on his desk. Its handle was a three-dollar gold coin inset with tiny diamonds and emeralds. The crop was a golden-amber color. I loved to go into Grandfather's library, pull those heavy pocket doors shut, sit at his desk, and play school. The crop was what I used as a blackboard pointer. I made believe it was a dueling sword, too. We had dueling lessons at school. They were supposed to teach young ladies to be lithe on their feet. During one particularly brilliant feint, I struck a small Tiffany lamp on Grandfather's desk with that crop and sent the lamp crashing to the floor."

"Did you get in trouble?"

"Not too bad. Grandmummy never made a big fuss about things like that. Mother was the opposite. She'd get angry or coldly disapproving and once a thing was broken it was never seen again. Grandmummy would glue it back and put it on a table or shelf in a lesser room."

"I notice a distinction between what you call your grandparents."

"What do you mean?"

"You call your grandfather 'Grandfather,' but you call your grandmother 'Grand*mummy*.'"

"Oh. Well, Grandfather was that way. It would have displeased him to be called 'Granddaddy.' He was old school and my mother, who adored him, was the same way. My mother had a barely contained disdain for her mother. Grandmummy was reputed to be a bit on the wild side ... but you know," Ann smiles, "as straitlaced as Grandfather was, he adored that wild streak in Grandmummy. I could see it peeking through his reproving frowns when Grandmummy said or did something Grandfather thought *irreverent*." She sighs. "I'm starting to think I may have some 'irreverent' in me—a notable example being that here I am—expecting a baby—which Max knows about because I told him on the phone when he was visiting his dad in Boston. Max was elated because he thought *he* had gotten me pregnant in Maine while we were spending Parents' Weekend with Edwin." Ann shakes her head. "Equally irreverent is my having had three physical relationships going on pretty much simultaneously."

Dr. Greenfield shifts in his chair. "I have a question, Ann. Two questions."

"Yes?"

"Why did you strike Max with Victor's riding crop?"

She hesitates before answering. "I struck Max because of something he said about Faye Graham. Well, no," she amends, "it wasn't what he said about Faye. It was what he said about me."

"What did he say?"

"He said that I was more upset about Faye's pushing me aside for him than I was about his having an affair with her."

"Was he right?"

"No, he wasn't. I cared about Faye, but Max and the children were virtually one with me. I lived and breathed them. And that wasn't why Max began speaking of Faye. He did it to dispel the intimacy that had arisen between us ... because Max has a love-hate relationship with intimacy. And he probably wanted to give Victor some competition. Max is an avid combatant and he relishes a victory." She sighs. "But the elation of victory and the spoils of victory are not of the same ilk. I found that out with Max in Maine."

"What happened with Max in Maine?"

"I woke up in the middle of the night and, according to Max, seduced him into making love." She shrugs incredulity. "He implied that I'd ravished him. I'd gotten violently ill from what I thought was too much lobster, but it was actually too much lobster exacerbated by being in my first trimester of pregnancy. Max had given me a shot for the cramping. It was strong and made me sleep, but I think it affected me mentally, too. I'd been dreaming about making love and then I woke up and actually made love to Max."

"Who were you dreaming about making love with?"

"A mysterious and dashing captain in a military uniform and wearing gleaming riding boots. He pops in and out of my dreams from time to time."

"Who is the captain meant to be?"

"I have no idea."

"You'll have to do better than that. The first person you think of. C'mon now."

She hesitates. "I started to say Maggie ... And then I remembered that Daddy used to call *me* his trusty little captain."

"Why Maggie?"

"She's akin to a woman dressed in an officer's uniform—a woman pretending to be a man—predatory and commanding like an officer on a mission. And, being in uniform, her face and body are—well, they're camouflaged because of the uniform."

"Did you dress her up as a man so you wouldn't feel conflicted about her being a woman?"

"I didn't dress her up. She came into the dream already dressed."

"But it was your dream. You were in charge of wardrobe."

"Perhaps so," she says hesitantly. She examines the crest ring on her finger and then looks up at him. "But perhaps not so. I told you in our last session that the way I viewed sexuality changed because of Maggie, but it was a comprehension that transcended my relationship with Maggie. I considered myself nonjudgmental about same-sex relationships but the truth was that I had never been tested. Being nonjudgmental is bandied about casually these days but I don't imagine that there are more than a handful who reside continuously in that state of consciousness."

"Well," Dr. Greenfield reflects, "we talked about being nonjudgmental last session. Would you give me your definition of nonjudgmental?"

She considers several possibilities before responding.

"Compassionate understanding unclouded by moral censure. I've had a taste of it ... just a taste ... but it was enough to make me aspire to it always."

"What was it like?"

She sighs. "How to put it in words. I tried to write about it in my diary, but it fell so pathetically short. Rapturous waves of all-encompassing affinity ... no fear ... totally free." She sighs again. "It's impossible to believe, much less to describe."

Dr. Greenfield observes her reflectively before speaking. "You said you had several unresolved conflicts."

"Well, my relationship with Maggie is pretty much ended. It culminated in a quarrel I initiated for self-serving reasons—one being that I didn't want to tell Maggie I was pregnant because I dreaded what her reaction would be. She might have badgered me about having an abortion. And then there was my having made love with Max in Maine. Maggie really dislikes Max. If I had told her, she would have torn me to shreds and walked out because of that. Of course I could have *not* told her but we had agreed that there would be no secrets between us. But the real reason we quarreled was because I was furious that she wouldn't stay with me in Hampton. Maggie lives with her mother and always has. It's an arrangement that precludes anything with Maggie apart from a 'catch as catch can' sort of intimacy. My cousin Cookie would have applauded the amusing irony of such an arrangement but I was devestated. I confronted her ruthlessly, and then blew her off by feigning an aura of cool disdain. I left and took the dogs for a long walk. When I came back, Maggie was gone. I haven't heard from her since."

"In other words—" Dr. Greenfield pauses to consider, "you walked out on Maggie before Maggie walked out on you so that you wouldn't be the one who was walked out on."

Ann nods grimly. "Yes, some poorly thought-out rationale like that, further rendered inept by the blinders of jealousy ... and ..." She puts her thumb to her mouth and nibbles it absently. "When I was young and my parents were ready to leave the house for yet another everlastingly long cruise, I'd wait until the trunks were in the taxi and then I'd scurry outside and hide behind one ancient tree or another—far enough away to not be visible, but close enough to hear my father calling his brave little captain to come to him. Mother would become impatient and insist that it was time to leave, but Daddy always waited and I always came to him. Perhaps in Maggie I was hoping for a daddy who always waited but ended up with a mother who didn't ... and yet ... and yet—" Her eyes soften and close in memory. "Maggie and I were happy together for a while. There was contentment ... and ... and joy between us for a while ...

for a brief while." She shakes her head from side to side. "March, April, May—" she counts on six fingers. "June, July, and August—six months in the fast lane."

Dr. Greenfield computes. "One hundred and eighty-four days, if you count August in its entirety, which is yet to come." He pauses in thought. "Were you content with Max in Maine?"

Ann's eyes open. She mulls over the question before speaking. "Max was secondary to Maggie that trip. My thoughts and emotions were constantly enmeshed in my relationship with Maggie. But Max was kind, charming, and emotionally supportive, not only with me, but also with Edwin, Edwin's new girlfriend, and Edwin's girlfriend's parents. I, on the other hand, was unkind, uncharming, and as mean-spirited as a just-poked-with-a-stick adder—so yes, I was dispiritedly content with Max in Maine." A half smile plays about the corners of her mouth. "I've neglected to tell you that Max wants to re-honor our marriage vows and raise Victor's child as his own."

"Hmm. Those are significant wants. What about Victor? What does Victor want?"

Ann stands up and begins to pace the room. "That's another unresolved conflict—a huge unresolved conflict. Victor doesn't know about the baby yet. I've just returned from spending a week in Portofino with him and his gracious mother. I went there with the intention of telling him and left without even dropping a hint."

The entire week had been magical—one fabulous event after another—including a masked ball. Mercedes had gone as Catherine of Aragon in an ermine-trimmed peau de soie gown and matching cape the precise blue of her eyes. Victor had worn an ancestral-crested breastplate over a leather tunic, and they had costumed Ann as Merlin in a red-silk magician's ruffled suit, studded with yellow rhinestone stars and with a tall pointy hat, a mask, and pointy-toed slippers of the same material. They had ridden to the ball in an open barouche—the winding narrow descent randomly spotted with onlookers who whistled and cheered as the carriage rolled by.

The elegant affair was rich with masked movers and shakers – the beautiful—the titled—the famous—voila Jacquie!...mais non! c'est sa soeur!—Prince Phillip—Caroline and Stephanie—Mick and a tall and bosomy blonde—Valentino—Donald—Ivana—one name after another—dropped—picked up—passed around—endless murmurs of where and with whom and no one knowing with unmasked certainty.

She had been momentarily caught up in the drama—envisioning a life there for Edwin, Amory, the baby, and herself, intuitively certain that if she told Victor, he would offer to marry her because of the baby and because Victor had gotten more than one taste of the impermanence of marriage—two or three tastes, Cookie had suggested.

Dr. Greenfield interrupts her reverie. "What kept you from telling Victor about the baby?"

The second time she came close to telling Victor was the night before she was to return home. She had determined she would tell him after dinner, after Mercedes had retired for the night.

As things had turned out, Mercedes had gone out that evening and Ann and Victor had dined alone—seated at opposite sides of the gleaming mahogany banquet table set with the crested silver flatware, service plates and candlesticks and with two liveried menservants who set before them a sumptuous presentation of lobster bisque flambé, escarole with curried prawns, veal tonnato and her favorite—zabaglione with hazelnut biscotti—followed by steamed honey and milk for her and brandy and espresso for Victor, served on the balconied terrace.

There were to be fireworks at the event Mercedes was attending—a supper party to herald the christening of the youngest scion of the venerable Rinaldi clan.

She and Victor had stood at the granite railing and watched the Portofino sky light up with elaborate fireworks of white, blue, and crimson and, for the finale, white plumes with the name "'Rinaldi" beneath a gold coronet trailing white ribbons.

"Ah!" Victor had murmured, "so very proud they are of their youngest heir."

"Now," she had thought, "I'll tell him now."

She returns to her chair and sits down, hands clasped in her lap. "I was certain that I would not leave Italy without telling Victor, but I was wrong. He and I had not touched intimately during my stay at Villa Blanca. We had embraced at the airport and often Victor would take my hand or wrap an arm around my waist or shoulders and there was a lot of wrist kissing—cheek kissing—ritual gestures of affectionate familiarity. I was a little surprised, given our night of intimacy in Kilkenny, but I attributed it to his traditional continental upbringing and our being at his mother's house ... an inherent respect for his mother's way of life. I didn't know how I would respond if Victor approached me amorously, but I wanted to know ... needed to know. Finally, that last night, after the fireworks were ended, he did kiss me."

Ann shakes her head in despair. "The very second Victor placed his mouth on mine, I felt an ache of unbearable loss. It came unannounced and it persisted. I thought of Maggie. She was between Victor and me like a...like a gaping wound and I knew I would never again *not* know. I would never again return to that innocence ... that *freedom* ... of not knowing. My lips accepted Victor's kiss, but my mind and heart were bound by those perceptions. And when Victor finally released me from that kiss, he smiled and whispered into my ear, 'Wunderbar!' That kiss I remember well!'

"But it wasn't wunderbar at all. It was ... I was ... as closed as a scallop in its shell—and Victor was ... oblivious." Tears gather in Ann's eyes. "Maggie would have never let me get away with a response like that. Maggie would have known immediately." Her mouth forms an anguished smile. "She would have said, 'Uh, excuse me, dearest, but am I keeping you from something in the kitchen?'"

She looks up at Dr. Greenfield and then down at her lap. "You must see how hopeless all of this is." Her voice breaks and she sobs quietly for several moments and then reaches for a handful of tissues and wipes her eyes. "This can't be good for the baby."

"Oh, I suspect something good will come of it," Dr. Greenfield says quietly. He pauses in thought. "What happened after Victor kissed you?"

"He took my hand in his, turned it over, pressed his lips to my wrist, and looked up at me. 'I would like for you to stay longer. Will you stay longer?' I closed my eyes, shook my head, whispered 'no', and walked into the hallway and up the stairs to my suite of rooms, where I paced all night, and in the morning I left Portofino looking like death warmed over. I felt lighter the moment the plane became airborne. I couldn't wait to get away. Here I was, pregnant with this man's child—a child I knew he would want but that I wasn't willing to share with him because, although I admired Victor, I didn't love him in even the tiniest measure and I didn't want to share the child or myself with someone I didn't love."

She draws a breath and exhales slowly. "I didn't want to hurt Victor but I didn't want to saddle myself with the charade of being one person pretending to be another." She gives a dry laugh. "That's the precise opposite of what my mother would have determined."

"What would your mother have determined?"

"Mother would have determined to marry the baron, of course," she replies in a haughtily measured tone, "and she would have thought the baron fortunate."

He observes her face with frank curiosity before speaking. "It's notable," he says, "that the trait you most deplored in your mother is so much a part of your demeanor when you speak of your mother."

"Mother was self-absorbed and I am too."

"There's a difference between self-absorption and self-awareness. I would say, Ann, that you're self-aware. You examine your thoughts and motives. You're like that where your children are concerned and in your relationship with Max. It's an integral part of self-determination."

She eyes him questioningly. "What trait do you think I most deplored in my mother?"

"Her exclusivity. In her it ran hard and deep. In you it's an affectation and it's subtle, unless you're discussing your mother. We all pay secret homage to the qualities we most affect. That's why we affect them. And—" He nods sagely. "That's why we so vehemently protest those same traits in others."

She balks and then gives a reluctant nod of recognition. "But exclusivity is an affectation with no redeeming qualities,"

"You've put it to good use with your art gallery. You search for and acquire fine art. That's an endeavor of multilayered respect—including respect for the craft of the artist. And then you offer that art to museums, to other galleries, to private collectors. I'd call those sublimations more than redeeming."

She sighs gratitude. "How generous you are."

"Not at all. I call it as I see it."

She looks at him reflectively. "You were right about my relationship with Maggie. It was of the same tenor as the relationship with my mother, but the crux of my dilemma was the anger I felt at not being *central* to their happiness. We tout universal love," she muses, "but what we really desire is to be loved above all others." She leans wearily against the side of her chair. "I have to say that this has been an exhausting session."

Dr. Greenfield looks at his watch. "I think this a good place to stop." He stands and pushes his chair under the desk. "I'll walk you to your car. Would you like to schedule another appointment?"

"Yes, but not tonight," she replies. "Let's see what evolves during my trip with Max to Amory's camp."

Dr. Greenfield locks his office door and they walk to Ann's car. The humid evening air is a shocking contrast to the frosty coolness of his office. Ann unlocks her car door and slides in. The leather seat feels hot against the backs of her knees. "It's time to forgive Max, too," she reflects. "No forgiveness—no freedom." She smiles, waves, and turns the key in the ignition.

"That's an enlightened perspective," He says. "Be sure you guard it well." He gives a goodbye nod and walks to his car.

Eleanor telephones to get an update on Belle, whose once-compact belly sways from side to side when she walks and who has the appetite of a carthorse. Ann relates this casually to Eleanor, aware that she has yet to tell Eleanor about the baby she's carrying.

"So," She reiterates, "Max and I will drop the dogs off at the gallery tomorrow morning at ten and you'll take Belle to Dr. Zuccaro if she goes into labor, right?"

"Of course!" Eleanor enthuses. "I got so used to having them with me while you were in Portofino. I can't wait to get them back. I've already moved all the art books and auction price lists back off my bed. And I've roasted marrowbones—Belle's favorite treat, besides which, she needs them for her teeth. Calcium," she adds knowingly.

"I hear you, o bountiful caretaker of animals of the land, fishes of the sea, and birds of the air," Ann intones, "but seriously, Eleanor, I'm grateful that you love them so. There's nowhere else I could leave them where they'd be content."

"I love having them. See you tomorrow."

The moment Ann puts down the receiver, the phone rings again. "Yes, Eleanor," she teases, "I'll remember."

"Why do you do that?" Max asks amusedly. "It's never the person you think it is."

Ann chuckles. "Oh, sometimes it is. I've been right with you before. So, what's the good news of the evening?"

"Not good news," he replies in a low voice. "I have another admission. I'm going to be at the hospital until late. Let's firm up the time. Is eight tomorrow morning early enough?"

"Eight is perfect."

"Then I'll say goodnight."

"Have you had dinner?" she asks, but the line disconnects while she's still speaking.

She turns off the lights and walks upstairs and into her sitting room. Belle is stretched out on the sofa, belly up. "Oh rats," she mutters. She forgot to tell Max that he'll have to park in the street behind her car because the driveway gates are jammed and won't open, even with a key. She picks up the phone to call him back, but the newly changed Hampton General extension is scrawled on the kitchen chalkboard and the very thought of going back downstairs is exhausting. She pulls an Amory and dials star-sixty-nine instead. A robotically modulated voice comes on the line. "The number of the last incoming call is 757-723-9193. You can redial by pressing two on a touch phone or by dialing two on a rotary phone. If you need assistance, please stay on the line and an operator will answer."

She puts down the receiver. The number she's just been given is not a number with which she needs assistance.

It's Faye Graham's number.

She tosses and turns, sleeps fitfully, awakens to total darkness, gropes the skirted night table until her fingers locate her grandfather's grande sonnerie carriage clock, and presses the repeat button. The gong sounds three times.

She reaches for the phone and dials Max's home number, allows ten rings, then turns on the light, redials, and lets it ring twenty times. He doesn't answer.

Don't do it. Please don't do it. Turn off the light and go back to bed. Try to sleep. He might not have heard the phone ringing. He might have gone back to the hospital. If you can't sleep, go downstairs and brew a pot of green tea. Take a brisk walk. Pace the seawall. But please— whatever you do—don't do that.

She throws on a pair of shorts and a T-shirt, grabs her sandals, and tiptoes past Belle softly snoring on the sofa and Liza curled up in her wicker bed beside the fireplace. Liza opens one eye, closes it, and sighs herself back to oblivion. She doesn't remember her sandals until the pebbled street painfully reminds her. She opens the station wagon door quietly so the dogs won't hear.

She is at Faye Graham's house in minutes. And there in the circular driveway, hidden from street view by the tall boxwood hedge, is Max's BMW. The air exits her lungs in a slow exhale and she presses a fisted hand harshly against tightly clenched teeth. And then that hard dry stab at the back of the throat—the precursor to salty stinging tears at the corners of the eyes.

She lifts her chin—narrows her eyes—blinks back the tears.

If you understand things are such as they are.

If you don't understand things are such as they are.

She sits in quiet contemplation for several minutes and then draws a resolute breath, nods comprehension, opens the glove compartment, and takes out a pad of paper and pen.

Max –

I'm taking the dogs to Richmond and then driving to camp alone.
I'll see you there.

Ann

Motor running, car door ajar, she walks over to his car, and leaves the note beneath the windshield wiper, where he'll be certain to see it, and then walks calmly back to her car and pulls slowly off—one hand on the wheel—the other cradling her belly.

Belle and Liza greet Eleanor at the gallery doors. "Good heavens!" Eleanor says. "It's only nine thirty." She takes in Ann's appearance. "You look like you just stepped off of a magazine cover!"

"I showered at the townhouse. I made it to Richmond by seven thirty."

"Why so early? And where's Max?"

"He's still in Hampton. We're not driving to camp together after all."

Eleanor looks at her suspiciously. "What's wrong? And if something's wrong, why do you look so—" She scans Ann's face. "So unworried?"

"Nothing's wrong, Eleanor, and I am unworried."

"It's more than just unworried." Eleanor's expression is pure perplexity. "You look radiant."

Tell Eleanor about the baby now. No, don't tell her now because she'll have a heart attack from shock followed by six trillion questions and you'll never get on the road plus she'll be anxious the entire time you're away. Just wait until you get back from camp and tell her then."

"For heaven's sake, Ann, where did you go? Tell me what's wrong."

"Nothing's wrong, Eleanor."

"I know something's wrong. How come you and Max aren't riding together like you said you were?"

"I don't want to ride up with him. I prefer to drive alone."

"What did Max say when you told him?"

"I wasn't present when—when Max took note of it."

"When Max took note of what? I'm not following you, Ann."

"You don't need to follow me, Eleanor. Max and I have been divorced for a long time. It's a choice I made—a self-determination I finally understand." She pauses in thought. "And respect." She walks over to Eleanor and kisses her on the cheek. "Stop worrying, for heaven's sake. You're such a Jewish mama."

Eleanor's face softens. Smile lines form at the sides of her mouth. "You're the Jewish mother and I'm the Jewish daughter. You worry for me so I don't have to worry about things myself. Just like you do with Edwin and Amory."

"Speaking of Amory, I need to get on the road. Do you have the travel route printed out?"

"Yep. It's on your desk. Courtesy of AAA. I'll brew you a thermos of coffee to take along."

"No need. It's too hot for coffee, besides which, I've limited my coffee to one cup in the morning with milk and honey."

"Since when?"

"Since I gave up my three cigarettes daily and alcoholic beverages, including wine."

"Must be time for an appointment at that Kushi macrobiotic institute in Boston." Eleanor looks at Ann for affirmation.

Ann shakes her head. "No, I'm determining for myself these days but I have great respect for Michio Kushi. Imagine! He can diagnose illness just by carefully examining one's face, hands, ankles and complexion." She glances at her watch. "I need to visit the powder room and head out."

Eleanor nods agreement. "You know, Ann, you never really told me what happened with Victor in Portofino."

"Nothing happened. We ate, drank, slept, swam, played baccarat and chemin de fer at a couple of casinos at St. Remo, went out on his yacht, and spent hours with his mother, who is a truly elegant woman. Her villa is magnificent, by the way. What else do you want to know?"

"Do you like Victor?"

Ann reflects before answering. "As a friend and occasional escort, yes—as a father figure—possibly—as a kindred spirit, a soul mate, I think not."

"How does he feel about you?" Eleanor presses.

"Victor doesn't reveal much," she replies. "He's intrigued with the Ann in his painting. It's flattering, but that woman doesn't exist. She's a figment of his imagination, a contrivance to satisfy his requirements for falling in love."

Eleanor shakes her head in exasperation. "Talk about skirting a question!"

"I don't really know how Victor feels about me. He asked me to extend my visit, but I know two things that Victor may not."

"What two things?"

"I know that I don't love Victor and I know that the feelings Victor has for me aren't compelling to me." She clasps her hands over her heart. *'It is you are the lonely bird through the woods; and that you may be without a mate until you find me,'* she recites in a fluting Irish brogue.

"That," she sighs, "would be compelling."

In her office, away from Eleanor's probing curiosity, Ann breathes a sigh of relief. She must hurry and get on the road. Amory's camp is a five-hour drive. But she lingers.

The room is redolent of Maggie.

Maggie, painstakingly snipping, with Ann's grandfather's cigar cutter, silver foil slivers of moon with which to frame a sidesplitting cartoon from *The New Yorker.*

Maggie—sprawled on the leather chesterfield, a lit cigarette dangling from the corner of her rakish grin.

Maggie—tender of face—fluid of voice—tracing the side of Ann's hand with her index finger.

Thank you—once unknown to me.

Thank you for loving me your way and for setting me free as you promised you would. And … thank you for being as you are—so that I never had to choose.

The serenity for which she had so fervently wished, beneath the starlit canopy of Portofino sky, descends as unexpectedly as midsummer rain on a parched sunlit day—merciful—pellucid—all-encompassing. How curious that serenity would follow in the wake of such a bittersweet reckoning.

And yet … *and yet …*

She walks to her desk, sits down, and extracts a card and matching envelope from the stationery drawer. Chin in hand, she considers a moment and then writes the words out slowly in black ink, encloses the card in its envelope, seals it, addresses it, and affixes a stamp to it.

Victor's painting stares down at her—contained—dispassionately watchful—otherworldly. How unfathomable destiny was! How unfathomable that she and Victor would meet and become irrevocably connected through such a seemingly random encounter—that life would begin through such a seemingly random pairing.

Plays within plays that we cannot see.

She cradles her body gently—protectively—with both hands and closes her eyes.

Your father painted that portrait of me. He painted it and then he and I made you.

I hope you're glad, because I truly am.

A pulsation in the center of her belly.

A tiny somersault of joy.

Eleanor is in the showroom chatting amiably with an art dealer from New Orleans. "He really likes the Boldini," she confides, "but he swears he can't afford it."

"That one not even Happy Rockefeller can afford," Ann whispers, "but she's mulling it over." She scans the travel route, puts on her sunglasses. "I'll call you this evening."

Belle and Liza follow her to the main entrance doors. "No, you're staying with Eleanor. She's roasted marrowbones for you. Be good girls, and Belle, please don't go into labor while I'm away."

"Drive safely," Eleanor calls out, "and follow the map."

"Yes, Mother. I promise, Mother," Ann teases in her most obedient-little-girl voice.

She kisses Belle and Liza on their snouts and walks out of the gallery and into bright midsummer sunlight. She continues past her station wagon and stops at the corner mailbox, removes the envelope from the pocket of the striped seersucker jacket of her sundress, holds it in the palm of her hand, and then opens the chute and drops it in.

The note is addressed to Miss Margaret D. Lambert and on the monogrammed card is written a stanza from a Theodore Roethke villanelle:

> *"Of those so close beside me, which are you?*
> *God bless the Ground! I shall walk softly there,*
> *And learn by going where I have to go."*

Ann awakening

About the Author

Mariah Robinson lives in Richmond, Virginia. Her first novel, *Love and Other Illusions*, was nominated for Best in Literary Fiction by The Library of Virginia. Her next work, a children's book, *Joseph Bottomley Squirrel*, is slated for publication in 2018.

Attributions

A Price above Rubies, adapted from a screenplay by Boaz Yakin, 1998.

Carroll, Lewis. *Through the Looking-Glass*. Macmillan, 1871.

Forster, E.M. *A Passage to India*, Harcourt Brace Jovanovich, Publishers, 1904

Greene, Graham. *The Quiet American*. Heinemann Publishers, 1955.

Lord Tennyson, Alfred. "Locksley Hall-Sixty Years After." *Poems of Alfred Lord Tennyson; Selected, with a Biographical Introduction and Notes, by His Grandson, Charles Tennyson*. New York: Collins, 1968. Lines 127-128.

Millay, Edna St. Vincent. *Fatal Interview: Sonnet II*. W. Harper and Brothers, 1931.

Roethke, Theodore. "The Waking." *Words for the Wind: The Collected Verse of Theodore Roethke*. Doubleday & Company, Inc., Garden City, N.J. 1958.

The Philadelphia Story, a play by Philip Barry, 1939.

White Squall, adapted from a book by Charles F. Gieg and Felix M. Sutton, 1996.